W9-ACE-909

PENGUIN BOOKS

The Second Time I Saw You

Pippa Croft is the pen name of an award-winning romantic novelist. After studying English at Oxford, she worked as a copywriter and journalist before writing her debut novel, which won the RNA's New Writers' award and was later made into a TV movie. She lives in a village in the heart of England with her husband and daughter.

The Second Time
I Saw You

PIPPA CROFT

PENGUIN BOOKS

PENGUIN BOOKS

Published by the Penguin Group
Penguin Books Ltd, 80 Strand, London WC2R ORL, England
Penguin Group (USA) Inc., 375 Hudson Street, New York, New York 10014, USA
Penguin Group (Canada), 90 Eglinton Avenue East, Suite 700, Toronto, Ontario, Canada M4P 2Y3
(a division of Pearson Penguin Canada Inc.)
Penguin Ireland, 25 St Stephen's Green, Dublin 2, Ireland (a division of Penguin Books Ltd)
Penguin Group (Australia), 707 Collins Street, Melbourne, Victoria 3008, Australia
(a division of Pearson Australia Group Pty Ltd)
Penguin Books India Pvt Ltd, 11 Community Centre, Panchsheel Park, New Delhi – 110 017, India
Penguin Group (NZ), 67 Apollo Drive, Rosedale, Auckland 0632, New Zealand
(a division of Pearson New Zealand Ltd)
Penguin Books (South Africa) (Pty) Ltd, Block D, Rosebank Office Park,
181 Jan Smuts Avenue, Parktown North, Gauteng 2193, South Africa

Penguin Books Ltd, Registered Offices: 80 Strand, London WC2R ORL, England

www.penguin.com

First published in Penguin Books 2014
001

Copyright © Penguin Books UK Ltd, 2014
All rights reserved

The moral right of the author has been asserted
Set in 12.5/14.75 pt Garamond MT Std
Typeset by Jouve (UK), Milton Keynes
Printed in Great Britain by Clays Ltd, St Ives plc
Except in the United States of America, this book is sold subject
to the condition that it shall not, by way of trade or otherwise, be lent,
re-sold, hired out, or otherwise circulated without the publisher's
prior consent in any form of binding or cover other than that in
which it is published and without a similar condition including this
condition being imposed on the subsequent purchaser
ISBN: 978-1-405-91704-9

www.greenpenguin.co.uk

MIX
Paper from
responsible sources
FSC™ C018179

Penguin Books is committed to a sustainable
future for our business, our readers and our planet.
This book is made from Forest Stewardship
Council™ certified paper.

To Charlotte, with much love

Chapter One

Hilary Term

It's dark. The kind of darkness you can scoop up in your hands or pull over your skin like a velvet cloth. Outside, the chapel clock chimes the first stroke of midnight, and after it, the other bells of Oxford join in, near and far, out of synch with each other. The chilly night air kisses my skin and the room smells of books and instant coffee and dusty radiators.

I can't move but I'm not dreaming, I just choose not to. I choose to lie here, naked on top of the duvet on my single bed, knowing Alexander is somewhere in the room. Maybe he's yards away, maybe only inches. He once told me that he could do that if he wanted to: break into my room and stand by my bed – and walk out again – and that I'd never know he'd even been there. He told me he was trained to do it and I told him he was talking bullshit, yet I remember the ironic tilt of his mouth as I laughed in his face.

The air shimmers a little. To my left, possibly a foot or so away, his voice cuts through the darkness.

'I want you,' he says. 'You drive me insane but I'm never going to let you go.'

And I say, 'Go screw yourself, Alexander.'

And he says, 'No, I'm going to screw *you*, Ms Cusack.'

I laugh but every nerve ending, inside and out, is waiting – no, screaming – for the moment when he touches me.

I lick my lips before I can reply. 'You can try, Mr Hunt, you can *try*.'

The mattress dips, the bed creaks, and his weight is next to me, over me, on me. His mouth comes down on mine in the darkness. I could stop him, any time I wanted to; I could end this thing between us but I choose not to.

'Good morning, ladies and gentlemen. We will shortly be landing at Heathrow Airport, where the local time is just after eight a.m. Can you please return your seats to the upright position and ensure your seat belts are securely fastened ready for landing.'

I lift the eye mask off my face and screw my eyes shut again as the light coming through the cabin windows blinds me. At home, my mother will be dead to the world under her down comforter. Even my father will be next to her by now, snatching a few hours' rest before he heads to the White House or some senate committee meeting. Around me, the other Business Class passengers are adjusting their watches to GMT and frowning because we're running late.

'Sweet dreams?'

The stewardess flashes me a smile that's way too

bright. I sure hope I haven't been acting out my fantasy as I dozed in the flat bed because *that* would take a lot of explaining. As for my dreams, I already consigned those to where they belong: to the boxes marked 'Big Mistake' and 'Don't Go There' and 'How the Hell Did I Ever Let That Happen?'

And yet . . .

And yet *nothing*, Lauren.

'Can I get you anything?'

'No, thank you, but I think I'll go freshen up before we land.'

'I'm afraid there's no time now. The seat-belt signs are on and we'll be on the stand very soon.' She tosses me an apologetic smile and hands me a wrapped mint by way of consolation for having to cross my legs for the next half-hour.

Rubbing some life back into my limbs, I pull off the cashmere blanket and push the button to raise the flat bed. So much for arriving in England looking fresh and relaxed. I planned on changing my crumpled Chloé pants in the washroom and slapping on an extra layer of NARS moisturizer. Now, I guess, I'll have to settle for arriving looking more like the girl in Degas's *L'Absinthe* than Blake Lively.

A couple of hours later, the limo reaches the centre of the city. Predictably, my father asked that Roger, his UK driver, be allowed to collect me from the airport again and it seemed a small concession to make. My parents have finally been forced to accept that I can look after myself and that my choice to study my History of Art master's at Oxford was the right one for me. After spending a term away from home in what Granny loves to call 'foreign parts', I haven't been abducted, arrested or died of starvation.

I did, however, fall for the most unsuitable man in Oxford, but that's something they're *never* going to know about. The six weeks I've been away from Alexander Hunt have been the Christmas gift I didn't ask for – but needed so much more than clothes or candy.

It's *over* and while I'm not normally superstitious, I'll take it as a good omen that pockets of watery blue sky peer out from among the clouds as we drive down the road past the University Parks towards Wyckham College. The branches are bare now, and on the shady side of the street their spiky fingers are tinged with frost. We pass the boathouse and through the iron railings I see the sun glinting on the river and the punts chained up on the slipway. The last time I saw this place, I was laughing and shivering as Alexander smashed the ice in the bottom of one of the boats, so he could punt us upriver to the pub.

Has it really been two months since we floated back downstream, him lost in some dark and distant place again, me wrapped in his coat, thinking that was the only way I'd ever get inside his skin?

Roger slots the limo into a parking space outside the

Porters' Lodge. The very first time I saw Alexander he was doing battle for a parking space – and winning, of course. Alexander always wins at everything, except perhaps this time.

'Do you want a hand with your bags, Miss Cusack?'

'No, thanks,' I say firmly. This term, I won't even waste my time trying to get Roger to call me Lauren. I've learned not to waste my time on battles that can't be won and before he's even pocketed my tip, I'm out of the door and grabbing my two bags from the trunk. The rest of the mountain of luggage I brought from Washington is locked away in the closet in my room.

'Bye and thanks again. See you at the end of term.'

I want to laugh at Roger's face as he reaches the trunk too late to do his duty. 'Miffed' is the word Immy might use, but no matter, I'm already on my way towards the Lodge. I'd forgotten quite how spectacular the Jacobean architecture is and the dark-gold stone seems to soak up the sunlight, lifting my mood. When I first arrived here, this place was alien to me but now, while it's not quite 'home', it comes with a familiarity that takes the edge off its austere grandeur.

As for the people hurrying in and out of the Lodge, wrapped in scarves and padded coats, I recognize most of them by sight and some well enough to say more than 'Happy New Year' to. They're all intent on getting their stuff into college from their parents' cars, or picking up schedules and mail from the pigeonholes. Everyone looks as if they're here to work, even if it won't last beyond First Week, and that makes me more determined to make the most of my final two terms here at Wyckham.

A few people nod as I schlep my bags around the Front Quad to my staircase and a couple stop briefly to ask if I had a good Christmas vac. My room is under the battlements on the top floor and despite my attempts to stay in shape over the holidays, I'm out of breath by the time I reach the third floor. The landing is silent as I drop my bags outside my door and delve into my jacket pocket for my key.

'Yay!!! You're back!'

The door opposite mine is flung open and its occupant leaps on me with a huge hug. 'Hey, I tried to keep away but I guess I just couldn't help myself.'

Laughing, Immy lets me go just before I pass out from lack of oxygen. I laugh but, to my horror and disgust, find tears pricking the back of my eyes. So I haven't been here five minutes and I'm about to blub? It's ridiculous.

'Are you OK?'

'It's bloody freezing here,' I joke, making a terrible hash of her English accent.

'Don't you have snow on the East Coast?'

'Sure we have snow, but generally nothing like New York and the skies are so much clearer at home. Does it have to be so gloomy here?'

She laughs. 'We aim to please but I've got something

6

to warm you up in my room. You get inside and I'll be back in a sec.'

I open my room and wrinkle my nose at the aroma: not coffee nor books but a cocktail of cleaning products. I hear the sound of a kettle being filled in the tiny kitchen at the end of our landing and dump my luggage by the desk. Outside the window, across the quad, the statues of the college founders stare sternly back at me.

'Yuk.'

I turn to find Immy pulling a face and carrying two mugs, with steam rising from them. 'My place reeked too. Had to throw open the windows. Shall I undo one of yours while you take your coat off?'

'Great.'

Ten minutes later, I'm sitting on my bed, cradling a mug of hot chocolate and Bailey's, Immy's 'welcome home' treat.

'How was your vac? Did you manage to have a good Christmas despite you-know-what?' She lowers her voice when she refers to the brief conversation we had on Skype over the vacation about my break-up with Alexander. Maybe she thinks I might burst into tears at the mention of him, but she ought to know me better than that. I genuinely have no intention of shedding a single tear more over Alexander.

'The vac was awesome; I hadn't realized how much I missed my family, even the grandparents – not that I'd tell them, of course – and it was so great to catch up with my old college friends from Brown.' My response, by now, is well rehearsed and sounds it. I'm not sure it will convince anyone, let alone Immy, who has a nose like a bloodhound for bullshit. I blow on my chocolate and steam rises in front of my face. 'How about you?'

'Oh, it was pretty good, considering. Once I knew George was on the mend from his op, I managed to get away to Verbier for a few days with Skandar.'

'Wow, that's almost long term.' Immy is famous for hopping in and out of relationships but Skandar, a gorgeous Viking-hotty-slash-tennis-Blue, has lasted a whole two months.

'Isn't it?' She rolls her eyes. 'I almost had to restrain my mother from trawling the Philip Treacy website. But enough of me, what I want to know is have you seen *him* since you got back?'

'Him?' I wrinkle my brow. 'You mean Professor Rafe?'

'You know *exactly* who I mean. I couldn't believe it when you told me about you and Alexander. I am *so* sorry I wasn't here when you got back from Falconbury. I assume that's when it happened?'

I nod because I don't want to tell even Immy the exact circumstances of the break-up. 'I think a brother with appendicitis takes priority over my love life. Is George still doing well? Sounded like it from your emails.'

'Oh, he's fine now. I can tell from the way he's back to being a total pain in the arse, and he's milked every moment of his "near-death experience". But forget George, I want to know when you're going to get back with Alexander.'

'Never.'

'No?'

'Not a chance.'

Her eyes widen. 'Really? I'm sure he'll have something to say about that. I can't believe he hasn't flown over to Washington to demand you take him back.'

'He didn't even call.' I swallow down my chocolate and regret it as it's still too hot and I burn my tongue. Do I wish he'd called? Part of me does, but this makes me even more annoyed. There's no point, anyway.

'Didn't even *phone*? What the fuck went on at the ball, Lauren, because this row must have been catastrophic to cause you to split up . . .' She pauses, eyeing me suspiciously. 'His cow of an ex wasn't there, was she?'

'Oh yes, Valentina was very much there.'

'Shit. I've only met her a couple of times but she seemed to assume I was pond-life and therefore beneath her notice.'

'Unfortunately, she decided I was *definitely* worthy of her notice. She was all over Alexander from the moment she got to Falconbury and she's made it very clear she wants him back.'

Immy snorts chocolate over my duvet but I don't mind. 'Cheeky cow! What does Alexander have to say about that?'

'He swore she means nothing to him any more, but

I don't care. I can't blame the split on her; the differences between us run a lot deeper.'

'Don't tell me you're fazed by the whole culture/ class thing! You're the sophisticated politician's daughter.'

'Am I?' I grimace. 'You said yourself that I'd probably want to kill most of the Falconbury hangers-on by the time I left and if there'd been a sword to hand, I might have. They're obsessed with tradition, most of them are blatant snobs and General Hunt was so frosty to me, I'm surprised the port didn't freeze in our glasses. Even so, it's more than that. Alexander and I – we seem to bring out the worst in each other and I don't think that's healthy.'

She wrinkles her nose. 'Well, he can be an awkward bastard, I'll agree, but I did think he seemed happier last term than I'd ever seen him. He must be under a lot of pressure, having to keep disappearing off to places with the army.'

'I suppose so, but I've given up trying to understand his moods and he certainly wouldn't want me to feel sorry for him.' I hesitate, realizing how well I know Alexander in some ways – and how little in others. Well, that's how it's going to stay so I lift my chin and add, 'I spent far too much of last term trying to understand him and I realized that it was sucking my time here away.'

Immy flicks her hair back, sips her chocolate, then says, 'You'll miss the sex.'

The vision of Alexander's gorgeous mouth doing insanely filthy things to me slides into my mind and I shift uncomfortably in my seat. The times when things were good between the two of us – when we had fun, when we made love every day and the sparks flew between us like a bonfire – were incredible. I can't deny I do miss them, and I spent too many nights over the vac reliving some of them.

My heart sinks a little. I may talk the talk, but I also need to walk the walk and resist any attempt of Alexander's to lure me back. Not that he will, after his reaction at the end of last term. I'll never forget the look of disappointment and anger on his face before he turned his back on me and marched away.

Aware that I've been slipping back into thoughts of him again, I harden my heart and my voice. 'I want to put Alexander behind me.'

Immy raises her eyebrows. 'I do hope that wasn't a Freudian slip.'

Fortunately there's a cushion to hand with which to bat Immy. After she's fended me off, she looks serious again. 'I still say that he'll be round here in a flash the moment he sets foot in Oxford.'

'You think?' I pick at a loose thread on the cushion. 'Have you . . . um . . . seen him around college since you got here?'

'Not yet, which is funny because I came up on Friday morning to do some extra reading and there's been no sign of him. I might have missed him or he could be at his house, of course, although Rupert didn't mention Alexander or the break-up when I saw him in the pub last night.'

I shrivel inside. Rupert was at the hunt ball and witnessed my champagne-fuelled 'moment' of vengeance on Alexander. The snake must be rubbing his clammy little hands together in glee if he knows that his cousin and I are history. He *must* know something is wrong because he was staying overnight at Falconbury the morning I rushed off.

It's tough; what he thinks is nothing to me now. Guiltily, I remember my tutor's warning words to me about not getting distracted by Alexander and his lifestyle. Professor Rafe is a grade-A creep but he marks my essays and, theoretically, he could kick me off my master's course in Art History. I wouldn't like to be at Rafe's mercy in any sense of the word, so I must make sure my work's top notch this term. With five long essays on the core subject and my optional topic, lectures, seminars and minipresentations, *and* a weekly Italian for Art Historians class, I have a lot to think about, without getting into Alexander's dramas, not to mention Alexander's bed.

Immy studies me intently, as if I'm some kind of interesting fossil she dug up on one of her Geography field trips. 'Lauren, what exactly *did* happen at the end of last term because I don't think I'm getting the whole story. If you want to keep this stuff private, then fine, but I'm sensing there's an elephant in the room here.'

Oh, there so *is* an elephant in the room, and he comes in the shape of a gorgeous hunky rower called Scott Schulze. Should I tell Immy about him, or the disaster involving the three of us on the last day of term? Should I tell her that when Alexander saw Scott and me kissing in the street, he glared at me as if I'd knifed him through the heart or, worse, shot his dog?

'Like I said, we bring out the worst in each other and things came to a head at the ball.' I cringe when I think about how I behaved, flirting with Alexander's friends in front of his family just to hurt him the way he'd hurt me. It was out of character for me and while I've been away from this hothouse I've realized that the way I acted is one more example of the fact that Alexander and I are a disaster together.

'Careful, you've almost unravelled that cushion.'

Glancing down, I see the thread is wound around my finger but Immy's voice softens. '*And* . . . ?' she asks.

'And . . . Alexander may have seen me kissing another guy in the middle of Holywell Street.'

After what you could describe as a deafening silence, she exhales. 'Oh dear. I can see how that might have pissed him off. Can I ask who this other guy is?'

'Just a friend.'

'Who snogged you in the street?'

'It wasn't a snog, just a kiss . . . It just kind of happened at the wrong moment.'

'And now this "other guy" is on the scene. I suppose you've changed your Facebook status to complicated?'

'That says nothing, like it always did and he's not on the scene, we're just . . .'

'Good friends?' Immy's voice drips with irony. I don't blame her because that phrase sounds so lame. It also happens to be true, at least for me. Scott may have other ideas, but I'm not going to fan the flames of Immy's curiosity any further.

I had half expected to see Scott while we were both back in Washington but for most of the holidays he's been in training with the Boat Race squad. I spoke to him once, briefly, just before he flew out to a rowing camp in France. He sounded about as excited as Scott can get but it sounded like torture to me. I told him I didn't want to talk about what happened at the end of term. I don't want to leap from one relationship into another, even though he does make me smile, is light-hearted and fun.

Fuck, that makes him sound perfect for me, which he is, but I'm not looking for perfect; I wasn't looking for anyone. After Todd and I split up, I just wanted to *be*, but Alexander Hunt exploded into my life like a hand grenade and I'm done with picking up the pieces.

Immy's watching me, chin on hand, and alarm bells go off in my head. There's no way I'm going to convince her that Our Thing is over, but time will tell.

'Are you going to tell me who this mystery man is?'

'Just a friend. I swear it.'

I cross my heart and she watches me for a while

before saying, 'If you ever need to share, I'm always here.'

'I know and thanks for not pushing me. Now, do you mind if we change the subject? How was your skiing trip?'

She grins wickedly. 'Sod the skiing, it's the après-ski you really want to know about.'

While Immy went off to the library to finish her vac essay, I resolved to go somewhere where I wouldn't be able to daydream. A few hours in the grad centre, surrounded by my fellow grad students, has focused my mind and the past couple of hours have been an Alexander-free zone.

When I step outside, it's already going dark. Winter in Washington isn't that different to here: it can be mild, or you can get heavy snowfalls, but it's the lack of daylight here that really gets me down. It goes dark so early; and on a dull day it never really seems to get light at all. I pull my scarf higher, and quicken my steps. My restless night on the plane and the jetlag must be affecting me; I need a good night's rest and everything will seem brighter in the morning.

The bright lights of the Lodge beckon and I drop by my pigeonhole, which is stuffed with invites from USSoc, the American students' society, from the Department of History of Art, from the dance studio, from the Dean wanting me to go to drinks and the Student

Union reminding me about meetings and the Wyckham Bop. Add the requests to go to birthday celebrations, and I could be out every evening. I stuff the invites in my bag and smile. While I might not be able to go to everything, I'm determined to do as much as possible in my next two terms because far too much time was spent in Alexander's bed last term.

The wind cuts to my bones as I walk back to my room, thanking my lucky stars that I'm not in Alexander's bed now, or pressed against his naked body in the shower, soaked, hot, shaking with lust, his mouth coming down on my breast . . .

No. I will *not* do this. As if I can outrun the rogue thoughts, I hurry towards the archway that leads to my staircase. An R&B track pumps out from a room on the second floor, the bass line so loud it makes the wooden steps tremble. I take the stairs two at a time, full of fresh resolution to obliterate every trace of A. Hunt from my mind.

'Lauren?'

A guy emerges from a door as I pass, raising his voice above the music. It's the physicist who helped with my bags at the beginning of last term.

'Had a good vac?' he grins.

'Great, thanks!'

'Good. Um . . . just so you know, there's a bloke outside your door. He's been there over an hour. I think it's . . .'

I'm already gone as he says the name I dread hearing.

Of course it's Alexander. My pulse races and every instinct tells me to head straight back down the stairs again. How could I have thought he wouldn't try to confront me after what happened with Scott? This is the man who told me he always wins and never stops until he gets what he wants.

I stiffen my resolve because *this* is the woman who spent the vac ready for this moment: it's over, no matter what he throws at me.

My heart thumps against my ribcage as I reach my landing and see the dark figure resting against the wall outside my door.

Then he lifts his face to me.

For the next few heartbeats, I half wonder whether the figure isn't Alexander after all. Because the guy slumped against the wall outside my door isn't the arrogant guy I last saw blocking the pavement in the street, the unshakeable, implacable man that other people had to go around. This man looks shapeless and beaten, a sack of bones in a black Crombie overcoat.

My hand freezes on the banister. 'Alexander?'

His eyes are red-rimmed as if he's been crying.

My stomach clenches. 'What's the matter?'

'It's my father. He's dead.'

Chapter Two

No matter what I thought about General Hunt, and no matter what I think about Alexander now, seeing him in this state makes my stomach churn. I touch the arm of his coat and he flinches.

'I'm sorry. I shouldn't have come here.' He gets up, raking his hand through his hair.

'Yes, you *should*.'

What am I saying? It's just the instinct to comfort another human being who's in pain. Standing beside him, with my arms wrapped around my chest, I don't know whether to touch him or stay well clear.

'Lauren . . .' His voice is so full of every kind of misery it physically hurts to hear it.

'Please. Just come inside.'

After I've closed the door behind him, he occupies the middle of my room, rubbing his hand over his mouth over and over, as if he's stuck at a crossroads and doesn't know which way to turn.

'When did it happen? *How?*'

'Last Saturday at Falconbury. He was thrown from his horse while he was hunting.' His voice is hollow, like a grand room now empty of furniture.

'Oh Jesus.'

'He broke his neck; the doctors said it was instant.'

'That's some consolation, isn't it? I can't imagine your father paralysed or dependent on other people.' I cringe as soon as the words leave my mouth.

'No, but ... if he hadn't gone so suddenly, we might . . .' He stops, and I see him swallow. 'The way I left him . . . before he went out with the hunt, we'd had another row.'

He steps forward and his arms tighten around me, in an embrace so fierce the breath is almost squeezed from my body. After a couple of seconds, his hold on me slackens a little but he rests his forehead on the top of my head, as if he doesn't want me to see his face.

'Alexander, I'm so sorry. What can I do?' I ask helplessly. Although I already know what the answer will be, his reaction stuns me with its ferocity. In seconds, he's ripped off his coat and dragged me on to the bed. He's above me, his mouth hard against mine, his body crushing me into the mattress. He wants to obliterate his pain and despite myself I want him just as desperately. Six weeks of pent-up desire and tension are unleashed and any resistance leaves me as we roll around the bed, clutching at each other like we're drowning. I grip his back, gouging the muscles with my fingers, not caring if I hurt him. He shoves his hand up inside my sweater and he drags my bra down and cups my breast in his roughened palm.

When I arch my hips to meet him, he scoops my bottom upwards and crushes me on to his erection. Then we're both fumbling at the other's jeans, me hurting my fingers on the fly buttons, him wrenching at my zipper as if he wants to tear my jeans in two.

'I'll do it.'

I pull off my boots and strip my jeans and underwear off while he kicks off his shoes and pulls off his trousers and boxers, almost tripping over in his haste to rip off the clothes. His shirt follows, pulled over his head before he's even got all the buttons undone. It's like our first time in its haste except it's not: this is desperate, frantic and essential. My inner muscles clench painfully when I see how hard and thick and desperate he is for me but then he's on the bed, kneeling either side of my legs, trapping me. We hold each other's gaze for a few seconds, before he leans down and runs his tongue right through the centre of me.

I almost take his head off as I buck my hips up and waves of sensation course through me.

He lifts his head and there's desperation on his face, and relief too. He plants his hands either side of my head and works his hips between my legs. As he enters me, I wrap my legs around his butt and urge him deep, deep inside me. Six weeks of emptiness are filled up in one swift thrust, and I cry out, unable to stop myself.

The headboard bangs the wall as Alexander drives into me hard, and my nails bury deep into his flesh. It's been so long – too long – since I had him inside me and the intensity is almost painful but I want it, I *need* it, and I squeeze my eyes shut so tightly as I come that stars pop out in front of me. I'm still coming down from my orgasm, still milking him as his body goes rigid and he groans in agonized release.

My breath comes in short bursts, like I've been running a hundred-yard dash, and my bare ass is squashed against the wall. Alexander is breathing hard too, his chest rising and falling rapidly, the hair between his pecs sheened in sweat.

His eyes are still shut because he can't bear to open them and remember why he's here and what has happened to him. I don't want him to come back to the real world either; I want to stay here and just be. I want to savour for ever the physical pleasure and forget the drama and the angst. All I cared about when he leaped on me was that I wanted his body on mine – in mine – as savagely as he did. I've missed the sex and I've missed the intensity and that already scares me.

Minutes have passed and neither of us has moved or spoken. The air has begun to chill my body and then I feel him stroking my hair. It should be a tender gesture but I get the feeling he doesn't know or perhaps care what or who he's touching. I just happened to be here.

'Lauren . . .'

'Uh-huh.'

'We forgot something.'

I hold my breath momentarily, then exhale. 'Should I be worried?'

'Not from my point of view. There's been no one since you.'

'Ditto.'

He shifts on to his back and rolls me on top of him so we're face to face. While I was away, I convinced myself that I'd imagined the raw sexuality and power of the man. Now he's here, there's no denying the way he makes me feel physically.

'That's the only piece of good news I've had since I last saw you,' he says and I know exactly what he means.

'Alexander, I'm so sorry about your father. And I know this will be the last thing on your mind just now but so you know, what you saw in the street the morning after the ball was a mistake. I was upset, I'd had no sleep and it really wasn't what it looked like . . .' I say, cursing myself even as the words come out. What happened to my well-rehearsed dismissal, the no-hard-feelings smile? The things I'd vowed I'd say and do when we met again?

'I can't think about that now,' he says distractedly, but his face has darkened, obviously reminded of the way we parted. I have the feeling that kiss is going to haunt us all for a long time.

'I didn't mean or want it to happen,' I try again. 'Scott's a friend . . . and does any of it matter now?' I shiver. I'm getting no response to any of my gabbling and his real feelings are impossible to judge. I'm cold and I know that the gulf between us *does* matter, and has only been temporarily put into context by his father's death. But he really doesn't seem to want to discuss it, and part of me is relieved.

'Hold on.' He reaches down and drags the bedcover over us. The warmth and hardness of his body is intoxicating and deceptive, as he pulls me tighter against him.

'Have I ever told you how good I am at fucking things up?' With my cheek on his chest, I can't see his expression and perhaps that's what he wants, so I stay still, as his voice continues into the air. 'I don't think a day went by when my father and I didn't blame one another for something and now it's too late to do a fucking thing about it.'

'Do you want to tell me about it?'

'Dad rode out with the hunt on the estate as usual. Apparently, he tried to jump a high hedge near the priory copse but the horse refused and threw him. He . . .' I hear the pause, louder than words. 'He hit the gatepost and broke his neck.'

I shudder.

'I should be used to death by now; Christ knows I've seen men snuffed out before – more than once – but I can't believe it. Maybe it's because I wasn't there when it actually happened and I should have been. I was supposed to be going out on the hunt with him; the field was one of the few places where we actually shared any kind of consensus on anything. But I didn't go.'

Finally he loosens his hold on me so I can shift my head to see his face.

'Why not?' I ask, sensing he needs to have the question asked, and to answer it.

'Because . . . because we had an almighty row. Emma was in a state about going back to school. She and Dad had another set-to about what she was going to do at university. I made some excuse about having to stay in and write my exam essay but really I wanted to talk to her while Dad was safely out of the house. I was going to take her into Henley to do some shopping and as we walked to the car, Helen ran up to us and told me there'd been an accident.'

I picture the normally unshakeable Helen's face. She and her husband Robert are housekeeper and butler to the Hunts and devoted to the family. 'She must be in pieces. All the staff must be so shocked.'

'I've never seen Helen like that but I had to leave her with Emma while Robert drove me to see Dad. You know, I kept asking him why the air ambulance hadn't been scrambled and when I got there, I realized why: because there was no point. There were so many people around him . . . Jesus, so many fucking people for no fucking reason.'

There's no point in me speaking either, or offering any comfort because I don't know how to do that. I also feel irrationally guilty because, while I'm physically sickened by the thought that Alexander and Emma have lost both their parents so young, I'm also grateful I'm not in their situation. I'm glad it wasn't me approached by some terrified servant with the worst news anyone can ever hear and that it wasn't me racing to the hospital behind my father's ambulance, knowing it was too late.

Despite the tensions still simmering between us, my instinct is to put my misgivings aside for now and do what I can to help Alexander. If the only comfort I can offer is physical, then who am I to hold back?

'I don't know what to say.' I curl myself around him, wrapping my leg over his.

He strokes my arm, idly. 'Maybe I shouldn't feel this way, because I lost my father a long time ago. We'd never been that close and after my mother died, we might as well have lived on different continents. I just thought . . .'

I say nothing in the pause that follows, waiting for him to continue.

'I thought that we still had time to resolve our differences. I kept hoping that things might change one day, or we'd come to an understanding. Maybe he might have realized that my mother's accident wasn't my fault.'

'Maybe he already knew that. He just didn't know how to say it.'

He laughs bitterly. 'Now we'll never know, will we?' He shifts and pushes himself upright, abruptly. 'I have to get dressed and get back to Falconbury.'

'So soon?'

'Yes. Emma needs me and there's still so much to do: funeral arrangements, a ton of bloody legal stuff . . .'

'Have you got people to help you?'

'Plenty. The staff, solicitors, but as an executor of Dad's estate, I have to make the decisions. Jesus . . . What are we all going to do?'

He sits on the edge of the bed, and rakes his hands viciously through his hair like he wants to rip the responsibility from his head.

'I know. I'm so sorry, Alexander. For everything.'

He turns to me, with an intensity in his eyes that almost scares me. I don't know what he's about to say but his face changes, taking on the armour that usually protects the man inside.

'It can't be helped now. It can only be dealt with.'

He gets up, and pulls on his clothes. We dress in silence but my mind is a whirl of conflicting emotions, thoughts . . . so many, all powerless to help him.

His phone rings as he shrugs on his coat and he frowns at the screen. 'Hunt.'

From his face and the few words on his side, I get that he's had more bad news.

'What?' I ask as he clicks off the phone and exhales heavily.

'That was Helen, worried about Emma. She's locked herself in her room with Benny, apparently, and won't accept anything to eat . . . Obviously the staff are concerned. Not to mention the bloody dog must be crossing his legs. Shit.'

'Poor Emma. I know she and your father didn't get on but she must be totally devastated.'

'She's not stopped crying. Despite their differences,

she worshipped Dad. She had more chance of getting through to him than I did. Can you believe he told me he might possibly allow her to go to Saint Martins after all, as long as she settled down at school and got good A levels? He mentioned it to me just before he went out hunting, and I think he hoped she'd get good grades and maybe take a gap year and go up to Oxford after all, like he wanted. I nearly fell off my chair and he promised to discuss it with Emma when he got back.'

'And Emma didn't know he'd changed his mind?'

'No, and it's too late now. Too late to change anything.' He snatches up his car keys from the desk and shoves them and his hands in his pockets. I've seen this defensive gesture before, when he saw me in the street, kissing Scott . . . *being kissed by* Scott.

'Alexander, be careful . . .' I hate the thought of him making the dark and lonely drive back to Falconbury in his current frame of mind, even though I know he has to go. He looks at me, a battle raging behind his eyes, then he says:

'Lauren, come to the funeral with me.'

This I never expected; this I don't know how to deal with. 'I . . . I . . . don't . . .'

His face shows something I've never seen in it before: desperation and panic.

'I need someone there with me, someone who knows me from outside the family. I want it to be you.'

This is the closest thing I've ever seen to a plea from Alexander. Everything else has been a demand or a request that he expects to be met. Looking up into his face, realizing what it's taken for him to ask me for help, my stomach turns over and over. Even if I wanted to, how could I refuse?

'Of course I will.'

On the morning of General Hunt's funeral, Immy stands by in my room as I button up my pea coat and arrange a dark-grey scarf around my neck. Outside, it's a bitingly cold morning and the wind rattles the sash windows. It's still only January, so I can hardly expect anything else.

'I brought these,' Immy says, holding out a fold-up black umbrella and a mini silver hip flask. 'Dad left them in my room the last time he visited but I think you may need them. They're de rigueur at English funerals.'

'Thanks.' With a brief smile, I take the umbrella and flask from her and lay them on the bed next to my handbag.

Immy shoots me a sympathetic look, as if I'm the one who needs comforting. 'How are you, hun?'

'I've had happier occasions to look forward to but I guess I'll get through it, and I can't imagine how Alexander and his sister are feeling. I expect he'll hide his feelings in public, like he always does. You know, I think there are two hundred people invited to the house, let alone all the villagers and officials.'

Immy sits on the bed. 'Have you seen much of him lately?'

'Not since he came round to tell me the news about his father and that was almost a week ago. He's called me, mainly to talk about arrangements for today, although he has confessed he's worried about Emma. I think I'm the only person he feels he can talk to.'

'That's because you're an outsider and let's face it, he has no one else left, unless you count Rupert, and we both know he's not the most sympathetic of people.'

Actually, I'm thinking, General Hunt's death gives Rupert de Courcey the perfect opportunity to drive a bigger wedge between Alexander and me. Rupert is Alexander's cousin and studying at Wyckham with us. He's also an old schoolfriend of Immy's and she knows there's no love lost between us, but he's the last thing on my mind now.

'Alexander has insisted I travel in the family funeral cortège. I've tried to say I'll meet him in church but he won't have it.'

'Eww. Travelling in a family car will be horrible.'

I shrug. 'I know but he's steamrollered all my objections so I think I'm travelling with an aunt and uncle on his mother's side. He did hint that I could share the same car as him and Emma, but I flat refused. Imagine if I turned up in church behind the coffin with the two of them?'

Of course I want to support him, but I'd hate

anyone to feel I was inveigling my way into the family on an occasion like this. Even Immy looks surprised at this revelation. 'Well, Alexander must think an awful lot of you to ask that, but I can see exactly why you've said no.'

'Of course I refused. I don't even know what's going to happen to us after the funeral is over. We haven't begun to sort things out between us, after The Scott Thing, but how could I leave him to face such a horrible time on his own?'

Immy jumps up and hugs me. 'You couldn't.'

My room phone rings and I pick it up while Immy hovers next to me.

The hail clatters against the window as I put down the phone. 'That was the Lodge. My cab's here. Wish me luck.'

I pull on a pair of dark-blue leather gloves, while she picks up the umbrella and flask.

'Don't forget,' she says, with an encouraging smile, 'there's plum vodka in the flask and if I were you I'd make good use of it.'

'Lord Falconbury, please accept my sincere condolences . . .'

'I am so sorry, Alexander, this is a truly awful thing for you and Emma to bear. I just thank God your mother isn't here to see this day.'

'Sorry, mate. Shitty thing to happen. If you need anything, you know where I am.'

My feet are numb, I can't remember how long I've

been standing next to Alexander in the ballroom at Falconbury as, one by one, the mourners offer their own brand of sympathy. At the end of last term, this grand space had been decorated with swags, balloons and flowers for the hunt ball. The panelled walls pulsated with bass and everyone glittered in ballgowns and diamonds.

Today, it's black tie again, but of a different kind, alleviated only by odd touches of scarlet and gold braid on the army officers' khaki uniforms. Tumblers of whisky and china cups of tea have replaced the champagne that flowed at the ball. If anything, there are even more people here now, talking in hushed tones or huddling in front of the fire that's been lit in the huge stone hearth.

Briefly, Alexander touches my hand, as if to reassure me, although I thought that was my function here. Actually, I don't know what my function is, since from the moment I arrived at the house I've felt like a fraud, and there's no mistaking the glances of confusion as relatives and family friends greet us.

I'm travelling with an aunt and uncle in one of the other cars. I've discovered they're actually cousins of the late Lady Hunt, Alexander's mother. I'm not sure they knew quite how to deal with me, an impostor in their midst, but mercifully it was only a few minutes' drive from Falconbury to the church and we spent most of it staring out of the window.

I was still shocked to find that a place had been reserved for me in the pew directly behind Alexander and Emma. Rupert was only feet away and studiously ignoring me, just as he had at the house. That suits me fine but I hope he isn't going to use this occasion to score points off me. At any other time, I can handle anything he throws at me but I really don't want a scene or to make life any harder for Alexander today.

Apart from Rupert, many of the faces are the same ones I met at the hunt ball. The Master of the Falconbury Hunt is here, of course, along with many of the followers. There are also relations of Alexander's I can put names to; how could I forget Aunt Celia and the horsey mother and daughter who were grade-A bitches at the ball? How could I forget any of the weekend that finally ended my relationship with Alexander?

Never in my wildest dreams could I have imagined I'd be back here again so soon and in such different circumstances.

The people I don't recognize must be the local great and good, the business acquaintances and tenants who farm the land owned by the Hunts; by one Hunt now – by Alexander. Hearing him addressed as Lord Falconbury by several of the guests is surreal for me, and I know Alexander must hate it. He forbade anyone to use his courtesy title before his father died. He's done his best to fix his face into its usual mask, yet I can see the facade slipping when he hears, loud and clear from people's lips, that he is now the owner of Falconbury. The weight of this place is on his shoulders now, and he can't escape it any more, no matter what he does.

As if to reinforce that fact, the family portraits line the walls, including one of the late general himself, staring sternly down at us. A group of men, immaculate in army uniform, who carried the general's coffin into the church, stand by the fireplace, drinking whiskies.

'Do you think he'd approve?' I say to Alexander, who is sipping a whisky next to me during a rare break in the steady stream of people offering condolences.

A brief and bitter smile crosses his lips when he looks up at the portrait. 'He'd probably think it was a lot of bloody fuss over nothing, while scrutinizing every detail to make sure it was all done correctly.'

'I can imagine that. I'm also not sure he'd be too pleased that I was here.'

'Tough. *I* want you here and that's all that matters. Anyone who doesn't like it can go to hell.' Then his bravado slips a little and he lowers his voice. 'Emma's taken to her room. I know she's upset, and I don't blame her for not wanting to face this, but people are asking where she is. I'd go up and try to persuade her but I can't leave everyone . . . Do you think you might be able to get her down here?'

I'm taken aback. 'I'll try if you think it would help but she doesn't know me.'

'That's exactly why she might listen to you. I know

it's a lot to ask but if you don't mind at least giving it a go?'

Actually, it seems a small thing compared to what he's gone through but I still hesitate. 'If she kicks me out, and I wouldn't blame her if she does, don't be too hard on her, will you?'

He stiffens. 'Of course I won't. I've no intention of turning into my father, in any way.'

I soften and squeeze his hand. 'I'll give it a go, then.'

As I climb the staircase up to Emma's bedroom, I can't think which is the trickier task. I already needed my father's diplomatic skills to greet a bunch of mourners who are variously hostile and incredulous. Now I'm on a mission to persuade a devastated teenager to find her stiff upper lip and do her duty. I'm only five years older than Emma Hunt; what the hell can I do?

I pause outside the door, before knocking gently. 'Hello.'

'Go away.'

Great start. I knock again. 'It's Lauren.' Then I stand back, half expecting the door panel to shake as some object is thrown against it. Instead, I hear a low thump and eventually the door opens a crack and a face peers around the edge of the jamb. Two dark eyes, ringed with smudged mascara, peer at me like I've come to arrest her.

'I'm not coming down.'

I shrug. 'Fine. I just came to see how you are.'

She narrows her eyes suspiciously. 'Did Alex send you?'

'Yes.'

'Why didn't he come himself?'

'He wanted to but he's a little busy right now.'

She sniffs, then opens the door wider. 'Well, you can come in but don't think you can persuade me to come down and be nice to that bunch.'

'I won't.' As I say it, I mentally cross my fingers although I *have* actually told the truth. I really don't think I can persuade this determined girl to do anything she doesn't want to and, frankly, I don't blame her.

She closes the door behind me. Despite its obvious grandeur and the opulence of the furniture, it's still a young woman's room – not too far from what mine was like a few years back. The carpet is scattered with clothing and books, the dressing table almost obscured by make-up, costume jewellery and assorted 'stuff'. There's a dressmaker's dummy in the window, with an elaborate work in progress made up of gold brocade, purple velvet and black netting.

A laptop whirrs softly amid the crumpled bedcovers and discarded Kleenex, and the framed *Vogue* posters on the walls are in stark contrast to the Victorian prints of be-ribboned little girls with spaniels. At some point not too very long ago, Lady Emma Hunt stopped being Daddy's little girl.

She folds her arms and stands by the bed, as if I might try and drag her downstairs.

'I can't face all of this.'

'I don't blame you. I can't face them either. Can I sit down? These boots are killing me.'

She looks almost shocked, which I think is a good thing, then shrugs. 'If you like. Just sweep that stuff on to the floor.'

I lift an armful of dresses, a hat and a dog-eared Latin grammar tome off the dressing-table stool and place it on the carpet. Emma flops down on the bed and glares at me. Oh yes, she is definitely a Hunt. 'Go on then, what does Alex have to say?'

'That he'd like you to come and speak to people. Aunt Celia has been asking after you . . .'

She wrinkles her nose. 'Then I'm definitely staying upstairs.'

'I know it must be hard but people expect you to be there.'

'I don't give a toss what they expect.'

'Just for today, can you try and pretend you do?'

She gulps back a sob. Shit, I feel so bad about doing this but I also happen to think Alexander is right. 'I can't. I don't know most of them, and those I do are horrible.'

She snorts, and I have to admit I'd struggle to name anyone who I particularly warmed to, outside of the staff and a few friends, like Angus. I'm not sure what I can do to try to help this poor girl, or what to expect next, when she changes the subject and begins to look slightly less miserable.

'I like your boots.'

I resist the urge to do a jaw drop at this hairpin turn of conversation and instead wiggle my black suede toes, like a lure on one of my dad's fishing rods. Subterfuge is not one of my strong points but if it gets her out of her room . . .

'Prada, are they?' she asks.

'Chloé.'

'I suppose you bought them especially for Dad's funeral?'

'As a matter of fact, I did.'

She nods in satisfaction. 'At least you're honest. I bet every woman here has hit the shops for new stuff. Did you see that bony blonde with the big black hat and the Mafia sunglasses?'

'Blondes. What can you expect?'

She stares at me, looking worried, and then giggles. 'Oh, I don't mean *you*, of course. You don't count and you are incredibly pretty. I can see *exactly* why Alexander is so keen on you. I mean, as for Cousin Tom's new Russian girlfriend, someone should tell her this isn't the fucking *Sopranos* and why was she in floods of tears? She's never even met my father!'

I *think* I'm meant to be highly honoured by her conclusions though I actually feel pretty embarrassed. She starts to snigger, as if she's laughing at her own joke about the Russian impostor, but then, to my horror, starts crying again. I walk to the bed and put my arm around her and she clings to me. Oh Jesus, how do

I deal with this? Is it selfish to wonder how I got myself the role of surrogate big sister? I rip a bunch of tissues out of the box on the bed and hand them to her, sitting at her side.

She blows her nose noisily, and then glares at me. 'You're not just some bimbo, of course, although when I first saw your picture on Alexander's laptop, I did wonder what you'd be like because you look so American and perfect. Then he got "mentionitis" about you and Talia said you were really very OK so I was willing to be open-minded.'

I listen to all this, trying not to laugh. Talia is the Hunts' head groom and one of my allies at Falconbury, along with Helen the housekeeper. I get on well with the servants.

'You must have a brain and some balls for my brother to get so worked up about you because, believe me, he could have *any* girl he wanted.'

'Gee, thanks.'

She lifts her hand to her mouth. 'Oh fuck. I didn't mean to be rude.'

I smile. 'I'm joking, Emma.'

'Oh, really?' Her eyes widen as if she just discovered an exotic new species in me. 'I didn't think Americans did irony.'

'Well, irony is this American's middle name.'

'You're funny . . .' She hesitates. 'And most of all, you're not that vile bitch Valentina. I am so glad she couldn't come today, or I might have had to push her into the grave.'

'I don't think she's quite that bad,' I say, playing the most reluctant devil's advocate on the planet. I'm also still processing the fact that I gave Alexander 'men-tionitis' and that he 'got worked up' over me.

'Bollocks! She's a witch. You do know she kicks Benny when Alexander's not around? I've seen her do it once and Talia's seen her hit him too.'

'I don't think she'll be making donations to the Dogs Trust any time soon . . .' I begin, not daring to let on I saw Valentina hit Benny with her riding crop before the hunt last term. However, my curiosity about Valentina is piqued and since we're talking now I decide to explore a little further.

'Alexander told me she couldn't make the funeral. Her grandfather's sick, isn't he?'

Emma snorts. 'Not *that* sick. I think it's all a lie. Val-entina just didn't want all this shit to deal with, and I'm delighted about that.'

Privately, I must admit I was far too thrilled for decency myself when I heard Valentina wasn't going to be here.

'Did you see the bouquet she sent? The thing was so huge they couldn't fit it in the hearse. I heard Rupert say it had been flown in from her place in Positano spe-cially and delivered by her own driver to the house. Typical of her to be way over the top.'

'I think I saw it outside the church.'

'Did you read her card?' Emma makes a fingers-down-throat gesture.

Actually, I did and the fulsome message attached made me cringe. 'I don't think I noticed it.'

There's a silence and I wonder whether to dare ask her to come down to the wake again when she springs up off the bed and stands opposite me, her arms folded again.

'Suppose I could try and stand it down there for a few minutes.' She stops. 'Mainly because I'm hungry and there'll be food soon. I don't want to ask the staff to bring me something up here. They're busy.'

I try not to look relieved and delighted. 'I'm starving too. We can go down together.'

'I need the loo first and I want to wash my face.'

While she visits the bathroom, I cross to the window where the half-finished outfit hangs limply from the dummy. Unlike the guest room, Emma's overlooks the side of the house and the stables. I suppress a shudder at the thought that this must remind her of her father's death; maybe she can even see the horse who threw him. She comes out a few minutes later, and with her pale face free of the mascara and dark lipstick, she's even more ethereally beautiful. She shares the same aristo good looks as Alexander while also not resembling him that much. I guess she takes after her mother, but even after a tour of Falconbury's galleries when I was last here, I can't recall seeing a portrait of Lady Hunt.

She shuffles awkwardly across the room and picks up a grey hoodie from the floor, with the words 'Though she be but little, she is fierce' on it. Well, at least, it's Shakespeare . . .

'Alexander won't care what I wear now, will he?'

I'm surprised she's bothered to ask – the purple crushed-velvet Goth coat she wore to the funeral attracted pursed lips from some of the older mourners. Personally, I thought it was in keeping with the whole High Gothic air of the village church and Falconbury itself. 'All he really cares about is you coming to support him,' I say, crossing my fingers she won't sneer or change her mind.

The relief in her eyes is obvious.

'I never set out to cause Daddy any trouble, you know. Or Alexander . . . It just sort of happened . . .' She lifts her huge dark eyes to mine, and looks younger than her years and the picture of innocence, like some pre-Raphaelite heroine. So why do my antennae twitch?

'You haven't caused Alexander any trouble. Why would you think that?' I say.

'I don't know, really. Maybe you're right. I suppose I'm just being silly . . .' She flashes me a smile that turns into a grimace. 'Let's go and get this over with before I change my mind.'

Chapter Three

Heads turn as we enter the ballroom, where the waiting staff are laying out a buffet on long tables covered in white cloths. All my efforts persuading Emma to join the wake are made worth it by the look of relief and pleasure on Alexander's face.

'I'm glad you decided to come down,' he says.

Emma shrugs. 'I could smell food.'

Any frustration he may feel is well hidden and subtly, and he slips her hand in his. 'Thanks, anyway.'

When he squeezes her hand, Emma bites her lip, and I know she's fighting back tears. God, I want to cry again, remembering Alexander's arm around her at the graveside, him granite-faced and her quietly weeping into Alexander's handkerchief.

'Where's Benny?' I ask, in desperation to save Emma from any more tears.

Alexander replies as Emma dabs her eyes. 'He ran off towards the kitchens. I think he's hoping for some treats, wouldn't you say, Emma?'

She wipes a hand over her face and says, 'Any opportunity to steal food.'

Alexander is suddenly accosted by an older man in a spectacularly OTT uniform, who knits his bushy eyebrows together as he growls condolences at Emma and seems dumbfounded by me. I'm not sure what's disturbed him more: Emma's hoodie or my accent.

Emma rolls her eyes and steers me behind a huge aspidistra plant near a door in the panelling. 'Why do people have to have *so* much booze at a funeral? Helen was doing her nut about how many bottles of whisky Robert had ordered this morning,' she says, curling her lip at the mourners knocking back the drinks.

'I guess it gives people something to focus on and it's a horrible cold, damp day, and many of them have come a long way.'

'I wish they hadn't. I wish Dad could have a normal funeral like normal people, and not have all these hangers-on and strangers flooding the house. I hate it.'

'I can see what you mean, but your father was a well-known man. Lots of people want to pay their respects to him.'

'Respects? That's such a stupid phrase. They just want to be seen to be doing the right thing, and I'll bet not many of them truly respected him.'

'I think they probably did.'

'You didn't, did you? Alexander told me he behaved like a shit to you. That's what Dad was good at. Behaving like a shit, to me sometimes and to Alexander all the time.'

'I'm sure he didn't mean it.' She folds her arms and looks at me angrily so I qualify my claim, which I have to admit might have been over-generous to the general.

'I hardly knew him but from what Alexander told me, he loved you very much.'

'I suppose so.' She pouts but I guess I should cut her a whole load of slack today. And what do I know? I've no siblings, younger or otherwise, and at twenty-one, I've definitely no clue how to deal with a bereaved and angry teenager. That's Alexander's job, though God knows how he's going to do it. I don't think being in special forces will be much help.

The uniformed man has his hand on Alexander's arm.

'Yuk. Alex must want to barf. He fucking hates that man.'

Sure enough, Alexander has stepped away from the man and is standing stiff as a board. 'Is he an old army colleague of your father's?'

Emma stares at me and I half think she's going to laugh at my ignorance, which would be a change from the truculent pout. 'No. He's the Lord-Lieutenant.'

'I see,' I say, not seeing at all. At best, I'm a novice in the subtleties of English titles and picking up on my confusion, Emma decides to help me out – kind of.

'It's some boring ceremonial thing. I don't know what he actually does and I don't care. I bet Alex is desperate to get this whole thing over with. I know I am.'

She sounds bored but then I see her lip wobbling. 'Oh fuck, Aunt Celia's coming over. Please, can we get out of here?'

'I don't think we should, Emma.'

'Alex won't mind. You must hate it here just as much as me.'

'It's not my favourite way of spending a day, I'll admit, but your brother asked me to be here and I don't mind.'

She glares at me and despite her delicate, almost elfin features, the determined set of her chin reveals more than a hint of the Hunt stubborn streak. Alexander glances at us and I try to pour some oil on the troubled waters, not that I expect it to work.

'OK. Here's the deal. If you can stand to speak to Aunt Celia for half an hour, it would help out Alexander, and then I'll ask Alexander if it's OK for me to come out with you to take Benny for a walk. I don't think he'll mind that.' God, listen to me, speaking to Emma like she's about ten and I'm her mother, but the strategy seems to have worked.

'We can go into the stables.' Her face brightens. 'Talia keeps a stash of vodka in the office. Dad would never have it in the house and there's only whisky on offer today, which tastes like cat's piss to me. I fucking hate it.' There are a lot of things that Emma fucking hates today, but who can blame her? Following her father's coffin into church, listening to the eulogies and then standing by the grave while he was interred must have been the worst experience of her life, apart perhaps from when her mother died.

Aunt Celia bears down on us like a galleon in full sail. I've met her before and it didn't go well. Fortunately for me, and unfortunately for Emma, her attention is focused on her niece.

'Emma! You poor, poor darling. What you must be going through! Come here.' Emma is swamped in a mega-hug and I cringe on her behalf, but it gives me the chance to find Alexander, who's barely got a few yards from his original position. After grabbing two tumblers from a passing waiter, I wait patiently as he nods tersely to a couple I recognize from the ball. Eventually they walk away and I hand Alexander his glass.

'I thought you might need this.'

He blows out a breath. 'You have no idea.'

He drinks a good third in a couple of gulps, while I sip mine. It's probably some ludicrously expensive single malt but it still makes me shudder. If I could slip some of Immy's secret stash into my glass, I would do, but it's in my coat pocket in the hall cupboard. Alexander must have noticed my grimace. 'Sacrilege,' he says. His tone is sombre but there's a flicker of irony in his eyes that, strangely, encourages me.

He downs the rest of the tumbler and calls after one of the staff. 'Can you get me another of these, please? And make it a proper one, this time.'

The waiter nods and leaves, presumably to find the bottle.

He scans the room, frowning again. 'Where's Emma got to?'

I nod in Aunt Celia's direction. 'She's being consoled by your aunt.'

'God help her then, but at least she's left her bedroom. I don't blame her wanting to hide away but it would be better for everyone if she could stand to speak to a few people, even for a little while. They deserve that much from us.' He pauses then asks, 'I know she claimed she only came down because she was hungry but what else did you do to persuade her?'

Somehow, I don't think Alexander will understand that we bonded over a pair of boots. 'I don't know, but she can only stand so much more of this. She wants to leave again.'

He sighs. 'I can understand that, and I suppose she's made an effort.'

'She promised to stay a bit longer. I . . . uh . . . struck a deal with her.'

'What kind of deal?'

'I said I'd go out for a walk with her and Benny if she showed her face for half an hour. I hope that was OK.'

'It will have to be.' He touches my arm and his eyes tell me he's pleased. Even in the sombre suit and black tie, with a face that's grey with lack of sleep and grief, he looks pretty devastating. Is it wrong to stand here in the midst of such misery and want to make love to him? I think back to the way we leaped on each other when he came to my room at the start of term and forgive my rogue thought: there truly is nothing like sex to make you feel alive.

'I don't think I did much and she . . . er . . . feels that some comfort may be found in the stable block.'

He rolls his eyes and at first I think he's going to be angry with me, but then he sighs. 'Talia's cocktail cabinet . . . I might have guessed.'

'You know about it?'

'Everyone knows about it. The grooms are legendary for their parties. Can you make sure Emma doesn't get too pissed?'

Just then the waiter returns with a tumbler that's almost full to the top with whisky.

'What about you?'

'Oh, you can make sure I get absolutely pissed out of my mind.'

Robert, the butler, approaches. He's wearing traditional mourning dress like Anthony Hopkins in *The Remains of the Day* and I want to laugh but that's enough inappropriate thoughts for one funeral. Am I a bad person or have the nerves and tension got to me? It already feels like a very long day and it's only halfway through.

'Sorry to disturb you, my lord, but are you ready for us to announce lunch now?' he asks in a low voice.

'Of course, Robert, and thank you for all you've done so far. I don't know how we'd have managed without you and Helen. I'll thank the rest of the staff personally when this is all over but can you please pass on my appreciation in the meantime?'

Robert strikes me as a man who would rather die than blush, but even he struggles to hide his surprise and pleasure at this praise, which I'm guessing was not so forthcoming from General Hunt. 'It's a privilege to be of help to the family, sir.'

This statement is delivered without a trace of irony, and it hits me again that the Hunt staff seem genuinely to like and respect Alexander and Emma. I can't feel cynical about it, even though the whole 'serving' thing may seem ludicrously outdated in the twenty-first century. Robert lingers, as if he wants to say more, but can't find the words.

'I don't like to trouble you with this, sir, not today, but there's been a man on the house phone for you. I told him it was the funeral and he apologized but he did ask if you might call him as soon as you could. I think it's someone from the regiment. Said his name was Armitage.'

Alexander purses his lips in frustration. 'You did right to tell me. Excuse me,' he says to me and strides towards the door to the hallway. So the regiment are on the phone already, even today. I wonder how Alexander can possibly cope with studying for his master's, running Falconbury and his work. I'm still not sure whether he's in special forces or military intelligence, but whatever it is, I hope the army will give him compassionate leave for a while. What happens after that time, I don't know. He's always made it clear he wouldn't give up the service to run Falconbury. He and his father conducted their own personal war over the issue. I have no idea where that leaves him now.

After another attempt at the whisky, I swap my half-full glass for some orange juice and catch a glimpse of Angus's curly head. He's one of Alexander's more human friends, a lively, funny Scottish doctor. I first met him at a masked ball before I started seeing Alexander properly. Warmth rises to my cheeks when I also remember reeling with Angus at the Falconbury hunt ball. I'd had far too much to drink and I think I may have practically dragged Angus on to the floor. He had to leave later to attend an urgent call at the hospital. I'm not proud of what happened after that with another friend of Alexander's.

Emma is helping herself to some food from the buffet table and my stomach rumbles a little. Before I can join the line at the table, Rupert appears at my side. If I ever want to curb my appetite, I only have to look at him.

'So you decided to grace us with your presence again?' he sneers.

It was only a matter of time, I suppose, yet his proximity still makes the hairs stand up on the back of my neck, and not in a good way. How I want to wipe that arrogant smug expression from his face, but I keep my voice cool. 'I can't believe you'd want to create any more trouble for Alexander on a day like this.'

'I've no intention of causing trouble for my cousin. My aim is to make his life easier.'

'That would make a change.'

The smell of his cologne assaults my nose and there's

something feral about the glint in his eyes. 'I come in the spirit of reconciliation, since you and Alexander are so obviously an item again,' he says.

'He asked me to support him today; I came. That's all.'

He sniggers. 'So you'll be leaving as soon as the wake is over?'

'That's none of your business.'

'On the contrary, anything that may affect Alexander's ability to make decisions is my business. My father's an executor of General Hunt's estate.'

I'd sure like to execute Rupert right now. 'I was aware of that.'

His forehead creases in surprise.

'Alexander told me,' I add, with a smile of triumph. So much for vowing not to spar with Rupert today, but the guy must be the most obnoxious man in England, and he's on a mission to rile me in any way possible.

He arches his eyebrows dramatically. 'Well, well. You two are even closer than I thought.'

So many replies to this remark crowd into my head, but the truth is, even I can't work out which of them is true. 'This really isn't the time.'

'Oh, I don't know, I thought any time is the right one for Lauren Cusack. You seem to take advantage of every opportunity.'

'Well, you know me. Anything in pants, or in Angus's case, a skirt. Or rather, anything human in pants, which kind of rules you out.' I joke, while seething inside.

'Oh, I think you're doing rather well, without adding me to your tally. Let me see, Alexander, Angus, Henry Favell and that American I saw you with in the pub . . .' He ticks off the names on his fingers. 'Four men in one term is going some, although I suppose a girl as stunning as you only has to snap her fingers to pick up whomever she wants. However, I *did* think you might have had better taste than Favell. You do know that Alexander can't stand him since he shagged Emma?'

'What?' He tuts loudly and my stomach turns over at the revelation about Favell. *No wonder* Alexander was so monumentally pissed at me flirting with him at the ball.

'So you don't know everything about the Hunts? I expect sweet and innocent young Emma was dazzled by the force of Henry's personality. Fortunately for her – and him – once Henry got wind that Alexander was on his case, he turned all honourable and dropped Emma like a hot brick.'

'When was this?'

'Last summer. Emma's seventeen now, of course, but Henry's two years older than Alexander and me. You see, no matter what you think of me, even I wouldn't sink so low as to screw a sixteen-year-old.'

If he thinks I'm going to compliment him on his chivalry, he can take a hike, but at least I can console myself that Emma's no longer seeing Henry Favell. I also hadn't realized she'd had a birthday over the vacation.

'Are you saying that you and Alexander warned Henry off last year?'

Rupert smirks. 'It's a good thing that Alexander has some friends with his family's best interests at heart, don't you think? Lucky for Henry too, that someone warned him to keep away from Emma, otherwise, I think Mr Favell might now be talking in a very squeaky voice.'

My throat clogs with embarrassment at the memory of my drunken slow-dance with Henry Favell at the hunt ball, inspired, of course, by Alexander's flirting with Valentina. I spot Emma a few yards away, a forlorn figure drowning in a sea of sympathy. General Hunt, Alexander, Henry . . . it seems as if everyone had some kind of plan for her, both well intentioned and otherwise. No wonder she kicks against the traces so hard; however, in Henry's case, I think maybe Alexander's done the right thing.

'You have so much to learn about us,' says Rupert.

'I have to go. Emma needs me.'

He mimes applause. 'My, you really have wormed your way into the heart of the family, haven't you? But be careful what you wish for, Lauren, because if you threaten them, hell hath no fury like a Hunt scorned.'

I shake my head at him sadly. 'Get a life, Rupert, and stop trying to live Alexander's.'

I may have turned my back on him but inside I'm a little shaky from the confrontation. I can handle bitchiness and ignorance but Rupert's constant barbs come with an edge of malevolence. I'm not sure if he hates me because he wants to sleep with me – or possibly with Alexander – or because he just can't stand the idea of an 'outsider' playing any part in the future of Falconbury. Not that I have any ambitions whatsoever in that direction; I don't even know what will happen between Alexander and me tomorrow, let alone beyond. I also have no intention of telling Rupert any of this.

As I make my way over to Emma, she detaches herself from a group of relatives with barely a goodbye and I wince inwardly. I really don't want to be seen to be taking her over and I don't know why she sees me as some kind of ally, but I can't abandon her.

She holds out her plate. 'Would you like a pork pie? Dad loved them.'

'I . . . um . . . thanks.' Pastry wrapped around pig isn't really my thing but I don't want to offend Emma.

'I've survived half an hour. Can we get out of here now?'

I swallow down a lump of the pie. 'I'd like to let Alexander know we're going out.'

'Why? No one will miss us.'

'They may not miss *me* but you're a different matter. Can you possibly bear to stay a bit longer?'

She looks like the sky just fell in on her, which actually it has, to all intents and purposes. 'Do I have to?'

'You don't *have* to but it would be a massive help to Alexander.'

She considers for a moment, then nods haughtily.

'For Alex, I'll do it, but I want to get Benny in here as a distraction.'

I'm worried that if she leaves the room, she won't come back. 'Sounds like a great idea but why don't we get Helen to fetch him? Look, she's just over there.'

We catch Helen's eye and she gives in instantly to Emma's request, grateful I think that she's even emerged from her room. A few minutes later, Benny races into the ballroom, claws skittering on the parquet and tail wagging joyously in flagrant disregard of the sombre mood. Ignoring the mixed reception of smiles and frowns from the mourners tucking into the buffet, he makes a beeline for Emma. She sinks to her knees and throws her arms around his neck while he licks her face. I kneel down to ruffle his ears.

'Hey there, boy.'

When I look up, Alexander is crossing the room towards us, glass in hand. His face is sombre but then Benny scents him and homes in like a heat-seeking missile.

'Down, boy!'

Benny drops to his haunches instantly and gazes up in adoration at his master, tongue lolling. People have lost interest now and gone back to their food and networking. I drop to the floor and stroke Benny's ears while he licks Alexander's free hand, and Emma dutifully accepts the condolences of someone I've never seen before. I can see she's struggling not to cry but at least she's here.

'Emma wanted him here while everyone had lunch. I hope it was OK.'

'It's fine.' He sounds weary, as if he no longer cares about anything. I wonder if his phone call has made his day even worse.

I watch him carefully. 'You OK?'

He keeps his eyes on the dog. 'I don't really know. I don't feel anything,' he says quietly. 'And I intend not to feel anything for the rest of the day.'

An hour or so later, I clap my gloved hands together as we walk out of the woods and down the slope that leads to the stable block at the side of Falconbury. Benny sniffs at a tree stump and roots under the fallen leaves. At least someone is happy at Falconbury.

'Are you sure you want to walk by the stables?' I ask, still unsure that visiting somewhere so closely associated with General Hunt's death is such a great idea. 'It's getting cold.'

Emma's face falls. 'Don't you want to get a proper drink?'

'Yes, but we've been out over an hour. Maybe we should get back. Alexander might need you . . .'

'Oh, he'll just be glad I've not run away or killed myself. He won't mind you being out here and you must be happy to have avoided the rest of my relatives. Look! There's Talia. Let's go and get a drink.'

Benny barks happily when he spots – or sniffs – Talia,

the Hunts' head groom, who greets all three of us with a hug.

'Good to see you back,' she says as Emma roots at the back of a battered filing cabinet in a closet at the side of the stable office. 'I'd heard rumours that you and Alexander had split up, so I'm glad it was only gossip.'

I don't know how to reply but luckily Emma lets out a shriek of delight and appears at the closet door, holding up a bottle of Stolichnaya. 'I knew it. Got any tonic?'

'This isn't the Met Bar, you know.' Talia softens and shakes her head. 'I think there's some cranberry juice in the staff fridge.'

Emma skips up the stairs that lead to the kitchen above the offices.

'I'm surprised she wanted to come here, after what happened.'

'Jesus, I know. I was on duty that day. I tacked the general's horse up.'

'God, I'm sorry.'

Talia shudders. 'I've beaten myself up ever since in case I did something wrong, but the Master said there was nothing wrong with the tack. It was just one of those things.'

'It wasn't Calliope, was it?' I ask, goose bumps rising on my skin when I remember my own experience on the weekend of the ball. A bird scarer caused my horse to bolt and nearly threw me while I was hacking around the estate with Alexander.

'No, it was a stallion . . .' Talia looks down at her boots as if she might burst into tears, then she glances back at me and throws on a forced smile. 'Valentina didn't turn up, then?' she says. 'I was holding the fort here or I'd have come to the church.'

'No. Some kind of family illness kept her in Italy.'

Talia snorts. 'Typical! She'll wait until the dirty stuff is over, but she'll be here, I'd bet my job on it. There's no way she'll miss the opportunity to sink her claws into him now he's in charge of Falconbury. Watch out.'

I manage a tight smile because I really like Talia and I suspect everything she says about Valentina is true, but I don't want her or anyone to think I'm in some kind of battle to claim Alexander. I don't even know what's going to happen after today, and it bothers me that everyone we've met assumes he and I are an item again.

Emma brings out three glasses of cranberry and the bottle on an old tray.

'Will you join us?' I ask.

Talia grimaces. 'Love to but I'm working. Horses need looking after even when their owner has died. I'll have some juice but I can't stay long.' We chat about the horses for a while and it makes a welcome change from other subjects, then the ring of hooves reaches us from outside in the yard. Talia downs her juice. 'Sorry, have to go. That's one of the hunters back from his exercise and I want to see how his leg is doing.'

After Talia has gone, Emma flops down on the seat next to me and finishes her vodka.

'Want another?'

'I'm fine, thanks.'

She looks around the office and sighs. 'Alex is almost as bad as Daddy is . . . was.'

'Oh come on, you know that's not true. He supports what you want to do at uni.'

'He's told you I want to go to Saint Martins? There's a theatrical costume design course there I want to get on. I've applied but Daddy wanted me to have a gap year and try for Oxford. I got As in my Latin and Greek GCSEs but I hate them both. I love my Art and Drama classes, even though Daddy said they were a waste of time.'

It's on the tip of my tongue to tell her that the general had, possibly, relented on her plans to go to Saint Martins. It's not my news to share but I'll ask Alexander to tell her. Maybe it will give her some comfort.

'I wish I could be a groom.'

'I thought you wanted to be a costume designer.'

'Oh, I *do* but what I really meant was that I'd love to be like Talia.'

'Instead of what?'

'Instead of being on show all the time, like today. If Dad had been a normal person, we could have had a few people round the house or a wake at a pub and it wouldn't be in the papers and no one would expect me, or Alex, to be polite to everyone and act all stiff-upper-lipped when what we really want to do is shout and scream and tell them all to leave us alone so we can howl the place down.'

I try to picture Alexander doing just that and can't.

'They'll be gone soon. You can shout and scream then.'

She pushes her empty glass away from her. 'I don't want to do it now. I just want us to be together, Alex and me.' She looks at me. 'You can stay too. He really likes you, you know.'

I cover my awkwardness by drinking my vodka.

Emma jumps up before I've finished it. 'Shall we go into the stables?'

'If you like.' I don't know whether her restlessness is normal for her or she worries that if she keeps still for too long, she might think about what's happened.

Benny stays in the yard while we walk between the stalls. It's warm and the air is full of the sharp tang of horse, hay and dung. Emma stops outside Harvey's stall and strokes his muzzle.

'Hello, Harvey.'

I rub his nose. He was the horse I was supposed to ride on my hack but Valentina took him out, leaving me with the flighty Calliope.

'Where's Calliope?' I ask.

'On loan to the Huntmaster's daughter,' says Emma. 'She's going to be an Olympic eventing star and can handle her. Alex suggested it to Talia. I heard what happened to you.'

'It's OK. I was fine.'

'Alex said you could have been killed. He told Dad that Calliope was dangerous.' Emma pauses. 'Alex has already given away the stallion that threw Dad. It wasn't the horse's fault but Alex didn't want him here any more.'

'I can understand that.'

Emma turns to me, her lip trembling. 'I still can't believe he's gone.'

'No, I guess you can't.'

'At least Dad won't have to worry about me any more, though, will he?'

It seems an odd thing to say. 'All parents worry. They're hard-wired to. Trust me, mine do and I'm out of their hair altogether.'

'Yes, but I'm sure you haven't done anything to worry them like I have.'

I laugh. 'You think? I split up with a guy they thought was perfect for me last summer and I ignored their pleas for me to stay and study in the States.' I could add that I followed that up by getting involved with her brother, a troubled, difficult, arrogant guy who has cost me more sleepless nights in a few months than I've had in the rest of my whole life. Many of them were intensely pleasurable, however.

'Bet you never got threatened with expulsion from school.' Emma's voice cuts into my happier memories.

'Well, no . . .'

'Or threatened to leave? Or smoked weed on the

battlements? Or got so pissed outside a club that your friends had to carry you into the taxi?'

'I can't say that happened but I've had my moments at university.' A few hazing ceremonies spring to mind. Mine involved skinny-dipping in the fountains outside one of the faculty buildings at Brown, but I think I'll keep that to myself also.

'I bet you were never almost caught shagging someone in the cricket pavilion,' says Emma. I'm not sure whether she's trying to provoke me into my own confession or trying to shock me.

'We didn't play cricket at my school,' I say with mock solemnity. 'However, we do have a summerhouse at home.' I recall having sex in it with Todd, my ex, during my grandmother's birthday party. I'd forgotten about that.

'Alexander would kill me if he found out. He'd definitely kill the boy.' Emma has ignored me and her eyes throw down a challenge. She clearly wants to share something.

'He might be pissed off about the expulsion and the drinking but he's no need to know about this boy,' I say carefully.

'Yes, but it was Henry Favell, and Alexander can't stand him.'

I daren't reveal that Rupert has already told me this, and I feel sorry for her with so many other people interfering in her life, even if they think it's for a good reason. Thank goodness she's stopped sleeping with him. Thank goodness she doesn't know he tried to get me into bed during the hunt ball.

'I . . . um . . . This was some time ago, though, I'm guessing? Why would Alexander be mad at you now?'

She says the next words to Harvey, as if that makes it OK. 'Henry told me that Rupert and Alex had threatened to nail his balls to the wall if he carried on seeing me. I was *so* mad at Alex I almost left school there and then to get revenge on him! Henry did leave for a while, but' – she gives a little smile, nurturing the secret she just shared – 'we've started seeing each other again. He took me to the Ivy when I was last in London and he rented a room.'

I feel physically sick at this news. Why, why, *why* do I have to be the one to hear Emma's confession? Why *now*?

'You won't tell him, will you?' Suddenly there's panic in her voice. 'You're the only person who knows about us apart from a couple of girls at school. Alex really would kill Henry. He's never liked him and I know he doesn't trust him.'

'I'm sure he wouldn't *actually* kill him,' I say, although I'm not confident there wouldn't be some kind of physical pain involved. Henry's fate doesn't bother me; but Emma's does. Should I tell her that Henry hit on me at the ball? Oh help, was she actually dating him back then? Because if so, she has no idea what a slimeball he truly is.

'Don't say a word!'

'I won't tell him.'

'Promise me!' She grabs my arm.

'I promise, but maybe you should be . . . um . . . careful. Maybe Alex has a point.'

'Don't you start too. I thought I could trust you. I love Henry, and it's none of Alex's business.'

Emma also has a point; no matter what Alexander thinks of Henry, she has a right to see him. However, after my one encounter with him, I side with Alexander. He's a charming, manipulative bastard who'd do anything to get what he wants and now that Emma is, I assume, a very wealthy young woman, he might well be even more interested.

'It's none of my business either, but Alexander would never do anything to hurt you, I'm sure.'

'I know and I do love him to bits most of the time but he thinks he knows what's best for me. Just like Daddy did.' Her eyes glisten dangerously. 'Don't tell me to stop seeing him. Not now. I need him.'

This statement is heartrending and from the wobble in her voice, I think she really means what she says, which is even more tragic. Deciding that now is definitely not the moment to shatter her already fragile heart, I give her a hug. 'Come on, let's go back inside. Most people will have gone by now, with any luck.'

Chapter Four

The chandelier has been lit in the ballroom, making it seem darker outside than it actually is. The fire still glows in the hearth but it's growing chilly despite the heating. Our voices echo because almost all of the mourners have gone. A few closer relatives lingered after I got back with Emma but they've gone too. Finally, the room is almost empty and we're standing by the door, as Alexander kisses Aunt Celia goodbye and almost passes out from her floral fragrance. A few of the catering staff bustle about collecting glasses and plates.

After smiling politely during countless glances and remarks about Americans, I suddenly feel tired, and Emma's 'secret' is an added burden I never asked for. I know Alexander would hit the roof if he found out and that kind of news is the last thing he needs now. Fingers crossed, Emma will get bored with Henry Favell, or he'll think better of chasing her. I just hope she doesn't get hurt too badly.

Rupert approaches, knocking back the remains of his whisky.

'I'm off, then.' He embraces Alexander in a way I've never seen him do before, which makes me suspect it's for my benefit. 'If you need me, you know where I am.'

'Thanks.' Alexander's eyes seem a little glazed.

Rupert turns to me, ultra polite. 'Can I give you a lift anywhere, Lauren?'

'Thank you so much for the offer, Rupert, but I'll take care of myself.'

'She's shtaying.' Alexander slings his arm around my back and hugs me to his side. 'Aren't you, Lauren?'

I smile at Rupert. 'If you want me to.'

Alexander glances down at me, puzzlement in his eyes, although that could, of course, be the whisky. 'Of coursh I do.'

'In that case,' says Rupert, pulling on a pair of black leather gloves, 'I'll leave you to console each other.'

What a toad he is. Who else would use a funeral to score points off his own cousin, who's supposedly his 'best' friend too? Alexander, however, is wrapped in a fug of Lagavulin and hasn't noticed the irony in Rupert's remarks. Actually, in his state, I don't think Alexander would notice irony if it hit him over the head.

'Robert will show you out . . .' he says, tightening his arm around my back. I think he needs the support.

'There's no need. I think I know my way out of Falconbury by now.'

As Alexander turns away to pick up his glass, Rupert shoots me a glance of pure venom that makes me shiver inside, but I smile sweetly and give him a little wave. 'Goodnight. Have a safe journey, Rupes.'

*

A few hours later, Emma has gone to her room and Alexander slumps in the deep buttoned armchair in the library, staring into the embers of the fire. His black tie is unknotted and the top button of his shirt is open. I've been curled up in the chair next to him, trying to catch up on some reading for college. No one wanted dinner in the dining room, so the staff brought a tray of buffet leftovers into the library. I was starving but Alexander hardly touched anything, preferring his whisky.

The door creaks as Robert enters and places a tray with a fresh bottle of whisky, a jug and two glasses on the table between our chairs. 'I brought some water too . . .' he says, eyeing Alexander apprehensively. 'Can I get you anything else, sir? Some more food? Helen could make you an omelette or a fresh sandwich? What about some coffee?'

'Coffee? What would I want coffee for? I don't know about Lauren.' He flaps a hand in my general direction.

I give Robert a tight smile. 'I'm good, thanks.'

'Call me if you need anything.' Robert seems to direct this offer at me and I mouth a 'thanks' at him.

The door closes with a soft click as Alexander reaches for the bottle.

'See thish?' he says, ripping off the seal. 'This is a Glen Moray from the 1960 vintage.' He screws the paper into a tiny ball and flicks it at the fire but it falls short. 'It was bottled in 1988, the same year I was born.'

He unscrews the cap and sloshes the contents first

into one glass and then another, leaving a tiny puddle of amber pooling on the silver tray.

My head has started to throb. 'Not for me, thanks.'

He frowns, his eyes full of hurt. 'You have to try it. You have to drink it *now*, or when will you? Who knows when "when" will be. Here . . .'

The tumbler trembles a little as he hands it to me and leans over, his breath reeking of whisky. He's off his face already but who can blame him?

He holds the glass in front of him, and the crystal and amber liquid glisten like jewels in the firelight. I cradle mine in my hands and he sniffs the glass, takes a sip and leans back against the chair, with a dramatic sigh.

'Now isn't that the best fucking thing you've ever tasted?' He looks at me lustfully. 'Apart from me, of course.'

I take a sip and try to look as if I'm enjoying it for his sake, although by now I'm just wishing he'd stop drinking.

'I'm no whisky buff but I'll admit that it's good.'

'*Good?* Is that all you can say about a bottle of whisky that costs a grand?'

'I don't care how much it costs,' I say.

He laughs, and tosses back a third of the measure, which was generous in the first place. 'My father would have a blue fit, if he saw me glugging it down like lemonade,' he says, with a bitter laugh. 'He'd hit the roof.'

'Perhaps he wouldn't mind so much in the circumstances.'

'In the circumstance of him being dead?' I flinch a little as he raises his voice, then he seems to realize he's almost shouted and lowers it again. 'I *knew* him. I knew – fucking lived – every one of his moods while I was here. You know, he told me he'd bought this to celebrate me being born, but he never opened it for some reason. God knows why, he was obviously waiting for something more momentous than that.'

'Maybe he just forgot it was in the cellars . . .' I say, trying to deflect his rising anger.

He looks in my direction, but I get the impression he doesn't really care who I am any more. 'Maybe,' he says truculently, briefly reminding me of Emma.

'Or he might have been saving the bottle for you.'

'Why would I merit something so infinitely more precious to him as *this*?' He holds up the glass again and drinks it all down. Then he starts laughing, really loudly like I've just made some hysterically funny barrack-room joke. I put my glass down, wondering if I dare fetch Robert. I just hope Alexander passes out very soon before he can get alcohol poisoning.

He downs the rest of the glass and while I haven't been counting, I figure he must have had close on a bottle of whisky already today. How the hell am I going to stop him drinking himself into oblivion? Should I even try after what he's gone through?

He pats his lap and his eyes are hungry with lust. 'Why don't you come and sit here?'

'I was thinking of going to bed.'

'Why bother with a bed?'

'Robert might come in,' I say keeping my tone light. 'And I'm sure you don't want to be caught shagging by the staff.'

'Personally, I don't care but I'll lock the door if it bothers you.'

He gets up, or rather staggers out of his seat. I jump up and steady him with my arm around his back. 'You're pissed,' I say.

'Pished?' He tries to mimic my accent. At least I think that's what he's trying to do.

'Do you want to go and sleep?'

'No. I want to fuck you.'

He may be too drunk to stand, but he's still incredibly strong and when he half topples, half sits back down in the armchair, I overbalance and fall into his lap. As I get my breath back, our eyes lock. His breath smells like a distillery as he kisses me and his mouth is hard against mine. Drunk he may be, but I can feel how much he wants me. Besides, he can't drink and have sex with me at the same time so this is for his own good, I try to kid myself.

His hand is on my thigh, pushing up my skirt. 'Alexander, I don't think this is the greatest idea.'

'I do. If you hadn't noticed, I've had quite a day and I need to forget it.' He pulls my skirt up and his hand snakes between my legs. I'm turned on, even though he's drunk and someone might come into the room. I make a pitiful attempt to stop him, clamping my fingers around his wrist, but despite the whisky, he's strong and I *can't* lie, I want him too. It's been a hell of day for me too and I find myself kissing him back, my sheer lust for his body obliterating everything else. He tugs my blouse impatiently out of my skirt and his hands are all over my back, fumbling with my bra strap.

He frowns at me. 'What the –'

'It's front-fastening.'

He pulls his hand from my blouse and starts to attack the buttons.

'Hey . . .' I reach for his hand but it's too late and one of my buttons pings off and bounces off something as he almost tears my blouse open. I moan with pleasure as he snaps the fastening of my bra open and bares my breasts.

Something in his eyes changes and he reaches for the bottle from the table.

'Hey, no!'

He lifts the bottle pours several hundred dollars worth of single malt over my breasts.

'Alexander!' My cry is loud as my white blouse turns amber and the whisky runs down my cleavage. 'What are you doing?'

'This.' His mouth descends on my chest and he starts licking the whisky from my breasts. He closes his mouth around my nipple, sucking it hard, and I cry out in pain and pleasure. I push my breasts together into his face and, for a second, I think I can hear voices outside the door but they move on. I'm past caring anyway; this feels like the wickedest thing I've ever done. It's so, so wrong, so why do I want him more than I've ever done?

I climb off his lap and pull my panties down. His eyes devour me and he starts to fumble with the zip on his trousers.

I throw my panties on the sofa and close my hand over his. 'Here, let me.'

I loosen the knot on his tie and pull it over his head, trying to blot out the fact I'm about to have sex with a man in mourning clothes.

Alexander leans back against the chair, his hands hanging limply over the edge of the armrests, with his trousers around his thighs. He licks his lips as I strip off my whisky-stained blouse and shimmy out of my skirt. I climb into his lap and straddle him, and he rests his hands lightly on my waist.

I kiss him softly, savouring the bittersweet malt on his lips. When I stop, he looks at me. 'Lauren?'

'Uh-huh?'

'I loved him, you know. Despite the fact he was an awkward sod and he blamed me for my mother's death. I did actually love the old bastard.'

'I know,' I say.

'And from now on, I think we should be honest with each other. No more shecrets.'

'No more shecrets, eh?'

'No. I think we should be absholutely honest with each other.'

'Absholutely honest?'

72

'Are you laughing at me?' I think he's trying to intimidate me but it's more glazed than glare.

'I wouldn't dream of it.' Boy, am I glad he probably won't remember any of this in the morning, after what Emma confided in me earlier.

'Close your eyesh . . .' he says and I obey, happy to move on from a tacit agreement I can't keep and he probably has no intention of so doing.

His breathing gets louder as I wait for him to kiss me again or touch my breasts. I clench my bottom and wriggle against his thighs, still waiting. When nothing happens, and his hands drop from my waist, I open my eyes. His lashes flutter once or twice against his cheek before he passes out cold.

Getting dressed was simple; getting Alexander's trousers zipped up again wasn't. I'd half hoped he'd wake up but maybe it's far better he's unconscious and out of his misery temporarily. At least he still had his shirt on or I'd have had a hell of a time explaining that to Robert, because I had to call him in the end. There was no way I could get Alexander to bed and no way I wanted to leave him in that state all night. I'm not sure Robert believed my story that Alexander had spilled the whisky on me by accident.

After covering him up with a tartan rug – which I'm not sure Alexander will be too amused about when he wakes up – Robert offers to check up on him periodically so I can get some rest. I don't know when Robert gets any himself but I'm too exhausted myself to argue with the guy and anyway, he seems to consider it his duty.

I drag myself to the guest suite I had last time I stayed here and flick the light switch, expecting to find my bags on the bed.

'Miss Cusack?'

Helen walks into the room behind me.

'Hi, Helen. Do you know what happened to my bags?'

'They're in Lord Falconbury's room, miss.'

I can't believe this. 'I'm staying in the general's room?'

She smiles at me. 'No. You're staying in Alexander's room. He asked for your things to be moved in there while you were out for a walk with Lady Emma. Is that all right? I can move them back in here if you'd prefer.'

I blush, embarrassed at my mistake yet quietly delighted. 'No, thank you, Helen. Things are just fine as they are.'

So, the unthinkable has happened. An unmarried woman is sharing a room with a guy at Falconbury. The last time I was here, Alexander told me about the tradition, which I assume was enforced by his father, and even he agreed it was laughably old-fashioned, but neither of us wanted to rock the boat by complaining.

The room is even larger than the guest suite and, unsurprisingly, exudes masculinity. There's a sleigh bed that has to be six feet wide, a huge gentleman's chest of drawers and an oak wardrobe. The walls are panelled in dark oak like the guest room and the prints, predictably, are largely hunting and sporting scenes. What I didn't expect are the photographs – a dozen or more, framed in silver gilt, wood and brightly coloured plastic, all arranged on a large round table by the window.

There's a younger version of the general in one, leading a young Alexander on a Shetland pony, and one of the two children on a beach with fishing nets, on either side of their father. There are also two of Lady Hunt. I pick one up and look at the beautiful face that peers back at me. It's obviously a professional shot, taken in one of the rooms at Falconbury I presume. She can't be much older than me in the shot, and she's wearing a pearl necklace and earrings. I wonder if it was done as an engagement portrait.

I move on to another picture, a family snap of her and Alexander in the country, sitting next to a picnic basket. Alexander looks about ten. It can't have been long before the car accident that ended her life and from which Emma and Alexander were lucky to escape.

I replace it carefully and climb into his bed, wondering when – if – he'll join me.

I wake to the sun shining through the window and Alexander sitting on the edge of the bed. His eyes are red-rimmed with dark blotches underneath and his voice isn't so much cut glass as dragged over broken glass.

'That bad?' he growls as I stare at him.

I nod.

He manages a wry smile. 'I suspected as much but I'm avoiding mirrors this morning. I think I may have fallen asleep in the chair in the library. I was off my face last night.'

No shit, Sherlock. I sit up, wondering if he remembers exactly what he was doing before he passed out. 'It's OK. You'd had quite a day.'

'And a night. My head feels like it's under mortar fire. Helen greeted me at seven o'clock with a packet of paracetamol and a bacon sandwich.'

'And?'

'I needed the pills and I thought it was my duty to eat the bacon.' He grimaces. 'It's stayed put so far.'

'I'm surprised you haven't ended up in the ER.'

'It's probably a good thing you distracted me from the second bottle.' So, he *does* remember.

'As I recall, most of it ended up on us, not in you.'

His expression is stern, his voice rough. 'That was a very expensive bottle of scotch.'

'I know.'

'But I can't think of a better use for it,' he adds with the faintest of smiles, which sets my pulse racing again despite myself.

'No,' I agree. I wait for him to kiss me but he rubs his chin and sighs. 'I suppose I need a shower and a shave.'

'I'd like to take a bath. What time is it now?'

'Nearly ten.'

'Arghh. I missed breakfast again.'

'It's becoming a habit but don't worry, I missed it

too. How do you feel about getting out of here for some brunch? I existed on a liquid diet yesterday and the bacon sandwich won't keep me going long. I hear the full English is the only true cure for a hangover and I think we both need to get out of this house.'

'What about Emma?' I ask, remembering again, with a pang of worry, the confession she made to me. Should I tell him and risk making life even more difficult for Emma? Or am I making things worse by not telling him? Shit.

'She's going out with a friend while I see to the legal stuff but she'll be back tomorrow and I'll need to talk to her then. I'm not looking forward to it.' He lets out a breath. 'Do you mind walking into the village? I'm probably still over the limit and I need to clear my head before I deal with the lawyers later.'

While Alexander showers and I take a quick bath, I try not to panic too much about the fact I'm missing a seminar at the faculty later today. I managed to get my tute with Professor Rafe rearranged, and while he'd 'warned' me about getting involved with Alexander last term, he could hardly complain about me attending the funeral.

Yet he is my tutor and I really have to leave Falconbury on Sunday morning. Even if he wasn't pressuring me, I'd put pressure on myself to work hard and make the most of my master's. I only have one year here — with the vacations, it's less than six months. Much of my first week has been spent wondering how Alexander is.

77

I resolve to get some work done on my essay later while Alexander attends the reading of his father's will.

Wrapped up in a borrowed Barbour and Hunters, I tramp across the deer park to the village with Alexander, our breath misting in front of our faces. Alexander strides out, grabbing my hand and practically dragging me along and shooting out constant jibes about not being able to keep up with him. I have the feeling he'd like to put a million miles between him and Falconbury and never come back.

Even at a brisk pace, it takes over half an hour to reach the village from the house, and I don't think we've even left Falconbury land yet, but eventually Alexander pushes open the door of a tiny cafe in the centre of the village. On a January morning, the joint is hardly jumping, but there's a definite change in the atmosphere as we walk in. I get the impression they're amazed to see Alexander out at all, let alone with a strange girl. His shoulders are stiff as he thanks the cafe owner and one of the other customers for their condolences, but then he sets to devouring the plate of bacon, sausage and tomatoes, washed down with gallons of tea. I tuck into a smoked salmon and cream cheese bagel and some fresh juice.

We walk back to Falconbury at a much slower pace, Alexander stopping periodically to point out various landmarks to me, occasionally mentioning his father. He reminds me of Shakespeare's schoolboy, creeping like snail, unwillingly, to school. Our route back takes us up a hill with a round stone tower at the top. It looks like a folly to me, stuck in the middle of nowhere.

Finally, after a short, sharp climb, we reach the top. My breath comes in staccato bursts; I'm glowing with the effort.

'I really must do more running,' I say as Alexander stands with his hands on his hips, gazing over the view.

'The last time you went running, you know what happened,' he says reminding me of the start of last term when I tripped and sprained my ankle outside his house. I almost ended up in bed with him that day but I escaped.

'Maybe that's what I should do now. Run away from you . . .'

'Perhaps you should.' He keeps his eyes on the scene below us; the estate – his estate – is spread out in front of us, with Falconbury at the centre. 'But you won't.'

'Won't I?' He turns to face me. 'How can you be so sure?'

'Because you want me too much for that.'

I don't know whether to feel incensed at the return of his arrogance – or to secretly rejoice in it. He steps forward and flames me with a look. 'And I think we have unfinished business, Lauren.'

I couldn't agree more, but I also know that I arrived back here with such resolve to move on from the stormy relationship we had. This time I'm determined not to be a pushover. I'm here for him because of his father, I remind myself, and I'm not committing myself beyond that. 'It's cold out here,' I murmur, distracted.

'Then let's get inside. In fact, I'll race you back to Falconbury.'

'In these?' I point the toe of my wellington boot.

He folds his arms. 'Excuses already? I don't accept that from my men.'

'I'm not one of your men, if you hadn't noticed.'

He smiles. 'I need to make doubly sure and it will require you taking all your clothes off. Now come on! You're wasting your breath.'

Of course, I couldn't keep up with him. Not even if I was in Usain Bolt's golden spikes, maybe not even if I *was* Usain Bolt, could I have beaten him to the house but I have my own victory. I amble down the hill, waving at him as he stops a hundred yards ahead, hands on his hips, shaking his head at my refusal to play the game. Eventually, he walks back to me.

'You're no fun,' he says.

'Not at this game.'

His eyes flash. 'Is there another one you plan to play?'

'Maybe. If you're lucky.'

'I don't believe in luck.'

'Hey!'

My shriek as he sweeps me off my feet cuts through the still, cold air and I fling my arms around his neck to avoid falling, but after a few steps, he staggers, groans and I feel I'm slipping through his arms. He recovers just in time and lifts me back up to safety. I tighten my grip on his neck.

'Jesus, you almost dropped me!'

He grimaces, and seems to be breathing hard. 'I'm still hungover. Either that or you're heavier than I expected.'

'Youuuuu!'

The insult is snatched away as he sets off again, me in his arms, almost running now with no sign of the hangover whatsoever. I cling on for dear life as we get nearer to the ha-ha that separates the parkland from the gardens. It looms ahead, a deep hidden ditch. Surely he's not thinking of running down into it? I screw my eyes shut as he heads straight for it.

'Alexandeerrr!'

He stops and, gently, sets me on my feet. His forehead glistens and he really is breathing heavily now, but also grinning fit to burst.

'You really are the limit,' I say as he puts his arms around me. I don't know if it's the adrenaline or the endorphins but a bolt of lust hits me and when we kiss, and I push against him, he's rock hard for me through his jeans.

'Ready to play the other game you promised?' he asks.

'I never promised anything.'

'Whether you did or not, it's too late to back out now.' He lifts my hair off my face. 'Even if you wanted to.'

My skin prickles with anticipation and lust. 'Is that a threat, my lord?

'No, it's a bloody promise and if you call me that once more, I'll . . .'

'What?'

He folds his arms. 'Not take you to bed and shag you senseless.'

I hate – *really* hate – to admit it, but the state I'm in right now, a seething mass of sheer lust for him, I don't think I can face the prospect of being left alone to take care of things myself. Not that Alexander is going to make good on his promise, by the look and feel of him against my body.

He grabs my hand and we hurry over the little bridge that spans the ha-ha and down the path to a side door, grunting thanks to the few members of staff that greet him.

We run upstairs and finally he locks the door of his bedroom behind him.

'Is this the first time?' I ask.

'What for?'

'That you had a girl in here.'

'Rules are made to be broken,' he says. 'Now are you going to get your knickers off, or do I have to do it for you?'

I lick my lips. 'Oh, I think you're going to have to do it for me, my lord.'

I was half expecting it, but the speed at which I'm swept up and dumped on his bed snatches the breath from my body.

'I still have my boots on.'

'Not for long.' He pulls off the Hunters as I lie giggling on the bed. My jeans follow, and my knickers.

He kicks off his own boots and strips off sweater, shirt and jeans.

Wow. My throat is full.

I had forgotten.

Forgotten what the sight and smell and feel of his body did for me. But I'm remembering now, now that I have time to savour him, rather than fucking frantically with a desperate man or fumbling with a drunken one.

His shoulders are broad, his abs taut and hard, though he's somewhat leaner now than I remember. As for the scar . . . no matter how many times I see him naked, the angry white flesh on his shoulder fascinates and horrifies me. It reminds me that he's probably killed, and almost been killed himself, and I realize what I have taken on.

'Second thoughts?' he asks as he climbs, naked, on to the bed and plants his hands either side of my shoulders.

'Am I allowed any?'

'Like I said, you can't resist me.'

And I can't, not when he parts my knees and uses his mouth so skilfully to bring me to unconditional surrender. His tongue makes delicate little circles and flicks on me that have me clutching at the bedcovers and whimpering shamelessly. He blows gently on me and circles his thumb until I'm teetering on the brink of the mother of all climaxes.

Then he stops, climbs up my body and murmurs in my ear. 'I told you so.'

I can only moan in desperation. While I fist the

sheets, he settles himself between my legs and urges his way inside me in one smooth thrust.

'You're so tight, so wet, Lauren.'

I know this and I'm loving the way he fills me up, so much I can hardly take him even though I'm readier than I've ever been. Above me, his chest is still tinged with a summer tan, his eyes full of such intent as he drives in and out of me, in long, slow, deep thrusts that bury me into the mattress. It's not possible to be filled up any more but I want it anyway so I wrap my legs around his thighs and I dig my heels into his backside to drag him into me. Sensation builds again, radiating from my core through my limbs. His face is contorted in a kind of pain as he comes and it tips me over the edge after him, falling hard and fast.

Afterwards, I lie on my back, catching my breath, every part of me, from the tips of my toes to the roots of my hair, relaxed. Alexander lies next to me, flat out, his eyes closed, his palms turned upwards, fingers curled, all the tension washed from his face. I reach out and flatten my palm against his chest, feeling his heart rate slowing down and the light sheen of sweat under my fingers.

The rap on the door makes me twitch and stiffen.

Alexander's eyes open instantly. 'What the –?'

The knock comes again, louder and more insistent this time.

He sits up and calls out. 'Yes?'

'It's Robert, my lord. Mr de Courcey and your lawyers are here.'

Alexander lifts his wrist, peers at his watch as if he doesn't believe it, then hisses, 'Fuck.' He pushes himself off the bed and spikes his fingers through his hair.

Robert's anxious voice is louder now. 'They've been in the study for twenty minutes already. Shall I tell them you're indisposed?'

Indisposed? That's one way of putting it.

'No!' Alexander throws up his hands in frustration at losing his temper but crosses to the door and growls through the panel. 'I'll be down in a few minutes, Robert. Can you serve them some tea or whisky or something?'

'I'm afraid we don't have any decent whisky left, my lord.'

I clap a hand over my mouth to stifle a highly inappropriate laugh. Alexander reins in his irritation. 'Sherry then. I really don't care. Please, just keep them happy until I come down.'

'Of course, my lord.'

Footsteps retreat down the landing as Alexander stands motionless for a few seconds, staring into space. Then he shakes his head. 'It's no good. I can't put it off any longer.'

He pulls on trousers and a shirt and rakes his hand through his hair.

'Good luck,' I say as he opens the door.

'I'll need it.'

Chapter Five

The sky over the deer park is rosy as the sun slips closer to the horizon, but Rupert's father's BMW and a black Lexus that I presume belongs to the lawyers are still parked outside on the drive. The house has been eerily quiet while I've been working on some research for my essay. I also made a phone call to Immy to tell her how the funeral went. It's Friday afternoon, of course, and she'd been rushing to finish writing up some fieldwork before she gets ready for a night out at someone's twenty-first birthday party. The contrast has not escaped me.

Maybe I should go downstairs and try to find out what's happening, because I'm going stir crazy up in Alexander's bedroom and, let's face it, I'm dying to know how the meeting has gone.

As I reach the first landing, the study door opens off the hallway below me. I stop in my tracks as a man I assume to be Mr de Courcey comes out. I think it's him, judging by the country tweed and sandy combover hairstyle I can see from my perch. He's followed by a younger man and woman in sober suits, who I assume must be part of the legal team. Alexander emerges behind them but I can't see his face. I wait on the landing, not wanting to join him until they've gone. The lawyers shake hands with Alexander and leave first, but Mr de Courcey lingers.

'You will call me if you need anything,' I hear him saying in a gruff haw-haw voice. 'You know you can rely on Rupert, Letitia and me, any time. We are family, after all.'

I hear a clipped 'Thank you, I do appreciate your time' from Alexander and shortly afterwards the front door shuts again.

I run down the stairs and call after Alexander, who is already heading back to the study. 'How did it go?'

'Not now,' he growls, strides back into the study and slams the door.

So I'm left standing in the middle of the hallway, shut out again. I take a deep breath and tell myself that he's under a lot of pressure and that he's bound to be on edge, yet I'm furious to be shut out so abruptly and I remind myself why I've been so determined to keep my distance from Alexander.

Some time later, I walk downstairs again and spot Helen in the hallway.

'Hello, Miss Cusack,' she smiles. 'Can I help you? Would you like some tea sent up?'

'Not really, but thanks for the offer.'

The study door opens and Alexander appears, looking tired but calm. 'Lauren?'

'Yes?' I say coldly.

With a wry smile, Helen leaves us.

'I'm sorry, will you come in?' he asks, standing by the door to allow me in, like I'm being invited into the principal's office. I hesitate, and then remind myself the meeting was probably tough and move towards him.

'Sure.'

Inside the study, the huge mahogany desk is almost obscured by files and papers, illuminated by a brass desk lamp. 'I apologize for being a git earlier.'

'Yes, you were, but I'll forgive you this one time.'

That draws a faint smile but I wonder what nasty surprises might have been in the will. Debts, perhaps? Maybe the general had a secret love child? No, I can't imagine *that* somehow.

Alexander sweeps some files off the leather chesterfield by the window, sits down and pulls me gently into his lap. 'Was it worse than you expected?' I ask.

He traces circles on my thigh with his finger, almost absent-mindedly, although I don't think there's much that Alexander ever does without a carefully thought out purpose. 'No, it was precisely what I expected,' he says. 'My father left everything to me, including the estate, all the property and the investments. I've no choice about the bloody title, of course.'

'And Emma?'

'She's got her own trust fund to add to the jewellery and property my mother left her. The fund's substantial and will continue to grow. She'll never have to work if she doesn't want to but of course that's not the point. She has to do something.'

And, I think, it may as well be something she's

passionate about . . . 'If you expected all of this from the will, what's got you so rattled?'

'That I'm responsible for Falconbury and a small property empire and that I'm now my sister's guardian and in charge of her financial affairs until she's twenty-one. Lauren – how the fuck am I going to deal with all that and stay in the service? Then there's the little matter of my master's, which has gone completely to cock.'

'The university will give you a dispensation and surely the army will grant you some compassionate leave.'

'I don't want special treatment from anyone and any-way, that would just be a short-term fix. I want to get on with my fucking life,' he mutters.

'I can see this isn't easy,' I say, as troubled by his dilemma as he is. 'Perhaps you need time to yourself?' I try to get up but he pulls me back down.

'No, wait. I'm sorry. Fuck, I keep saying sorry.'

'Yes, you do,' I say, lightly.

'I'm . . . It's been a long day. *Another* long day and you didn't ask for any of this. In fact, I seem to recall, you didn't even want to be with me. Not at the start and not at the end.'

'I guess that part of the plan went horribly wrong.'

He frowns at me. Even exhausted and tetchy, he looks so sexy I can't help but want him right now. 'You do know you're the most infuriating girl I've ever met,' he says, with a faint smile.

'I'll take that as a compliment.'

His fingers encircle my thigh. 'And the sexiest . . .'

So, I underestimated him earlier. This clearly *is* the time. 'I bet you say that to all the girls.'

'You know full well I don't.'

I keep my voice light and teasing. 'Then, I guess I should feel singled out.'

'Unfortunately for you . . .' The slight twist of the lips evaporates and the tension returns to his features. 'Joking apart, things are going to get complicated for me.'

And they aren't already? I keep that observation to myself.

'I don't know what's going to happen this term. I'll have to spend a few more days here with the financial people, the tenants, tax lawyers, and I need to speak to Emma when she gets back.'

'I guess it's going to be tough for her to hear about the will.'

'It's going to seem very final. I hadn't expected it to feel that way but hearing his wishes read out hammered home the fact that he really is gone. I'm not sure I fully grasped what that meant until today. It's all up to me now and I'm not entirely sure I can handle it.'

This is a massive admission from Alexander and my stomach tightens as I see his face. 'I think I may have no choice but to leave the army.'

I am shocked at this; I know what it means to him. 'Are you sure? I mean, how do you know until you try that you won't be able to manage both in time? How much of the day-to-day management did your father have to do? Surely you can get people in to run things at Falconbury?'

'To a degree, but there's still so much to deal with in the overseeing of the estate, and decisions only I can make. At the very least, I'll be fielding calls from managers and lawyers and signing documents for months to come. I had no idea how much Dad did. But that's not what really bothers me.'

I get that feeling of something skittering up my spine. He glances at the window, and our reflection stares back at us.

'If I stay in the forces and something happens to me, who will look after Emma? There's no one else left.' His face falls. 'I can't just do what I want now.'

What can I say to this? It makes my blood run cold. 'Alexander, I have no answer to that. I'm sorry, I hadn't thought of it that way.'

'Funnily enough, neither had I, and to be honest it's the first time it's really hit me.' He stops and gives a sarcastic laugh. 'Look, this is getting us nowhere. There's nothing I can do now. I'll just have to see how things go, I suppose.'

'When will you talk to Emma?'

'Tomorrow, when she's back from her friend's. I'm glad you're here but I'm sorry that you've been dragged into all this . . .'

My kiss cuts off the rest of his words and when I've finished, I say, 'No one dragged me, I came of my own accord, remember?' Then I smile. 'Almost, but I do *really* need to go back to college on Sunday. I have a master's to complete too, and I've nowhere near your excuse for not getting on with it.'

'Not now though. You're going nowhere tonight,' he murmurs, his eyes darkening with desire. I respond instantly, shifting in his lap as I feel how much he wants me. He slides his hand up my thigh under the hem of my mini. 'I also promise that this time I won't pass out on you.' At this, I am lost.

Moments later, I hear the click of the key turning in the lock, shutting away the world, and the rustle of the heavy velvet curtains being drawn across the window. He walks towards me, unbuckling the belt on his trousers as I kick off my shoes.

Alexander pulls me to my feet and turns me round. He nuzzles the tender skin of my neck, and slowly draws down the side zip of my skirt and pushes it down my hips. I'm standing in my sweater, underwear and thigh-highs. He sweeps me up into his arms again, just like this morning, but this time there's no joking between us. His eyes hold such sensual, predatory intent that I shiver with lust. He lays me on the sofa and kneels beside me. With my head resting on the arm of the sofa, I lie back. His hand rests at the top of my thigh.

'I love it when you wear these . . .'

He obviously loves it even more when I don't because the next moment, he starts to peel the stocking down

92

my thigh. It's a slow, measured process, as if he wants to savour the exposure of every inch of skin. He rolls the nylon over my heel and over the sole of my foot, then holds it in mid-air before he lets it fall to the floor.

My eyes are riveted on my other leg as he removes the other stocking, just as carefully, giving my calf and thighs the same sensuous attention. By the time my legs are bare, my panties are damp and I'm struggling not to squirm against the slippery hide.

'I'm a little worried about your sofa . . .'

'So? It's my sofa. My house. If I have the burden of it, I may as well enjoy the benefits.'

Taking my hand in his, he helps me to my feet. When I'm not wearing heels, he's a head above me. Cupping my face between his hands, he kisses me deeply, exploring my mouth with his tongue, as if he has to be inside me. I want him to be inside me too; I want him deep in me so I press my lips harder on his, and pull his hips against mine. When the kiss ends, he threads his fingers through my hair and my scalp tingles at the gentle yet insistent pressure of his fingertips.

'Do you know how much I need this?' he whispers. 'You help me forget the world.'

I gasp because, without warning, he tugs my hair, not that sharply, just enough to make me gasp in surprise, but far from making me want to stop him, the shock turns me on more. He turns me around so that the front of my thighs butts against the smooth hide of the chesterfield and with his hand on my back he tips me forward over the rolled edge.

He pulls the crotch of my boy shorts aside and enters me without any foreplay, easing in until I open for him, then lifting me on to my tiptoes. His cock is hot and silky and my hips bang against the sofa as he deepens his thrusts. My fingers slip against the hide of the seat pad, sliding into the button pockets, my nails scraping the leather as he takes me to the brink. He pulls the hair at the base of my neck again, sharply, and though I cry out in shock, I am throbbing like crazy.

Now he's driving into me and the fullness of his cock and the friction of my sex against the sofa ramps up the tension in my core to an unbearable level. It's a life-affirming fuck, a statement of intent in his father's study. I feel his fingers grip my hips, his body tense, suspended, as he comes hard – almost violently – deep inside me. I claw at the leather and grind myself against him, loving the sensation of him releasing all he has, for good and bad, into me.

His grip on my hips slackens and, slowly, he pulls out of me. I stay over the arm of the sofa, almost but not quite there.

'That was selfish of me.'

His hand is gentle on my back and he helps me to my feet. He pulls me to him and touches my forehead with his face. 'I am a very bad person.'

'And yet you don't look very sorry,' I murmur. My body twitches, and I push against his pelvis, teetering on the edge of coming or losing it altogether if he – or I – don't do something soon.

'I didn't say I was sorry, I said I was selfish, but I want you to feel the way I just did. It's your turn.'

When he presses his fingers against me through the damp lace of my shorts, I almost take off through the roof. 'Oh my God.'

Alexander has now slipped his hand inside my shorts, while I'm still standing up. I bunch his shirt as he massages my clit with one finger until I want to scream. I was on the edge anyway, and before I know where I am, I'm clawing at his back and his butt and my body spasms like someone plugged me into the electricity supply.

When, eventually, I open my eyes and release my death-grip on his shirt, he's looking down at me with the satisfied expression of a guy who knows he just blew my mind and every other part of me.

'Better?' He holds me a little tighter and I'm grateful for the support because I'm a little wobbly on my feet.

'Uh-huh.'

He kisses me, a slow, deep kiss that goes on and on and there finally seems a moment of truce between us, even peace; even if it is only post-sex lassitude, it feels mighty fine. Only now do I notice my skirt tossed on the rug by the sofa and my thigh-highs, one draped over a side table, the other curled on top of a document wallet on the floor.

'It's been a hell of a day,' he says, as we survey the debris, 'but it's beginning to look up.'

'It could get even better,' I say, running my finger along his jawline, sliding it over the freshly shaven skin. He smells divine, of Creed Green Irish Tweed. 'I have something in mind to soothe your troubled soul after dinner,' I murmur.

'You think I'm a troubled soul?' he says, challenging me with a sexy glare.

'If you're not, you won't need soothing, so it's your call.'

He rests his big palms on the cheeks of my bottom and nuzzles the side of my neck with his lips. 'Oh, I need soothing. Very badly, but . . .' He pulls gently away from me, the fleeting smile dying on his lips. 'I'm afraid I have a large pile of paperwork to read through first. This afternoon's meeting has made me realize just how much time I'm going to have to spend here this term. God knows how I'm going to get my work done and I don't think I'm going to be able to see you as much as I want to.'

'We'll have to work around it,' I say lightly, trying to hide my disappointment while reminding myself that nothing has changed between us.

He picks up my clothes and hands them back to me. 'Now, that's the kind of work I think I actually will enjoy. Thanks for the distraction. I needed it and I look forward to more of it later.'

'There?'
   'No, higher.'
   'How about *there*?'

96

'Almost, but perhaps a little to the right . . .'

'OK, Mr Awkward, what about *here*?'

'Oh fuck, yes . . .' Alexander's groan is part pleasure, part pain, as I sink my fingers into the flesh between his shoulder blades. The massage was my idea and after the evening he spent poring over papers in the study after dinner, he needs it.

I tip a drop of massage oil into my palms, rub them together to warm the oil and then apply it to the muscles around his spine. Candles flicker in his room and the spicy scent of the oil fills my nose. Luckily, I had a little bottle at the bottom of my overnight bag. It was meant to be used on me, a gift from a friend at Brown, but I think Alexander needs it more right now.

'What's that smell?' Even his voice sounds relaxed, freed from its knots of formality and edginess.

'That is not a "smell", that is a "fragrance"; a high-end lavender and chamomile massage oil to be precise. Do you like it?'

'Anything would smell good with you sitting on me naked.' He moans again as I knead his skin with the heels of my palms and drag them down his back. I shuffle lower down his legs until my bottom rests on his calves. His butt is bare and it's pretty magnificent. I don't know what he gets up to to develop an ass like that but I've no intention of discouraging the activity. My palms sweep over the swell of his glutes and the muscles glisten with oil.

'Lauren, you're wriggling your arse.'

'And you object to that?'

'No.'

'Then shut up, Captain Hunt. You're supposed to be relaxing and that's an order.'

'I'm trying not to get a massive hard-on at the moment. Believe me, that's not comfortable while I'm lying face down on a Falconbury mattress.'

I tsk and slap his behind sharply. 'You should have your mind on higher things.'

'I do but I can't see them from this position.'

I plant a kiss on the middle of his right butt cheek.

'Jesus. I can't take much more of this.'

'Shh.'

I carry on massaging his backside and the backs of his thighs, luxuriating in the solidity of his glutes and hamstrings, the softness of the hair, slick with oil, under my fingers. The truth is I can't stand this much longer either and after I've worked my way down the tightly bunched muscles of his calves, I lie on top of him, with my breasts pressed against his back and my cheek resting on his shoulder, on the thickened ridge of the gunshot scar.

I rake my toes down his calves.

'Ow, that hurts.'

'Wimp.'

I wriggle a little, grinding my pelvis against his butt. Despite the heat from his body, goose bumps pop out on my skin. I lift myself up a little and run the tips of my fingers over the white flesh. 'Does this hurt now?'

'No, but it hurt like fuck at the time and it's not something I want to repeat, for all kinds of reasons.'

'I heard you got shot while you were dragging one of your men from a bombed-out house.'

His body stiffens beneath me. 'Who told you that?'

'Valentina. Was she telling the truth for once?'

He shifts so that I slide off him to the side. He turns over, lying face up on the white towel. 'Come here,' he says. I let pass the fact that he hasn't answered my question about Valentina or how he was injured. I decide now is probably not the time to push the issue, particularly when he looks totally edible.

I kneel astride him and he balances himself on his elbows, lifting his head high to kiss me. I lower mine to meet him, revelling in the sweep of his tongue inside my mouth. It's hot and frantic, a prelude to what he's going to do to me any moment now. When he's finished kissing me, his hands stray lower and I thrust my hips forward as his cock hardens between my thighs. He lifts my hips up and steers me over his erection.

'Why don't you take a seat?' He lowers me down on to him without any more warning, forcing me to take the whole length in one fell swoop. I whimper a little at being speared with so little preparation but then my muscles ease to accommodate him and he thickens even more inside me.

'Good?'

'Uh-huh.' I almost pass out with pleasure.

He smiles at me. 'I aim to please.'

'No . . .' I pant. 'You don't.'

'In this case, I do.'

I have to support myself by gripping his thighs while he circles his hips, stretching my inner muscles to the limit. My fingers dig into his thighs in discomfort and pleasure. He pushes upwards, lifts me so I'm sliding up and down his cock, wetter by the second, thrilling at the full, tight feeling of having him inside me.

Our eyes are intent on each other and his voice is hoarse. 'Fuck, but this is so good. You drive me insane.'

'I . . . do . . . try.'

He drives up hard, lifting me higher. The thrusts are harder and faster now and I have to grip his legs tight to hang on. The friction of his erection stokes my own climax and I close my eyes as he drives into me. When his muscles go rigid I'm held almost in mid-air, every muscle taut, taken to my limit in every way. I literally ache with desire and the nerve endings have me almost delirious. Just as he's coming down, my own orgasm tears through me while he's still rigid inside me.

Afterwards, we lie, naked, glistening with oil, in a tangle of bedsheets and towels, the world a million miles away. I try to stay awake, and relive the intimacy we shared earlier today and tonight, but after the sex and the emotion of the past few days, my hold on consciousness is slipping . . .

'*No!*'

I awake with a jolt that feels like I just avoided being run down by a truck.

Next to me, Alexander is face up, his eyes screwed

shut, murmuring random words. 'Sorry . . . not my fault . . . blame me.'

I've seen him in the grip of these nightmares before but the anguish etched on his features still shocks me. There's such intensity in the way he speaks and looks, it makes the blood chill in my veins.

I also don't know how to stop the agony he's clearly going through. I slide out of my side of the bed and stand a few feet away from him, because he's started to thrash at the covers and I don't want to be in the path of his arm swinging down. It's obvious he feels guilty about something, but whether it's the accident that killed his mother or the bad feeling between him and his father I don't know. If I even mention the nightmares when he's awake, he slams me down.

I hug my body while he cries out again.

'I didn't mean it!'

Are those footsteps outside in the corridor? Have Robert and Helen heard him? I don't think that's possible because their flat is at the other end of Falconbury and it has to be the middle of the night.

I exhale, slowing my breathing, because Alexander seems to have slipped back to sleep, although his lips still move in a silent, desperate plea. I tiptoe closer to the nightstand by his side of the bed and pick up his watch, an old-fashioned, wind-up piece. Its hands tell me it's three-fifteen and I know it to be accurate to the second. I wonder if it was passed down to Alexander by a grandfather or a gift from his father.

'Jesus!'

Alexander lashes out, and his eyes are open. He has my wrist in his fingers with a grip like iron.

'Alexander. Let go, you're hurting me.'

'It wasn't my fault. I'm sorry.'

My wrist feels like it's in a vice and the way he's looking through me, not at me, I know he's not conscious.

I try to wrest my hand from his but his grip tightens.

'Shh,' I whisper, my pulse racing and my wrist burning. 'It's all right. I know you didn't mean it.'

He still stares at something or someone beyond me. If he doesn't let me go in a moment, I'm going to have to slap him, but that might make him lash out more. I could reach the glass of water by the bed and throw it at him but I don't want to resort to that.

'I'm sorry.'

Thank God. His fingers suddenly loosen, fall away and his arm is left dangling over the edge of the bed.

I scoot backwards until I'm well out of reach, and rub my throbbing wrist. The room is cool, but I feel flushed yet shivery. Again I ask myself: just what have I got myself into here, and with whom? What does it mean for the rest of term? I shudder, too afraid to get back into bed.

I arrived here barely a week ago, with every intention of not even speaking to Alexander Hunt, and yet here I am: back in his bed and at the centre of the drama of his life. I know his deepest fears and his sister's secret. Even if we get through this term, what lies beyond, with him tied to the estate and me planning to pursue my own career? I want to curate a gallery or work in a museum or art auctioneers in the States or another part of Europe.

Lying there, the covers tangled around his limbs, his chest bared and his handsome face at rest, he's as quiet as a baby now. His eyelashes flutter on his cheek, his chest rises and falls steadily, like nothing ever happened, and I could almost laugh at my fears. I'm getting way too ahead of myself with Alexander, I remind myself; the only way to live is in the moment and that's what I'm going to do.

I made it to breakfast but Alexander didn't. Finally exhausted by so many sleepless nights, he was still dead to the world when I crept out of bed this morning. I'd been awake for some time anyway, still disturbed by what I'd seen in the night. My wrist is a little bruised from where he grabbed me so I've put on a long-sleeved top.

Robert's face is a picture when he sees me enter the breakfast room so early, so I give him a cheery greeting. 'Morning, Robert.'

'Good morning, miss. You'll have to forgive me. I haven't finished putting out the breakfast things yet. I wasn't expecting you and Lord Falconbury just yet.'

'Alexander's still asleep. He's worn out.' I rapidly qualify that statement in case Robert thinks I'm bragging. 'It's been a very trying time for him.'

'Of course, miss.'

While I take my seat at the breakfast table, he disappears briefly before returning with another covered serving dish, and the aroma of cooked bacon fills the air. It amuses me that this ritual is carried out even though there are only the two of us here, but Alexander told me he hadn't the heart to ask Robert to stop. Apparently the general was a stickler for a traditional English breakfast and I suspect Alexander can't face ending this link to his father either, for his sake and Emma's.

After Robert has placed the dish on to the sideboard, he asks me if I want tea or coffee.

'An Earl Grey would be good,' I say, knowing better than to ask for anything 'newfangled' like chamomile.

'Very good, miss.'

'Um . . . Robert, thanks for helping me take care of Alexander the other evening.'

I half think he's going to bow and if he does, I'll die of embarrassment, but instead I see the trace of a smile tug the corners of his mouth. 'Glad to be of service. I'll bring your tea and the newspapers.'

I don't really want a full English but I feel obliged to taste something after it's been cooked. After he's brought my tea and left a bundle of newspapers on the table, I help myself to some scrambled eggs, bacon and toast. Outside the sun is full up, and the formal garden behind the breakfast room shimmers in the early light. The frazzled leaves on the copper beech hedge are rimmed with frost, now melting rapidly. I can see a few roses that ventured out during a recent mild spell, now withered on their stems. I picture my mother's face, and think how she would love to tend this garden. My parents still know nothing about Alexander, and I've confided that I had a 'fling' with only a handful of my friends back home. Once again, I wonder just where things are heading for us and immediately stop myself. I'm going back to college, to work and to have some *fun*.

I crunch a piece of toast while leafing through a piece on a new Klee exhibition at the Tate Modern. I love Klee and vow to arrange a trip to see it with some of the guys at the faculty. I wonder if Immy can be persuaded to come. At the thought of her in the Tate surrounded by what she calls a 'bunch of sad hipsters', I smile. She may as well try to get me to go digging for fossils with her and camp in a tent. Outside the sun is bright; if the courts back in Oxford aren't icy, we could get in a game of tennis. I'll text her when I get back up to my room, if Alexander is awake.

'Sorry I'm so bloody late . . .'

Alexander strides into the breakfast room, in jeans and a T-shirt, rubbing his unruly brown hair into submission. My stomach twists. He looks heart-stoppingly gorgeous but I also can't forget last night's violent dreams.

I lay down the newspaper. 'Hiya.'

He leans down and kisses me on the lips. 'Morning.'

Despite the nightmares, the night's rest has done him good and he looks better than I've seen him since I got back from Washington and found him slumped outside my door.

'How are you?'

'Not too bad. You should have woken me.'

'What for?'

'What do you think?' His eyes glint.

'I thought you needed your beauty sleep.'

He shoots me a glare. 'More importantly, I need to get my strength up. That breakfast smells good.'

After he's piled his plate high with the contents of the breakfast dishes, he takes a seat next to me. Robert brings him a pot of coffee and he drinks it black while talking to me about his plans over the next few days. He won't be back to Wyckham until later in the week, after meeting with the lawyers and financial team, and with some of the tenants who farm the estate. Then, he says, he has some 'regimental business', whatever that means. I'd like to know more, and if it has anything to do with the mysterious Mr Armitage who called during the funeral. I know better than to ask and as he helps himself to seconds, I conclude he seems to have no recollection of the violent nightmare, or else he's in denial again.

'When's Emma going back to school?' I ask as he butters another piece of toast.

'Tomorrow. She has to get back into her work for her exams. She's missed too much already but she's bright. Too bright . . .' He smiles. 'I hope she can settle down for the rest of this term and there's no more drama. I don't think I can handle running to and from the school on top of everything else, and Emma needs some peace and quiet, if that's possible.'

I smile, but mentally I'm crossing my fingers, hoping

that Henry Favell will keep away from Emma while she's at school. I wish she hadn't told me she was seeing him again. It's something I really don't want to deal with.

'More toast before I eat the lot?' He pushes the rack towards me.

'No thanks.' My appetite is sated and anyway, the pangs of guilt are stirring again at my promise to Emma.

'Alexander?'

He dollops marmalade on his toast and looks at me with mock seriousness. 'Yes, Lauren?'

'Do you really think Emma will be OK when she goes back to school?'

'I don't know, but the staff are going to keep a close eye on her and she has to get her head down again sooner or later.' I sip my tea as he spreads the marmalade and goes on. 'Thanks for being there for the funeral. You've made quite an impression on her.'

'Really? I didn't do anything.'

'You listened to her, which is everything. She really needed someone from outside the family to talk to.'

I force another smile and drink my tea while he demolishes the toast in a few bites. When he's finished, he sits back, with a sigh of relief. He looks, if not happy, then at least calm. I decide not to add to his worries by telling him about Emma, but to respect her privacy and hope things will settle down.

'Are you OK?'

He rests his hand on mine.

'Yes, I'm fine. Just thinking about all the work I have to catch up on.'

'That's my fault.' He rubs his thumb over the top of my hand and then his expression darkens. He pushes the edge of my sweater further up my wrist.

'What's this?'

The bluey tinge of a bruise is clearly visible.

'It's nothing.'

'You didn't have those marks last night.' His voice is hard.

I put my hand in my lap, lost for words because it's pointless to lie to him.

'Did I do it?' he snaps.

'Let's just say I didn't tie myself up for a bit of nocturnal fun!'

'Oh Christ.' His voice is low now, edged with something like panic.

'You didn't know you were doing it.'

'That's no excuse,' he says quietly. 'Has it happened before?'

'The nightmares or you lashing out?'

'Both.'

I take a deep mental breath. 'You've had the dreams a couple of times while you've been sleeping with me, but I think you know that. Things have gotten pretty animated but nothing as rough as last night. I just happen not to have got in the way before.'

The silence seems to stretch on and on before he murmurs, 'What did I do?'

'I was standing by your bed, looking at your watch, and you grabbed my wrist and cried out. You kept saying you were sorry and it wasn't your fault but you wouldn't let go for a while.'

His fingers move to the strap of his watch as I speak and from the look on his face, there's a battle raging inside his mind.

I touch his arm. 'Hey, I'm fine and you could cut yourself some slack after what you've gone through the past couple of weeks . . .'

'Once again, I can only apologize. It won't happen again,' he says in a voice that's turned so icily polite, you'd think I was someone he'd accidentally bumped into on the pavement. 'Come on, let's get you back to Oxford,' he says abruptly. 'I've taken up far too much of your time already. I'm keeping you from your work.'

'You are but I don't have to leave right this minute!'

He snaps to attention so fast you'd think his commanding officer just entered the room. 'You've been put to enough trouble. I'll get Robert to have the car sent round while you pack.'

Chapter Six

I've spent the past few days since I've been back at Wyckham in my room or the library trying to catch up with the work I've missed. Falconbury seems like another country and another age. Alexander disappeared off somewhere while I packed but finally turned up to carry my bags downstairs. He tried to joke about how little stuff I had this time and I went along with the charade, teasing him about being strong enough to manage my vanity case. Inside, however, I had very mixed feelings about the abrupt way in which he'd brushed off my sympathy and practically bundled me out of the house, even though I knew I absolutely had to get back to college.

He saw me off with a brief kiss and a promise to call me, before General Hunt's Bentley — Alexander's Bentley now, I guess — whisked me down the drive and back to college. Was I disappointed that Alexander didn't drive me back to Wyckham himself? Not really; he has a lot to do and I can understand that. Was I upset that he slapped down my attempt to play nicely? Actually, numbness had become my main feeling by the time the car purred up to the Lodge. It's probably self-preservation because the truth is I do need to try to focus on my work and make the most of a term that's already whizzing by – in no time I'll be halfway through my time at Oxford and there's still so much I want to do and experience.

It troubles me, too, that I've become embroiled in Alexander's life again against all my better judgement and that all our old issues are still there, lying like rocks beneath the surface.

It's Thursday morning now, and I've just staggered out of a bruising tutorial with Professor Rafe, during which he picked apart my vacation essay like Kay Scarpetta dissecting a corpse, looking for evidence of my intellectual shortcomings.

Immy is sheltering from the rain under the porch outside the JCR when I dash down the steps after my tute, hoping to avoid another chilly deluge. She pulls a face when I skitter under the porch.

'My God, you look like you've seen a zombie.'

'It's worse than that. I just finished my tute with Rafe and now I feel like my brain has been taken apart.'

'Did he keep his hands to himself?'

'Yes, but he said something about being "extra hard on me now I'd found my feet". I don't think it was a euphemism.'

Immy screws up her face. 'Eww. He's such a perv. Did you see he'd made the paper this week? *Cherwell's* "Hot Don" of the month.'

'You're kidding me?'

'Nope. I don't know what some of the undergrads see in him.'

'Top grades?'

'That's mean, Lauren, and I thought you were such a nice girl.' She laughs.

'I've never been a nice girl.' And I'm definitely not one now, I think, not since fate threw Alexander Hunt into my path. Not that I fought very hard to avoid him, not hard enough anyway . . .

She grins. 'Glad to hear it. Now that's over, shall we get out of this place? If you don't tell me the latest between you and Alexander, I think my brain will explode.'

'Do I have any choice?'

'None whatsoever.'

I laugh and as it's nearly lunchtime, we head out of the Lodge into the real world. The quads of Wyckham insulate you from the rest of the world, and while Oxford is hardly the metropolis, the buzz of the traffic and bustle of its streets, even in January, always strikes me after the cocooned hush of the college. Sometimes, that timeless charm can be soothing, but it can also be claustrophobic.

I button up my funnel-neck jacket and we scoot down New College Lane to the High. A few minutes later, the heat from dozens of bodies hits us from the inside of an ancient cafe on the corner of Queen's Lane. There's one tiny table vacant, wedged into a corner.

'Get that,' she barks above the din of chatter. 'I'll see if they have anything organic and innocent for you.'

There's no time to shoot back a riposte because a couple of rugby players have opened the door behind me and are eyeing up the table. The smell of the Turkish coffee is incredible but I've maxed out on caffeine over the past few days to keep me going through my essay crisis. Immy returns from the counter with a satisfied smile on her face and shortly after the wait staff bring a couple of hot spiced-apple drinks that have my nose twitching in delight.

'So, it's all on again?'

'Oh hell, I don't know what I've got myself into,' I sigh.

Thinking back to the way I was bundled out of Falconbury, I'm even less sure what we are up to, though I have had a couple of texts.

She shakes her head. 'Well, never mind the whole flowers and roses thing; have you at least shagged him again?'

My face heats up and it's not the steam from the spiced apple.

She laughs. 'I'll take that as a yes. I told you you'd miss the sex and I knew you wouldn't be able to resist the onslaught for long but I never dreamed it would take something like this to get you two back together. Poor Alexander; whatever I think of him, he's had a horrible time.'

'He needed some comfort. What's a girl to do?' I try to make light of a horribly difficult situation.

Immy follows my lead. 'Best therapy there is,' she says with a grin, before getting back to business. 'Was the funeral horrendous?' she asks, screwing up her nose.

'Are they ever anything else when someone dies pretty young? The general was only in his early fifties.'

'I must admit the Hunts have had a crap time.' She quotes Oscar Wilde: '"To lose one parent may be regarded as a misfortune, to lose both looks like carelessness."'

'I know, and Alexander is poor old Emma's guardian now.'

She winces. 'Poor both of them – he's only twenty-five. What a responsibility.'

'I know and she's going to be quite something to handle I think! I do like her but Alexander seems to think I can be some kind of big sister to her and I don't have the qualifications or the experience, *and* I'm just not sure I want to get tangled up in all of this just now. I'm not sure it'll do any of us any favours in the long run.'

'Oh God, don't ask me for any tips. George and I used to fight like cat and dog and although I love him to pieces, we only get on better now because we're not in the same county most of the time. I know Emma can be a handful; George went to the same prep school and they've still got a few friends in common. It's not going to be an easy time for either of them.'

'She's hard to fathom out. Half the time she acts like a little girl and the other half, it's like dealing with some kind of teenage Machiavelli. Tell me what I did to deserve running into the Hunts.' Make that literally running into one of them. My senses stir into life at the memory of my first encounter with Alexander in the cloisters. He was arrogant, magnificent, maddening . . . 'Arghh!' I drag myself back to the present and remember something I meant to ask Immy.

'Immy . . . do you know a guy called Henry Favell?'

'Henry? Yes, I know him. He went to Eton with Alexander. He wasn't at the funeral, was he? I didn't think Alexander and he got on.'

'That's the impression I got at the hunt ball, and he wasn't at the funeral, but I'm pretty sure his parents were. However, I think he gets on just fine with Emma. According to her, they're seeing each other.'

Her eyes widen. 'You're joking? He's got to be about ten years older than her. Does Alexander know?'

'No. Henry had started to see Emma last summer but Alexander found out and got Rupert to warn him off. After the funeral, Emma decided to go all confessional and told me she's started seeing him again. She says she's in love with him.'

'Oh. My. God. Poor deluded girl. Are you going to tell Alexander?'

'No. Or . . . maybe. I decided not to for now, but I don't know what to do. Emma made me swear not to say anything but I know Alexander will go postal if he finds out I knew and kept it to myself. I'm not entirely sure that Emma won't tell him herself and drop me in it. What do you think?' I ask, agonized.

'Do you want me to make sure he hears by other means?'

'Jeez, no!'

'It would get you off the hook.'

'But Emma would be devastated and probably blame me. I'm really not sure who else she's told except me.'

'OK.' She makes a zipping motion. 'These are sealed, but what a pain for you. When's Alexander coming back to college? He must have so much to do.'

'I'm not sure. I think he'll be back this weekend but I have no idea what will happen long term. He's trying to do some work at home but he's got the lawyers to deal with and a lot of stuff to sort out relating to the running of the estate. I'm not totally sure he'll finish his master's.'

'Really? That's tough,' Immy says with a sigh. 'What about the army?'

'He thinks he might have to leave that too,' I say, miserably.

'Oh dear.' Immy's face falls as she sees my own. 'Although that may not be a bad thing, you know . . .' she adds softly.

'In his book, it's the end of the world.'

'Poor Alexander, but where does this leave the two of you?'

I shrug. 'God knows. I know I should get right out

of this for my own sanity, but I'm not sure it's going to be as easy as that.'

She shakes her head. 'He asked you to go to his father's funeral. I'd say you were right about that.'

We make small talk while the waiter arrives with a BLT for Immy and a Moroccan chicken salad for me. Afterwards, I tell Immy more about the wake and we talk about Immy's boyfriend Skandar and some of our plans for the coming term. Immy's determined to get her head down for her Geography Finals (I've heard that one before) and I've decided to sign up for a new term of contemporary dance classes. By the time lunch is over, I have to admit I'm feeling more relaxed than I have for ages, maybe even since the middle few weeks of last term, when Alexander and I first started seeing each other. I feel the familiar kick of desire for him as we pull on our coats and walk out of the door into the High.

'Can I just pop into Ghost before we go home? I've seen a gorgeous dress in the sale.' Immy's voice is wheedling and there's no way I'm going to pass up the opportunity to shop. There are some cute and quirky fashion stores along the High.

'However, before we do shop, I need to pop into the OUP first to pick up a textbook I ordered,' she grimaces.

'Sure. That's fine. I'll take a look in the new accessories boutique that opened last term.'

So we cross the road and while Immy goes into the bookstore, I wait outside on the pretext of browsing in the shop's window display. The truth is my attention has been claimed by the people coming and going through the Lodge of St Nicholas's College, aka St Nick's, which is only a few yards away. St Nick's is Scott's college and he's studying for a master's in Water Policy there, when he can spare the time from his rowing. He's hoping to make it into the final eight of the Boat Race crew. He lives in Washington and is a cousin of my ex, Todd. Half expecting to see him emerge from the St Nick's Lodge, I feel a pang of guilt. I didn't return his call while I was in Washington and wrote him a card promising to be in touch when I got back to Oxford.

My feet seem to take me towards the Lodge, while I debate whether I should do the old-fashioned thing and drop a note in his pigeonhole. He was so lovely to me after I ran away from Falconbury the morning after the hunt ball. He found me wandering the meadows, not knowing what to do with myself, while I waited for the car to take me to Heathrow. I can't forget how kind he was, how warm and safe being in his arms felt . . . and to my surprise, I can't quite forget that kiss either. It wasn't quite as intoxicating as my kisses with Alexander, but I know that my life would be easier with a man like Scott, that's for sure.

'Lauren?'

'Immy. Sorry.'

'I thought you were going to take a look inside that new boutique or has St Nick's opened a Kate Spade franchise?'

Immy has found me lolling outside St Nick's. 'I decided to pop a note in someone's pigeonhole.'

'Does this have anything to do with the mystery man?'

'Might do.'

'Are you sure that's a good idea, running with the hare and the hounds, as they say.'

The hunting allusion is so apt, and Immy knows it, that we both laugh. 'If there really was anything going on between me and Scott, then it would be dangerous, but he's a good friend – a very good friend – and he was kind to me when I needed someone. I owe him.'

'Never a good position to be in,' she says wryly.

'I know . . . but . . . let's just pop inside and I'll send him a quick note.' It feels a more personal means of contact but also less furtive than a text or email. I pull myself up. 'There's nothing going on and anyway, I won't allow Alexander to control my life and who I want to see. I'm not some naive ingénue. Come on.'

So I march determinedly into the Lodge with Immy in tow. The more I think about it, the more I feel I want to and should keep up my friendship with Scott. He made me laugh when Alexander made me cry, and I'm not one of those girls in books who lets some alpha guy dictate their life choices. No man is ever going to do that. No matter how amazing he makes me feel in bed, or how many butterflies he stirs every time I see him, or how dangerous and exciting every moment with him is.

'Got a pen?'

Immy rolls her eyes and pulls out a biro with the end almost chewed off, and the St Nick's porter finds me an envelope. I rip a piece of paper from the Moleskine in my bag and scrawl a note to Scott. The faster I write it, I figure, the less time I have to think about the consequences of sending it. 'Sorry I've been AWOL. Things have happened but it would be great to see you some time soon. Thanks for you know what.' Actually, I'm not sure what you know what is but I hope he'll get the gist.

While Immy walks out of the Lodge to speak to someone she's spotted, I locate Scott's pigeonhole and shove the note in.

Immy's waiting under the Lodge porch, chatting to a girl with a bike and a racket bag. The girl laughs and says 'See you on Monday' when I reach them, before wheeling her bike away.

'Ready?'

'Sure you don't want to see if he's in?' Immy asks mischievously.

'I doubt he will be. He's always on the river or training with the Blues squad.'

Immy's mouth falls open. 'He's a Blues rower?'

Shit. I walked into that one. 'He's in the final squad.

I don't know whether he'll get into the First Eight for the Boat Race yet.'

'Oh my God, even if he doesn't make the First Eight, he's a good chance of being in *Isis*.' From my conversations with Scott, I know this to be the reserve boat, which will also be racing on the Thames after the end of term. Immy is almost hopping about in excitement. 'Hang on a minute. Scott Schulze . . .' she goes on. 'I think I saw him in *Cherwell*. There was a feature on the Blues team training. He's blond, isn't he? And American, of course. And unbelievably fit. Oh yes, I remember him. Who could forget him?'

'How do you know his name?'

She rolls her eyes. 'You wrote it on the envelope.'

I sigh. 'So I did. But we're not going to stalk him.'

'Rubbish. You need a bit of light relief and I'm sure he'll be thrilled to see you.'

'I'm not sure.'

'I hope you're not worried what Alexander will say?'

'Of course not!'

'Then you can have no further objections, Miss Cusack. It sounds to me like it would be rude not to call on him as we were passing. Now shall I ask the porter for his room number or will you?'

'They won't tell you,' I say, with a smug smile.

'The young Geordie porter will.' She taps her nose. 'Trust me.'

With a wink, she sallies into the Lodge office and in

seconds is back out with a grin as wide as the Potomac on her pretty face. 'Staircase VIII, Room 15. Top floor in the far garden quad. Come on, the exercise will do us both good.'

And grabbing my arm, she practically drags me. My God, she is fiendish.

'He won't be home,' I say, hurrying to keep up with her.

'Maybe not but there's a good chance. I reckon he'll be back from the river and lectures by now and be knackered. He'll probably be getting some rest before he does some work and some more training.'

'How do you work that out?'

'One of the girls from my field trip lives on a narrowboat opposite the Blues boathouse. She knows their routines inside out. She and her friend have binoculars trained on the place. Sometimes they pull the exercise bikes into the open doorway and cycle for an hour in the sun, the Lycra rolled down to the extent that they're barely decent.'

'Is your friend studying anatomy as well as Geography?'

Immy laughs. 'She is now. You *have* to introduce me to him. Let's go and see if he's in.'

I'm not sure whether Immy wants to see Scott because she fancies him or is just nosy, or both, but she's definitely a woman on a mission and maybe she's right. I *do* owe Scott a visit – and an apology for avoiding him – and it might look more natural if he thinks I was 'just passing by' with a friend and then decided to drop in as well as leave the note.

After marching through the quads, Immy locates Staircase VIII with the skill of a bloodhound and takes the steps that lead to Room 15 two at a time.

'He might be asleep,' I hiss, trotting up the stairs behind her.

'He might.'

Finally, we reach the door. There's a notepad stuck to it, with a pen hanging down. Someone's scrawled, 'Scott, you tosser, where the fuck are you?' on the pad. I guess it's a term of affection.

'I'm not sure we should disturb him,' I say, my feet growing colder by the second.

Ignoring me, Immy raps on the door and executes a deft move whereby she's standing behind me and I'm just a foot from the door. Shit. Why am I so nervous? It was only a friendly kiss, a comfort kiss, nothing sparked between us, did it? Then again, is it a great idea to have company if I have to tell him I've seen Alexander again despite my determination not to?

'Yeah?' The door opens and Scott appears, in boxers and a tee, rubbing his dark blond hair and blinking.

'I knew you'd be asleep.' I grin, embarrassed. 'Shall we leave you to it?'

'I was.' His scowl morphs into a grin. 'But it doesn't matter. To what do I owe this honour?'

'It was Immy's idea,' I blurt before Immy cuts in.

'To disturb you, she means. We're so sorry. You must

be exhausted after all that hard physical exertion but Lauren and I were passing by and she mentioned you're at St Nick's and she wondered how you were and I thought it would be a shame if she – we – didn't at least see if you were here. I've heard so much about you.'

Scott seems surprised but definitely not unhappy and he opens the door wider.

My God, I am going to *kill* her when we get out of here but for now I grit my teeth and do the introductions.

'Scott, this is Immy, Immy, Scott.'

'Hey there, Immy. Cute name.'

'Short for Imogen.' She pulls a face. 'Scott is short for Scotty, I assume.'

He laughs. 'Come on in, ladies, if you dare to step into the bear pit. I don't have much time for the chores.'

We follow him in, picking our way over kit bags and sports shoes in the semi-darkness. There's a pungent smell, kind of spicy and medicinal. When Scott turns his back on us to open the drapes, Immy pinches my elbow and mouths, 'OMG.' I give her an Alexander-style glare before Scott turns round.

'It's a bit of a dump, isn't it? Sorry about the smell. Embrocation.'

Immy sniffs the air. 'Really?'

'Well, it's not my cologne,' he says, 'and luckily for you, I got my laundry collected this morning so you don't have a pile of sweaty kit to contend with.'

'Nothing wrong with a bit of healthy sweat on a

man.' I want to melt through the floorboards as Immy raises a suggestive eyebrow. Good job Skandar isn't here now.

While Immy starts to interrogate Scott about his Blues training, I stand by awkwardly, forcing a smile to my face. Scott focuses on Immy and I can tell he's enjoying the attention and is amused by her blatant flirting, but I can't miss the subtle glances in my direction, and the slight look of confusion.

He tells Immy an outrageous rowing anecdote and we all laugh but then, out of nowhere, there's an abrupt silence and a gap in the conversation like the Grand Canyon. After the banter, it's like we're all staring into the abyss of why we – I – decided to seek him out in this way. I can't blame it on Immy totally; I could have simply walked out of the Lodge and ignored her protests. The thing is, I'm not sure I can explain without giving him the wrong idea. Oh hell, have I done the right thing?

'I should have offered you guys coffee. I don't have any beer. I'm supposed to be dry for the rest of the term.'

'Don't worry. We only just had lunch,' I say.

'Was it good?'

'Great.'

Scott's eyes are on me. 'So you're feeling OK?'

'Sure. I'm doing . . . great.'

'Oh, I appear to have a text.' We both glance at Immy, who fishes her phone from her bag.

'I didn't hear anything,' I say.

'It's on silent,' says Immy. 'And I need to call him – I mean her – back. Excuse me while I go outside. I'm sure you don't want to hear me wittering on.'

She lets herself out, and the door closes behind her with a soft click. Scott and I are alone and the smile on his face has been replaced with something else I can't quite fathom. Annoyance? Concern?

'I know, I know . . . I've been a very bad girl,' I say, keeping my tone light, while squirming inside.

He raises an eyebrow, still looking a little pissed. 'I know that much.'

'Scott. I did mean to call you but things got . . . complicated.'

The smile is back as if he's enjoying me digging a hole for myself. I can hardly blame him.

'After I split up with Alexander and you and I . . . uh . . . kissed, I needed some time to sort out my life. I needed time on my own.'

'I worked that one out. So what are your conclusions?'

'I have no idea, to be honest,' I confess, unable to look him in the eye. 'But I haven't been finding it as easy as I'd thought to stay away from Alexander . . .'

Chapter Seven

Once I've delivered this bombshell, Scott glances away out of the window as if he wants to spare my embarrassment. I'm really hating this – he's gorgeous and he's like a centre to my life, a reminder of the normal things, the fun things I sometimes think I've let go by plunging into Alexander's world. I also think I'm going to need his friendship during my time in Oxford so I really hope we can get back on track.

'Then good luck to you,' he says, meeting my eyes again and giving me his usual cheery smile.

'I know what you're thinking,' I say, mortified. 'You think Alexander is going to chew me up and spit me out and that I should walk away.'

'Really? You acquired telepathic skills since you arrived in Oxford?' he teases me.

'That's not fair!'

'No. You're right. Look Lauren, I like you a lot and I just don't want to see you get hurt.' His body relaxes and he takes hold of my shoulders lightly. 'More than you already have been.'

I take a deep breath. 'I'm a big girl, Scott, I know what I'm getting into. And to be honest, I don't know if I'm even getting into anything at all, it's so complicated.' I give him the same cheery smile back.

He looks down into my face thoughtfully. 'I'm sure you do. I'm not going to try and persuade you that this Alexander's wrong for you. That would be arrogant and controlling and I'm not that kind of guy.'

And Alexander is? I think that's what he's implying but I say nothing.

'You might think you're cool and sophisticated but in reality you're just as prone to falling in love as the rest of us mortals. I saw how you were with Todd.'

'Alexander is not Todd.'

'No, he's far more dangerous.' I laugh out loud and so does Scott. 'I wouldn't dream of getting in the guy's way. I might end up tied to some chair in a dungeon, minus my balls.'

I roar with laughter at this, so relieved that we are on safer ground and the old easiness with Scott is returning.

'Listen,' he says, still smiling, 'if you need a friend, I'm here, you know that. We Americans need to stick together, even if Alexander might not like that!'

I smile back. 'I know and don't worry, I would never let Alexander stop me seeing my friends.'

'Well, I'm happy to hear that,' Scott teases. 'So you'll come to the next USSoc mixer? It's just about the only time I'll get let off the leash these days.'

'I'd love to.' And I realize I *really* would.

'You could bring Immy along too.' His eyes twinkle

in the roguish way that I guess has most women melting.

'She'd love that.'

He opens the door and Immy appears to have just finished her call. 'Good to meet you, Immy,' he says, kissing her on the cheek. I then see something I've never seen before: pink stealing into Immy's face. I fear the weight of a massive crush on Immy's part.

Scott brushes his lips over my cheek too and whispers, 'Take care of yourself with his lordship.'

I try not to rise to the bait but can't help smiling as I picture Alexander's face if he were here. 'See you, Scott.'

'Good luck with the training!' Now recovered, Immy waves cheerily and we're on our way downstairs.

The moment we're out in the quad, she claps her hands together and squeals with delight. 'Wow. Wow and wow!'

Oh God, this is worse than I thought it would be. 'You liked him, then?' I say.

'He's OK, I suppose.' She shrieks, 'He is *completely* gorgeous. I can see why Alexander would have gone totally batshit insane if he saw you kissing Scott. I'm amazed Scott hasn't been found dumped in a skip, minus part of his anatomy.'

I'm a little surprised myself but I shrug in what I hope is a nonchalant way. 'Alexander knows that the kiss didn't mean anything. Scott's hot and so much fun and a breath of fresh air sometimes, but I don't really know if I fancy him . . .'

'Yeah, right,' says Immy gleefully, as we reach the Lodge.

'Oh, shut up. It's just so different with Alexander. I crave him, like you might crave something that's addictive but not that good for you.'

'Are we talking the Jägerbomb kind of not good for you or the crystal meth kind of not good for you?'

'Somewhere in between?'

She blows out a breath of exasperation. 'I give up.'

'Before you get too frustrated with me, I have news. Scott asked if we were going to the USSoc party. I said I'd ask if you could fit it into your busy schedule.'

She heaves out a sigh. 'We-ell, you know I am sooo busy . . . Of course I can bloody fit him in, I mean fit *it* in. Come on, I think that some while ago we'd planned to do some shopping. I think I need a new top for this party.'

'What about Skandar? Won't he mind?'

She winks. 'I haven't done anything yet for him to mind about.'

Some of Immy's favourite stores are along the High and I think we did them all by the time we got to the top where Cornmarket and St Aldate's join the street. The History of Art Faculty is only a few minutes' walk away.

'Thanks for a lovely lunch. I feel a lot better but I'm going to drop by the faculty to visit the archive before I go back to Wyckham,' I say as we're about to go our separate ways.

'OK. Glad you enjoyed yourself, and thank you for

introducing me to Scott, even if I did have to drag you there.'

'I'm happy to have cleared the air.'

'See you tomorrow for a game of tennis, if it's dry?' she asks.

'Sure.'

Immy saunters off down Cornmarket, swinging her Ghost bag, while I scurry down St Aldate's towards the faculty. I end up doing some work in there and it's dusk by the time I come out. The streetlights are on and a grey mist hangs in the air that seems to cling to my exposed skin. I take a short cut down Turl Street, and pop into one of the antiquarian bookshops to check if they still have a pair of beautiful Victorian lithographs of Wyckham and its gardens that I saw last term. It's my mother's birthday in a couple of weeks and I think I'll have them shipped over to Washington.

Luckily for me, they do still have the prints in stock and while the bookseller takes down my details, I get my credit card ready.

'I'm sure your mother will love these. They're very fine,' he says, waiting for my payment to go through.

'I'm sure she will.'

Outside the window, my attention is drawn by a black limo that has stopped by the kerb opposite. I'm wondering how it managed to get this far up the narrow street and am amused by the irritated students weaving round it on their bikes. The driver dodges one of them and scoots around to open the rear door. Must be someone important, if he's in that much of a hurry.

'There, that seems to have gone through. I'll just write you a receipt.'

'Uh-huh.' The bookseller must think I'm rude paying so little attention to him, but I don't care because I can't quite believe my eyes. A tall thin figure swathed in a fur coat has just climbed out of the limo.

'Here you are, Miss Cusack.'

'Sorry?'

I glance back at him and he holds out the piece of paper. 'Your receipt.'

'Oh, thanks.'

'I hope we'll see you again soon if there's anything else you might be interested in . . .'

'Yes . . . thanks. Bye.'

I dart to the door, trying to see where the woman has gone. Was that her just disappearing round the corner under the glow of a lamp? Out in the street, I weave my way through the students and shoppers and on to the Broad. Looking left and right, straining my eyes, I try to spot her among the other pedestrians but she's nowhere to be seen. It *is* dark and very misty, I tell myself as I walk back to Wyckham through the gloomy streets, and I *might* be imagining it – but here's the thing: if it *was* Valentina getting out of that limo, what the hell is she doing in Oxford?

*

A couple of hours later, I'm enjoying the view as Alexander bends over to rake the embers of the fire in his sitting room. I had a call from him when I got back to Wyckham, saying he was back in Oxford and inviting me to go round to the house he owns in the city. Despite the way we parted at Falconbury, I agreed. I've calmed down now, and although I still have misgivings about him practically bundling me out of the house, his invitation to dinner – and more – was way too tempting to resist.

As it happens, he had me even before hello. As soon as he had the door open, he practically dragged me into the sitting room and started to take off my clothes before I could catch my breath. The fire was already burning down, and the carpet spread with tartan rugs and scatter cushions.

Now, I'm watching the tiny sparks from the fire fly through the air and enjoying the way the orange glow lights up the angles and contours of his body, the muscles of his magnificent butt and everything else below. He drops the poker into the hearth with a clatter, turns around and gets back under the rug, beside me on the floor. Now, as I lie here, glowing from the delicious sex and the heat from the fire, my fear that I saw Valentina earlier seems a world away. It's clear that I've been working too hard; I may have eye strain and it was a gloomy afternoon.

'That was some view,' I say, as he slides his arm back under my head.

'Not as good as the one I have. God, I've missed these.' He traces a circle around my nipples with his index finger. 'Have I ever told you, they're the best ones I've ever seen?'

'Actually, you said they were the best in Oxford, or possibly the county.'

'I've revised that opinion. On reflection, I think they're definitely the best in England.' My breathing quickens as he circles the other nipple with his tongue.

'Why, thank you, your lordship.'

He pulls his mouth away from my breast and frowns at me. 'Don't say that.'

'Why not? It's true.'

'Only at Falconbury. Nowhere else and totally banned here.'

I now wish I hadn't teased him because the moment is over. He lies back and sighs.

'How have things gone at Falconbury?' I prop myself up on one elbow next to him.

'I've got some stuff sorted but it's only the start,' he says.

'And, um, how's Emma?' I ask, walking my fingers down his chest, as if the answer to my question isn't really important. Even now my pulse picks up a little.

'She's back at school and seems OK but her housemistress and teachers are keeping a close eye on her.'

'Good.' Secretly, I'm hoping it's a *very* close eye.

'In fact, I spoke to her on the phone this morning when I got back here.'

I look down into his face. 'This morning? I thought you didn't arrive until late this afternoon.'

'No, I left Falconbury straight after breakfast. I would have phoned you but I didn't want to interrupt your work.'

'Oh, OK. I had a tute anyway . . .' I say, feeling super guilty because of my visit to Scott – and then annoyed that I feel guilty about it. I need to start dealing with the situation as I mean to go on. 'Alexander, we both said we'd be honest with each other so I need you to know now that I saw Scott this afternoon.'

I hold my breath and he strokes my hair. 'And?'

'Immy and I went to lunch in the cafe opposite St Nick's and we – I – decided to drop him a note.' I'm not going to use the excuse that Immy wanted to meet Scott; Alexander is just going to have to deal with our friendship.

'And do I get to know what this note was about?' His voice is edged with tension now but I refuse to be drawn into a row.

I pull away from him and sit up. His jaw is tight as we face each other.

'The note was an apology for not calling him over the holiday, but I needn't have sent it because we – Immy and I – saw him at St Nick's anyway. He'd just got back from rowing practice.' I decide not to tell

Alexander that we virtually stalked Scott to his room and dragged him out of bed.

Alexander gives me the intense look I suspect he reserves for some out-of-line squaddie, and my hackles rise.

'I sure hope this isn't going to turn into an interrogation.'

He snorts. 'Don't be ridiculous. As if I'd want to know why you went to visit another man . . .' He leaves the next part unsaid, but I know what he means; he wants me all to himself.

'Well, tough. Scott isn't another man. He's a good friend *and one I intend to keep.*'

'A friend who'd sell his place in the Blues boat to get inside your knickers.'

'Actually,' I say, imitating Alexander's cut-glass accent, 'he's not in the Blues boat yet, only in the squad, but I know he'll make it.'

'I'm sure he will. Mr Schulze won't stop until he gets what he wants.'

'Then you two have more in common than you think,' I snap.

'Wrong. I *am* the man who gets in your knickers.'

His arrogant smirk makes me want to hit him and I say the one thing guaranteed to piss him off. 'Get over yourself, Lord fucking Falconbury. Sometimes I wonder why I have anything to do with you.'

'What about the other times?' His eyes glitter dangerously in the way that makes me bubble with a lethal combination of lust and anger.

'I wonder a little less.' My body, which ought to be sated, zings with desire for him, even though I hate the confrontation.

Alexander gazes at me and for a moment I think he may explode with anger but then he reaches out and touches my cheek. It's a gentle gesture, one that ought to be tender and calming; instead it makes the hairs stand up on the back of my neck. I joked with Immy about my addiction to him; at moments like this I believe it may actually be true. Yet I swore I would never be one of those girls, caught in a relationship I can't leave, that I don't want to leave.

'We did say we would be honest with each other, so I won't lie. I don't like you seeing Scott, even as a friend. I'm jealous but I won't try to stop you,' he says gruffly.

'That's good to hear because I wouldn't stop anyway. There's nothing between us, and that's exactly why I will keep seeing him. You don't control me, Alexander Hunt. You never have and you never will.'

He gazes down at me, intimidating, intense . . . 'You do know what happens when you speak to me like that, Lauren?'

'It gives you a hard-on?' I challenge.

My breath is snatched away as he sweeps me down on to the rug and pins me there. His face is above mine.

'As I said before, I'm the one that's here with you now and I'm going to make sure you know it.'

It turns out he's only back in Oxford for a few days so I decide I'd better make the most of him being here. Later, after dinner – a steak grilled by Alexander – we're drinking red wine by the fire while he sends some emails and I try to get stuck into something fascinating about the theory and methods of art history.

He holds up the empty bottle. 'Shall I get some more wine?' he asks.

He gets up but before he's halfway out of his seat, his mobile rings. He mouths an expletive and I can tell from the instant tightening of his jaw that the caller is either from Falconbury or his regiment. I wonder if it's the mysterious Mr Armitage again.

'Relax. I think I know my way to the kitchen and I can handle a corkscrew.' Leaving him to answer the call, I head for the wine rack in the kitchen. After I've peeled off the foil of a bottle of Nuits-Saint-Georges, I step on the foot pedal of the trash can to throw the foil inside. There are only two pieces of trash in there so far; Alexander's kitchen is as neatly kept as if he were still at Sandhurst, although that may be mainly down to the cleaner. The lid bangs down but then I stop.

I open the trash can again. I wasn't mistaken. There is an envelope on top of the empty meat carton and there is something odd about the writing on the envelope. Something familiar about the thorny tendrils of the elaborate, flowing black script . . .

I reach into the inner liner and pick out the envelope between my forefinger and thumb. It's a heavyweight cream affair with a deckle-edged seal, now smeared with blood from the steak carton. My mind goes back to the card attached to the flowers that Valentina sent to the general's funeral.

Valentina sent this envelope; ergo Valentina sent Alexander a card. So what?

I lay the envelope on the countertop and pull out the cork from the bottle, laughing at my paranoia. So she sent him a sympathy card. Of course she did; what else would I expect?

In fact he's made no attempt to hide it because it's staring at me from the wooden letter rack a foot away on the counter. I know it's from Valentina because the painting of Positano faces outwards, almost demanding to be seen.

The corkscrew abandoned, I pick out the card from the rack. I know I really shouldn't open it but I can't help myself. The same spiky handwriting fills both sides. '*Tesoro*, you are always in my thoughts. I am here for you now and always . . .' After that, the general is mentioned, and something in relation to his death, so it's clearly arrived since then. Then there is something that I can't make out. My Italian is sketchy at best, and mostly confined to a lexicon relating to art, but even I can see the words '*Ti amo* . . .' and the signature, of course, is Valentina's.

It would not matter; it does not matter. She's sent him a message of condolence, that much I might have expected, and yet . . . The envelope was still in the bin, clean and barely crumpled, and there was no address and no stamp which means he must have received it personally.

'Having trouble with the corkscrew?'

With the card in my hand, I turn round to face Alexander.

He clocks it briefly, his eyes full of annoyance, and before he has chance to reply, I can't help myself. 'I knew I wasn't mistaken. I *knew* it was her I saw in town this afternoon. Was she here before you called me?' Oh shit, it just came out. I've made myself look like the jealous bitch that Valentina is. Now he's going to laugh at me and say I'm living in fantasy land and I'm deluded. Please, let him say that and have an explanation why this handwritten letter is here.

'Yes, she was here,' he says calmly.

I try to stay calm while fighting a cocktail of emotions: anger, jealousy, confusion. All the kind of feelings that I never thought I would feel, that I hate feeling and only have ever felt since I met Alexander.

He folds his arms. 'Before you jump to conclusions, she simply dropped by to offer her condolences.'

'Well, hey, that's one name for it.'

He takes a step into the kitchen. 'She came to the house, I made her a coffee and she left. The cleaner was here most of the time. If you want to interview her under oath, I can try to persuade her.'

'Why should I care anyway?'

'I was going to tell you.'

'Were you? What was she doing in Oxford? Don't tell me she came all this way in her private jet just to offer you her "condolences"?' I bracket the word with my fingers.

'You clearly think I'm more important than I actually am. She's in London to buy some paintings and got her driver to bring her. She stayed here about an hour and then she left.' His voice is ice cool yet I can feel the impatience bristling from every pore. 'Lauren, I seem to recall us having a conversation about being honest with each other.'

'So do I.'

'Which is why I'm glad – but not happy – you told me you'd seen Scott. Believe me, I have enough on my plate at the moment without taking any kind of drama from Valentina. I told her I'm trying to persuade you to make a go of it with me and she's accepted it. That's an end of things, as far as I'm concerned.'

While I can't imagine Valentina ever accepting that Alexander has moved on from her, I don't want to start another row with Alexander because neither of us needs the hassle now. Yet she must be up to something. Taking a mental deep breath, I decide to act as peace-maker. My father would be proud.

'OK, let's forget Valentina. Was your call from home? Is Emma OK?' I ask.

'Actually, it was the regiment, but don't worry. I'm not going anywhere for a while.'

'Good,' I murmur.

'But I have heard from Emma today. She seems to be coping well. In fact she asked if you wanted to go to an exhibition at the V&A with her.' He seems a little embarrassed but goes on, 'You two seem to get on so well and I thought you might be able to use it for research. I want things to go well this term. It may be difficult but, after the start we've had, it would be good if things quietened down. I can't promise to be here as much as I'd like but we should make the most of . . .'

'Which exhibition? The "British Drawings" or the "Malay Silver"?'

'Neither. I believe it's called "Club to Catwalk". Some fashion thing or other.'

I burst out laughing. 'I saw it and I was thinking of going anyway but, Alexander, surely you're simply desperate to see that yourself? All those eighties and nineties outfits, Betty Jackson, John Galliano. I heard they had some of Adam Ant's costumes . . .'

He comes towards me and holds my arms lightly. 'Frankly, I'd rather be bayoneted.'

I can't help but smile. 'Now, now, I only asked you to go and see them, not wear them. Though I think you'd look great in legwarmers and a frilly shirt.'

He shakes his head. 'Lauren, you're asking for a serious . . .'

He stops, but I'm fizzing from the sensual threat in his eyes. A bizarre image slides into my mind and sends a jolt of desire right through me. I see myself standing naked in the kitchen with my hands tied behind my back with a black silk ribbon. My face fires up instantly and I rub my clammy palms on my jeans.

Alexander's eyes laser into me, then he smiles briefly. The bastard. I know he's guessed I was thinking something pretty kinky and I blush even more.

'So you will go with Emma?' he says coolly, while I take two fresh glasses out of the glass-fronted wall cabinet. 'We can go to the Ivy for lunch afterwards if you like. I need to meet my legal people anyway.'

My voice sounds shaky to me. 'OK. Yes, I'd love to. When do you want to go?'

'Emma has an exeat next weekend and the exhibition closes soon, so is next Saturday OK?'

I throw him a smile and start to fill the glasses. 'It's fine, but will we get a table at the Ivy at such short notice? I thought they were booked up for months ahead.'

'I'm sure they'll squeeze us in.' I turn to push the cork back in the bottle when his palm lands on my behind. He strokes my butt cheek deliciously and I close my eyes.

'I thought you wanted more wine . . .'

'I need other things more.'

The timbre of his voice changes. It's deeper and rougher. Without turning me round, he starts to unzip my jeans. I push away the bottle and let my head drift to one side. His lips brush my neck and he kisses my throat. I close my eyes, while his fingers slip inside the fly of my jeans and press down on me through the fabric of my underwear. He smells of the Creed aftershave he keeps in his bathroom and the scent of arousal. Or is that my arousal? I try to turn my head but he pushes my cheek away.

'*Don't* look at me.'

His command is like an electric shock. I grip the countertop, half fearful, half eager to know and feel what he has in store for me.

'Eyes front,' he whispers, dropping butterfly kisses on the side of my neck that counter the harsh command. He reaches round to hold his finger to my lips. 'And *no* talking.'

I may not be able to talk but I sure as hell can moan and whimper as he returns his hands to my jeans and tugs them down my thighs, along with my knickers. As he slips his hand between my legs from behind, I want to turn around, I want to know what he's going to do next, but I dare not. I close my eyes. Every sound is magnified in the big kitchen: our breathing, his boots on the tiles and the sound of him unbuckling his belt.

The muscles of his thighs are iron hard against my behind, and I can't resist wiggling my tush against him. I also can't resist reaching back to touch him, wanting to feel how hard I've made him but his fingers close over mine and return them to the countertop.

'*And* no touching, either.'

I bite back a retort, deciding to play along with him, amazed at how much I'm enjoying the game. At how wet I am, and –

My knuckles whiten on the edge of the counter as my panties are ripped down further and he parts the cheeks of my butt with his fingers. My breathing quickens and my palms are slippery. I try to focus on the espresso machine, my face distorted in the chrome like some weird fairground mirror. He nudges his cock between my cheeks and my body tenses.

Then, suddenly, he's kissing the back of my neck, telling me I'm hot and gorgeous and I drive him wild. Gently, he scoops his hands under my bottom and pushes into me, filling me to the hilt. All the tension in my body is released with a cry of relief and insane pleasure. I was so wound up, so on edge, that the pleasure of him inside me now is intensely good.

'You bastard. You wicked, evil bastard.'

'Thanks,' he says, nuzzling my neck, nipping my shoulder, then resuming the rhythm of his thrusts until we both come, him not long after me, his groan of release echoing through the kitchen. Boy, am I glad the walls are thick.

It is the calm after the storm, Alexander taps away on his laptop while I flick through the pages of a book on

Van Eyck. I must confess my mind is not wholly occupied by what may have happened to the stolen panel of the *Adoration of the Mystic Lamb*, but by Valentina, and Emma and our trip to the V&A. Of course I want to see the exhibition; who wouldn't? However, I'm also uneasy about keeping Emma's secret, about seeing her with Alexander present and possibly being dragged further into the intrigue. One Hunt sibling drama is more than enough for me.

I have wondered if I should tell Alexander – and after our honesty pledge, maybe now is the time, *but* I'm really not sure that it extends to other people's secrets. If I'd been Emma at seventeen, I'd have been furious that my parents – let alone a brother, if I had one – would try to control who I dated. And maybe she's not even seeing him any more, I tell myself. Then again, even on a short acquaintance, I know Henry Favell is not a nice guy; hell, even *Rupert* thinks he's a scumbag.

'Alexander?'

He glances up from the screen and I notice the dark circles under his eyes and the line deepens between his brows before he manages a tight smile. 'Sorry. What?'

'I just wondered if you'd like a coffee?'

'Thanks. That would be good.' His eyes return to the screen and he carries on tap tapping away. My confession dies in my throat; he has so much on his plate, I can't bear to add to it. All I can do is keep my fingers crossed.

*

A few days later, my grip tightens on my racket bag as Professor Rafe stops me halfway round the quad. He's really rocking the hipster-don look today, having ditched the cords for dark-red chinos and added a baby-blue scarf to the tweed jacket.

'Ah, Lauren. I'm so glad I bumped into you.'

'Oh, hi, Professor Rafe.'

'Nice to see you're enjoying yourself.' He glances at the racket bag on my shoulder. Why, oh, why does he have to 'bump into me' when I'm on my way back from a game with Immy, instead of when I'm hard at work in the Sackler Library or the Bod?

'Oxford has so many distractions, doesn't it?' He peers at my tennis outfit from over his geeky wire-rimmed specs in a way he thinks is intimidating yet sexy. Mercifully I have on my Lululemon tracksuit over my tee and shorts. He seems jaunty, so maybe he's been shagging the 'female friend' he mentioned to me at the end of last term; it would make a change from hitting on his students.

'I've been trying to ignore them but I needed some fresh air and exercise,' I say, already aware that I'm apologizing for something I have no need to regret. On the other hand, I did miss some of the first week of term and an important tute at the end of the last one to go to the hunt ball at Falconbury. Rafe warned me off Alexander and made it clear that I shouldn't let our relationship interfere with my studies. I was pissed at being patronized and at the personal intrusion but I can't deny I've had a lot of time off.

'Exercise *is* good for the brain but I'm glad to hear you've had your head down. I was going to ask you this at our next tutorial but as you're here, *carpe diem* and all that. Who knows what fate has in store for us . . .'

'*Carpe diem.* Of course.' I'm not totally sure what he's referring to, but it doesn't take Patrick Jane to surmise it has something to do with Alexander. Rafe was his pastoral tutor while Alexander was an undergraduate at one of the other colleges. His leer flicks over my body like a lizard's tongue and I suppress a shudder.

'What did you want to ask me, professor?'

'There's a showing of Bertolucci's *Il Conformista* at the Phoenix.'

'Oh, OK . . .'

'You do know it? It features thirties Fascist art and design. It's the supreme example of the relationship between architecture and film.'

'Isn't it also about a student planning to assassinate his tutor?'

He smirks. 'That is one of the themes, yes.'

'So it's a faculty trip? Who else is going?'

'Well, I was rather thinking of making it a one-to-one, a sort of off-site tutorial. I know you're interested in that era and the film is set in Rome. It's only on for one night, if you're not doing anything on Saturday.'

Just the two of us? 'Well, thanks so much for inviting me and I'd have loved to, but I've already got tickets for the "Club to Catwalk" exhibition at the V&A on Saturday.'

'"Club to Catwalk"?' Rafe looks even less impressed than Alexander did.

'Yes, with Emma Hunt, Alexander's sister. She's planning to do a theatrical costume course at Saint Martins. I feel obliged to go with her, to be honest.'

He smiles but his eyes are as cold as a lizard's. 'In that case, if you're forced to go . . .'

'I wouldn't say "forced" but, in the circumstances, I think she needs the support and encouragement.'

'Of course. I suppose I can ask one of my other students to come with me instead. I know that they'd all jump at the opportunity, but it's sad that we won't have chance to enjoy some extra time to exchange ideas. Still, I understand you feel you can't possibly let one of the Hunts down.'

'I don't *want* to let either of them down . . .' I qualify, annoyed at myself for implying that I've been forced to go to the exhibition.

'How *is* Alexander coping by the way? He's a volatile character at the best of times and losing his father so young, on top of his mother's death, must be very traumatic. You're not suffering from the fallout, I hope? After missing the first seminar of term, I was hoping you'd be able to refocus on your exam essays and research.'

'I have refocused and I've worked very hard to catch up. You saw my last essay? I hope it was up to standard.'

'It was very well written and researched, of course, but I was rather hoping for more than "standard" from a girl with your intellect and abilities, Lauren. I think we can push you a lot harder, now all this business with the Hunts is over. In fact, I've decided to demand more from you from now on.'

I swallow but he smiles serenely and continues, 'For your own good of course, and I hope you won't mind me being a stern taskmaster and cracking the whip.'

Eww. The professor as Dom. My stomach curdles.

He frowns. 'Many of my students respond well to a little firm handling; in fact, it's the most promising ones that ask for it.'

'I think you're quite firm enough how you are. Now, I must get out of the cold and take a shower.'

'Yes, you must . . .'

I give up. You couldn't read the phone directory without Rafe turning it into an innuendo. 'Bye and see you later. I have to work. Really hard. Right now.'

Chapter Eight

On Saturday morning, after a week of lectures and tutes plus the nerve-wracking short presentation I had to give to my seminar class on the Alfred Jewel in the Ashmolean, I'm more than ready to get out of Oxford. However, I have to confess I'm a little embarrassed when the Bentley arrives outside the Lodge to take me to London, especially as Immy insists on coming to wave me off in the style of the Queen. There's also no chance of getting the Hunts' chauffeur to speak to me like I'm a student rather than a dowager countess, so I decide to suck it up and enjoy the sights as he whisks me to South Ken. As he opens the door outside the V&A, Alexander and Emma are already waiting on the steps. Alexander picked her up from school in the Range Rover.

'Hello!'

Emma throws her arms around me like we're old friends and whispers, 'This is going to be *brilliant*!' while Alexander's expression is one of relief. Emma is rocking a long black Goth skirt and emerald metallic DMs, and her dark hair is piled messily but artily on top of her head. She has more colour in her cheeks than at the funeral, and somehow the quirky outfit looks sensational on her coltish figure.

When she finally releases me, Alexander gives me a quick kiss on the lips, then stands aside. I can tell that he feels too awkward for public displays of affection, or possibly there's been some tension between him and Emma on the way here. No, make that 'probably' and 'a lot of tension'.

'I've asked Brandon to pick you up at one. Two hours should be enough, shouldn't it?'

'We'd have been fine getting over to the restaurant by tube,' I say.

'Yes, I think we can make our own way to the Ivy,' says Emma sarcastically. 'Preferably by way of Camden Market.'

'I'd rather not change the plans now,' says Alexander firmly.

Emma slips her arm through mine. 'There's no point arguing with him. See you later, Alex!'

She sweeps me up the steps through the Grand Entrance to the museum. When I glance back, Alexander is already pulling into traffic.

'How do you get away with it?' I ask Emma.

'Get away with what?'

'Calling him Alex? I thought he hated it.'

'Oh, he *does*. Mummy was the only person who used to call him Alex, even though Daddy hated her doing it – maybe precisely *because* Daddy hated it – so I started using it too, partly to tease him and partly to annoy

Daddy. There's not much either of them can do about it, is there?'

'I guess not.'

'It won't do him any harm. He needs someone to pull the poker out of his arse now and then. Alex thinks he's been put on the earth to protect everyone: me, the estate, not to mention the rest of the world, of course; but the reality is that *he's* the one who needs people like you and me. He needs protecting from people like Valentina and from himself.'

Wow. I'm not sure I agree with all of this but it certainly shows some insight on Emma's part, and it also puts me on my guard. She is an explosive mix of little girl and wise woman: volatile, clever, vulnerable.

Even though I've visited the V&A recently, the scale and grandeur of the place takes my breath away. I make Emma stop so I can get a better view of the intricately decorated dome and the Bocci chandelier suspended above the reception desk. The coloured spheres are mesmerizing.

'Alexander doesn't know what he's missing,' says Emma, a smile on her face, when I eventually tear my eyes from the chandelier.

'Oh, I think he does.'

'Yes, and I'm glad he isn't here because he'd only stand about checking his watch and looking miserable. Can we go straight to the "Club to Catwalk" thing? We can check out some of the other installations and galleries afterwards and I'll tell you all my news.'

'Sure.' I manage a weak smile. Judging by the mischievous glint in her eye, this news is sure to involve Henry.

The exhibition captures all our attention over the next hour and has Emma almost popping with delight over the costumes worn by iconic eighties and nineties bands and artists.

'Some of them actually went to Saint Martins, you know,' she says, stopping in front of a John Galliano creation. 'I can't wait to go there, even if Daddy didn't approve.'

'Are you sure he was so set against you going?'

She snorts in derision. It's clear Alexander still hasn't told her that their father had resigned himself to her choice. After we've wrung every last drop out of the exhibition, we head to the Theatre and Performance Collection, where some of the dance costumes are beyond beautiful. It's while we're looking at a stunning ballet tutu designed for Princess Aurora in *Sleeping Beauty* that Emma nudges me and lowers her voice.

'I'm *so* excited. I'm seeing Henry later. Alexander thinks he's dropping me at a friend's house for a party but I'm actually going to spend the night with Henry. He booked a lovely hotel nearby.'

My stomach churns a little at this news. I have no idea why Emma has chosen me to go all confessional to; I guess it's her way of rebelling against the strictures of her life, but I don't want to be part of her strategy.

'Maybe you shouldn't be telling me this.' I'm only half joking but she laughs.

'Why not? You're not going to run off and tell my brother, are you?'

Her eyes challenge me and I wonder if she actually *does* hope I'll tell Alexander, just to get a reaction from him. Maybe she wants me to tell him, just to get his attention.

'I won't tell him anything you don't want me to but it does put me in a very awkward position. I know he would hate you seeing Henry. Are you sure you know what you're doing?'

'Oh, I know you won't, and don't worry, I know how to look after myself. It is nice to have someone to share my secrets with though.'

'What about your friends? Surely they know you're seeing this guy?'

'Allegra does, but I can't trust anyone else at school. They're so immature and some of them are real bitches and would love to go out with Henry themselves. They'd probably go straight to the teachers and *they'd* call Alexander. I know the head has got me on some sort of "bereavement watch" since Daddy died, and I hate it.'

'I guess they're only trying to help.'

'I think it's just an excuse to keep me away from Henry. We're hardly doing anything illegal: I'm over sixteen and it's not as if Henry's shagged me on school premises, apart from the cricket pavilion thing, of course.' She glances around her and giggles. 'Quite a memorable place for a first time, don't you think?'

My first reaction is that I hope they used protection. My second is to cringe when I think back to the way I flirted outrageously with Henry at the hunt ball. I can see Alexander's furious face now and his relatives' expressions as I slow-danced with the guy. OK, I was drunk *and* upset that Alexander hadn't exactly been fighting off Valentina's attentions, but I wish it hadn't happened now. For one thing, Henry followed me out of the room and tried to have sex with me. If I hadn't managed to escape into the orangery, I think things might have got pretty nasty.

Instead, I ended up having an enormous row with Alexander and left first thing in the morning without telling him. It wasn't only the argument and the flirting, it was the whole weekend at Falconbury – it brought it home to me how far apart Alexander and I had grown – or how different we'd always been. How different we still are.

'You don't approve of Henry, do you?'

When I drag my eyes from the display case in front of me, Emma is treating me to a laser stare that would put Alexander's to shame.

'I've only met him once . . .'

'But you don't think I should see him because Alexander can't stand him?'

'Like I say, I don't know him well enough to make up my mind, but why would you think you need my approval?'

She shrugs. 'I don't know. It's just . . . I'm sick of

doing things that other people don't like. I'd love it if, for once, I did something that my family were proud of, but it's too late for that, isn't it? Daddy's gone now and he'll never know or care what I do ever again.'

I'm not going to offer some platitude about her father looking down on her but I *am* going to ask Alexander to tell Emma that her father had relented about her choice of course. If he won't, I will tell her myself, no matter how much he thinks I'm interfering.

'I'm one hundred percent sure that Alexander cares what you do and is incredibly proud of you. I'm also sure he won't like you seeing Henry, whether his reasons are fair or not, and I won't tell him but, please, be careful. The only thing Alexander is bothered about is you getting hurt, and you can laugh at him for that if you like but it's true. Now, we've got ten minutes. Shall we grab a coffee?'

She pulls a face. 'I'd rather have wine.'

'Fine. Come on.'

A short time later, Emma chatters away excitedly as the waiter seats us for lunch at the Ivy. Alexander was waiting outside when his chauffeur dropped us off. He seemed tense, but that's to be expected, I guess. Against my expectations, lunch is a fairly battle-free zone and after we've eaten and Emma has gone to the bathroom, I ask Alexander how his meeting has gone.

'It went as well as these things can do, I suppose. It's still uncharted territory for me.'

Wishing I hadn't mentioned the meeting, I try for neutral territory. 'I'm surprised they could see you on a weekend.'

'As they charge by the half-hour, they seem to be eager to see me any time. They'd have come to the Oxford house, if I'd wanted them to, but Emma needed some time away from school and this seemed like a good opportunity. Has she been much of a pain this morning?'

'Not a pain at all.' Not in the way he thinks, anyway. 'I had a good time.'

'Thanks for coming with us.' He manages a smile and takes my hand.

'No biggie.' I take the plunge. 'She was a little upset about your father not approving of her going to Saint Martins. I guess you haven't told her what he said about that yet?'

'No, not yet. I'm not sure how to broach the subject.'

'I think it would give her a bit of comfort. I think she wants your attention.'

'My attention? I thought she was desperate to get away from my attention. I don't want to interfere in her life.'

I smile.

'What's funny?'

'Um, nothing. What the heck do I know about handling sisters or teenagers?'

'Probably as much as I do, but I will speak to her

about Dad if you think it would help. Not today though; it's probably better if I mention it when I'm alone with her, and I don't want to spoil her afternoon by talking about him when she seems happy.' He sips his water and it occurs to me that he can't face another emotional conversation with Emma on top of his other worries or he would have told her before. 'I've sent Brandon back to Falconbury. I'm going to drop Emma off at her friend's house on our way back to Oxford.'

'OK.' I swallow a tinge of unease that I know who this 'friend' is.

He leans closer and whispers in my ear, 'Then I'll take you home and shag you senseless.'

Beneath the shelter of the tablecloth, his hand rests on my thigh and my body tenses, not only because I'm turned on but because of Emma and Henry. Oh Jesus, I can't keep this up.

My pulse beats a little faster. 'Is that a threat or a promise?'

'With me, they're the same thing.'

He removes his hand as Emma breezes up, a sly smile on her face. 'Tut tut. You guys *do* look guilty. I hope you haven't been talking about me, or have I interrupted something? Hey, do you two want to get a room?'

Alexander never blushes but his expression would be worth capturing in oils. 'Actually, I was just suggesting to Lauren that you might like to pay the bill,' he says sarcastically.

'Why not? I can afford it now I have Mummy's money.'

'Not yet,' says Alexander in a voice as chilly as the iced water he's been drinking. 'Don't forget I have to approve your allowance until you're twenty-one.'

Emma curls her lip in contempt. 'Has anyone ever told you you can be a complete arse sometimes, Alex?'

'All the time.'

'I tell you what, I'll pay,' I say and before either of them can object, I slap my credit card on the silver tray and hold it out to the waiter.

While we're waiting for the Range Rover to be brought by the parking valet, Emma whispers in my ear, 'Now you can see why I don't tell him anything important. He can be such an arse!'

Since I agree with this to an extent, there's not much I can say and now Alexander is opening the door for Emma to climb inside. There's no way they'll talk while I'm here. I could tell Alexander that reminding Emma that he's in charge of her inheritance and ergo her life is not the best way to gain her confidence. I won't, because it won't help.

An hour later, he pulls up on the drive of a rambling stone manor house. Emma climbs down and Alexander retrieves her backpack from the trunk. The journey has largely been silent, Alexander intent on the road, worrying no doubt about Emma and the estate and his work. I've kept my eyes on the scenery while wondering how I can get out of playing double agent to Alexander and Emma. I can't see Emma's face but from her silence, she's still pissed at Alexander, or maybe just intent on her phone.

Alexander hands her the backpack and suddenly she flings her arms around his back. He hugs her tightly and they linger for a few seconds. She says something to him and he kisses her briefly and then she's off, marching up to the front door where Allegra has appeared.

He climbs back into the driver's seat and rests his hands on the wheel, watching as Allegra lets Emma inside.

'Everything OK?' I ask.

'I don't know. Emma's behaving strangely. She's up and down like a yo-yo, even more than usual.'

'Isn't that understandable? It's still early days.'

'Yes, and she's always been hard to fathom but she seems to be on edge about something and I don't think it's all due to losing Dad. Maybe I shouldn't have risen to the bait and wound her up about her inheritance in the restaurant but I'm worried about what will happen to her in the future. There are plenty of bastards out there who would do anything to get their hands on a fraction as much as she's worth. I feel responsible.'

He's under huge pressure, and I guess occasionally lashing out and behaving unreasonably is understandable. I can also see through his relationship with his sister that he is really a good guy, that there is substance there, that he is troubled and hurting and sometimes unbearably arrogant, but fundamentally he's a decent guy. I find myself wondering for the first time since I arrived back in the UK whether Alexander and I really could actually make a go of it. I've not been able to stay away from him, that's for sure, but up till now, in my head, it's just been sex. Perhaps I've been kidding myself about that anyway, because I'm becoming increasingly addicted to him and I'm not sure I could walk away even if I wanted to now, despite all the tangles that make my head ache just thinking of them.

He stares thoughtfully at the manor house and as he speaks, I am jolted out of my thoughts. 'At least I know she's safe tonight.' My stomach lurches; surely I have to tell him she's going to see Henry. He grips the steering wheel. 'I'd kill anyone who hurt her.'

A lump settles in my throat, knowing I'm damned if I do tell him and damned if I don't. I think I'm going to have to somehow get Emma to tell him herself because hoping she'll drop Henry is the coward's way out.

'I don't mind helping Emma.'

He turns to me. 'You've done your duty today and now I'm going to drive you home and take you to bed.'

'It isn't my duty. I like her.'

And it is true: I do like her, she's feisty, bright, doesn't want to conform to what people expect and I understand that so much, but she's also vulnerable.

He frowns as if he can't believe I'm serious, but then

says, 'I love her but I'm out of my depth with her. I'd rather have a whole platoon to deal with; none of them ever give me the trouble Emma does. I thought my father had no idea how to deal with her but now it's all my responsibility, I think I might be doing an even worse job of it.'

'I'm sure you're doing ten times better than other people would . . .'

He puts his finger on my lips. 'Enough, Ms Cusack. Not another word unless it's about the blow job you're going to give me when I get you back to Oxford.'

'That's beyond presumptuous, Mr Hunt.' I pretend to be outraged.

'However, it is accurate.'

'You are just . . .'

'Right?' He raises a sexy eyebrow.

'Arghh.'

OK, scrub that about him being a gentleman – and I can't hit him because he's in the process of reversing out of Allegra's drive. No matter how outrageous he is, however, I can't deny I'm relieved to have the distraction of a little sparring.

Now, back in the warmth of his bed, there's nothing in my head but the gentle rasp of his tongue on me and the sensations radiating through my body while I dig my nails into his sheets, my resistance in shreds. He's going down on me, in return, he says, for me doing the same to him.

Even if I wanted to stop him, I can't because my wrists are bound with curtain cord to the posts of his half-tester bed. Being tied up is a new experience for me, and I confess I got a swishing feeling in my stomach when Alexander suggested it, even though I'd fantasized about it when we were in the kitchen the other week. It's hardly perverted but it is my first foray into kink, although not, I suspect, Alexander's. Yet I can't deny the incredible sensation I have now, lying here, totally helpless to stop him doing whatever he wants to me. He varies the pressure of his mouth on me, skimming his tongue over my swollen nub and teasing me until I beg for mercy.

'Please . . .'

He glances up from between my legs. 'What was that again?'

'Please . . . Alexander!'

'Please stop or please go on?'

'Yes, no . . . I don't know . . . Oh . . .'

He renews the assault on me with his mouth and I can't do a damn thing about it. The bonds looped around my wrists aren't that tight but I don't think I can free my wrists and so I clutch the cord in my palms and writhe against the bed. The insistent lapping of his tongue is a torture, and my climax ramps up to a new level. I'm a mass of nerve endings, electric . . . I close my eyes.

The pressure has stopped and Alexander is kneeling now, one thigh either side of my legs. While I'm still tied to the bedposts, he edges inside my slick heat and then plunges into me. I want to dig my nails in his butt and urge him in but I can't. He's so tight, so big, that the pressure of his penis on my sensitized clit is enough to send me over the edge. I hold on while he drives into me, the rhythmic pulsation of him inside me and the rigid muscles of his neck tell me he's out of this world. I hope he enjoys watching me come as much as I like seeing him lose control completely. It makes me feel powerful and mysterious, even though I know it's just biology.

Smiling to myself, I lie still with him beside me, clearly too whacked out to move. I can't see him but his fingers creep over mine and squeeze them.

'I hate to say this but I do believe you're good for me, Ms Cusack.'

Thinking of Emma, I'm not sure I am, so I reply with something that *is* true. 'And you're bad for me, Mr Hunt. But somehow I can't seem to stay away.'

He laughs and for the first time since way back in last term, he sounds happy again. So what if he thinks I'm joking; I'm not about to change that.

Chapter Nine

Almost a week has passed since we went to the V&A. I haven't heard any more from Emma. I haven't dared ask Alexander how she is too often, in case he suspects I know something he doesn't. However, I can tell he's quietly pleased when I do ask after her, which makes me feel even guiltier, but I know I have to try to put her love life to the back of my mind and get on with my work.

It started snowing in Oxford not long after we got back on Saturday evening, although the streets are now thick with grey slush. Alexander has been in lockdown since then, desperately trying to catch up with the work for his course. He's been offered a dispensation by his tutor, but he's adamant he doesn't want any special treatment. He hasn't had to go back to Falconbury again nor, as far as I know, has he been summoned by his regiment again, so I hope now that things can settle down between us.

I've also needed the time to get some of my own work done. Professor Rafe has been cracking his whip, taking apart my essays 'for my own good', he says, and suggesting huge piles of reading, journals and pieces to study in the Ashmolean and Modern Art gallery. I think his strategy is to leave me with no time for anything other than work; maybe he hopes I'll be too exhausted to shag Alexander. By the time Friday morning comes, I'm trudging back from the Faculty of Art History, wondering if I can get away with taking Saturday off from working, when my phone beeps.

> So has Alexander given you one yet?
> I x ☺

I roll my eyes at Immy's message, then again as I almost do the splits outside the Lodge. Slush on top of sixteenth-century flagstones is a lethal combination.

> Not in the way you think.
> Has Skandar put anything in
> your pigeonhole yet?

Moments later, I get a reply.

> Yes, *and* I got an enormous card.

I text back:

> See you outside the JCR in 5. L x

En route to the JCR, I decide to check my pigeon-hole in the Lodge, not because I'm expecting an enormous card or an enormous anything (other than the obvious) from Alexander today. Valentine's Day is not a big thing for me, and it definitely won't be for Alexander, so I'm not the *least* bit envious when I see a friend called Isla picking up a huge bouquet of red roses from the porters' desk.

'Wow. They're beautiful.'

'Aren't they? Not that I was expecting anything, of course,' she says in her cute Scottish accent. 'But my boyfriend's in Edinburgh and I do admit I'll miss him today.'

Just then, her face changes and suddenly she shrieks, bursts into tears and rushes off, leaving the roses on the desk. When I turn around, she's launched herself at a guy carrying an overnight bag.

The Head Porter shakes his head and smiles like he's seen this scene a thousand times.

'I expect you'll have tons of cards,' he jokes, as Isla and her boyfriend walk off, hand in hand.

'I doubt it,' I say and it's then I realize that, no matter what I tell myself or anyone else, part of me wouldn't be too heartbroken if Alexander did send me a card. Which he won't, because he hates any kind of vulgar commercialism, of course, and you know what? I don't need a giant teddy bear or a bunch of overpriced roses anyway, and all that pressure to plan the perfect romantic evening is ridiculous. In fact, I thought I'd be able to avoid the whole Valentine's craziness we get in the States, with gifts and cards in the stores on New Year's Eve. However, having seen the stores full of what Immy calls 'pink tat' for over a month, I realize it's almost as bad here.

I slither along the Back Quad at Wyckham on my way to the JCR. Against one wall, in a stray patch of sunlight, tight buds of crocuses shiver in the wind.

They look too terrified to open yet and I shiver as the raw chill seems to clutch at my bones.

'Lauren!' Immy is standing in the JCR porch in crimson Hunters, a huge scarf wound around her neck. Her cheeks are ruddy from the sharp air but she has a warm smile on her face. 'Hi there. Are you still on for tennis later?'

'You are kidding me? In this weather?' I lift my soggy boot from the snow. 'I think my toes are about to drop off.'

'Yes, they'll have cleared the courts by lunchtime. Should be fun.'

'I . . . um . . .'

She eyes me suspiciously. 'You're not going to be a wuss, are you?'

'Of course not. What time?'

'I booked the court for two-thirty but we need to allow a bit extra for cycling while the roads are so dodgy. Meet you at two in the Lodge?'

'Sure,' I say, as a wet patch seeps through the toes of my tights. 'I can't wait.'

'Great. Want a quick coffee?'

'OK.'

We find a corner of the JCR that's not obscured by dismembered newspapers and sit down. 'So what have you and Alexander got planned for tonight?'

'Nothing.'

'What?'

'I'm not even seeing him, as far as I know. He's been

burning the midnight oil trying to catch up with his work since we got back from London. He called me last night but he didn't say anything about going out tonight.'

'Typical, but maybe he's planning on cooking you a surprise meal.' Immy uses the tone of someone condoling me on a bereavement.

'To be honest, I need to work too, unless you want to go and see a movie and get away from it all?'

She looks sheepish. 'I would have loved to but Skandar booked a table for dinner at a restaurant. Sorry. I know it's a bad night to go out, the service will be terrible and the place will be full of loved-up people sharing spaghetti and paying a fortune for the Prosecco but . . .'

'Hey, don't worry. Valentine's is even crazier in the States. It's a wonder they don't dye the Potomac pink. People send cards to their friends, family and even their teachers. Yes, I used to do it too.'

'Really?'

'Uh-huh. Last year, one of Todd's co-workers even sent a barbershop quartet to his girlfriend to serenade her at her workplace. Mind you, it was a law office.'

She pulls a face. 'Eww. That would be too much. I don't feel quite so guilty about getting a card and adding to the restaurant owners' bank balance now.'

'You shouldn't. Go and enjoy yourself. I never expected Alexander to even remember the day. He's so wrapped up in his work, worrying about Emma and the estate, and I have more than enough to do. I have another of these mini presentations to do for my seminar group tomorrow and I should be working on that.'

Immy finishes her coffee. 'We could go and see a film tomorrow. There's a director's cut of *Shame* at the Phoenix and there won't be people snogging everywhere. We could go to Po Na Na afterwards.'

'That sounds cool.'

She dumps the empty cup in the bin next to her and sighs. 'I've got a tute with Dr Scary before lunch. You know, the one who called me a bimbo when she found out I'd taken my eyelash curlers and bikini on a field trip?'

I laugh. 'See you at two. I'll just go look out my thermal underwear for the game.'

When I get back to my room, I fire up the laptop and check my emails, knowing it's only a displacement activity before I start actual work. There are a couple of messages from girl friends, and one from my mother to tell me 'a mysterious parcel' has arrived, with a message not to open until her birthday. That must be the prints I bought on the day Valentina 'dropped in' on Alexander. I make a note on the iMac to set up a Skype chat on my mother's birthday. There's also a message from Professor Rafe, entitled 'Italian video to watch before next tutorial'.

Sigh. Is this something about *Il Conformista*, the movie he wanted us to go to see together? I click on the link, waiting to be gripped by the scenes of Fascist architecture and interior decor.

What I actually get are two naked people writhing on the screen, moaning and groaning.

Instantly, I close the window. I'm going to *have* to go to the Dean with this. Rafe has sent me a link to a porn site and it cannot be an accident unless his email has been hacked. And yet . . . the subject line – 'Italian video to watch' – is so specific.

My finger hovers over the delete key, and then something makes me re-open the window and replay the video.

It can't be. It's not possible. My heart thumps like crazy. Surely I'm mistaken. *Surely*.

My fingers are trembling as I sit back in my chair, dizzy with shock.

When I open the link again, the naked woman tied to the posts of the bed with curtain cord opens her mouth and groans. Her long black hair spreads over the pillow. The guy, also nude, is kneeling beside her on the bed. He has his back to me but I don't have to see his face. I recognize the scar on his shoulder and the powerful glutes. As he leans forward to go down on her, and she turns her face to the camera and smiles in triumph, the bile rises in my throat.

The moans and shrieks grow louder as the clip runs and I can't tear my eyes from the screen.

With Alexander's head between her knees, Valentina shrieks, '*Dammelo, Alexander!*'

Even with my limited grasp of the language, I can tell she's not asking him for a fucking pizza.

'*Ah, sì, bene cosi va . . .*'

I dry-retch into the bin, while the groans and shrieks and a string of Italian expletives spew from the laptop. When I stagger back to the screen, Alexander is astride Valentina. I stand there, my hand over my mouth.

'*Ah, sono proprio arrapato per te. Succhia la mia grilletto.*' What happens next, while she is still tied to the bed, is so inevitable yet so horrible that I slam down the lid of the laptop. I stand in front of it, shaking like a leaf yet unable to move a muscle.

It's no good. I *can't* ignore it. Maybe I'm dreaming, or high or something, but when I open the lid again, the clip is still running and Alexander is still screwing Valentina as she writhes on the bed and wails like a banshee. Do other people *really* make that kind of noise when they're having sex? Do *I*?

And then the *killer*. Alexander thrusts himself into her and cries out, '*Ti amo!*'

Abruptly, the clip ends, with Alexander's bare butt a frozen blur and Valentina's mouth open so wide in a scream of ecstasy and triumph that you could do a tonsillectomy on her.

I should delete the video; I should run out of my room and not stop until my legs collapse from under me. I should rush out into the quad and scream at the top of my voice – but I don't.

I click on the clip again.

I'm like a junkie, compelled to OD on the thing I know will hurt and torment me, and yet I have to burn the images into my mind. I have to make myself believe that what I've seen is real and not some nightmare or hallucination, even though watching it feels like a cold hand squeezing my stomach time after time after time.

I don't know how long I've lain here, curled up in a ball on my bed. There's a lead weight in the pit of my stomach and a numbness in my limbs.

There's a knock at my door.

'Lauren! Are you in there?'

Immy. Oh fuck. I forgot I was supposed to be meeting her in the Lodge to play tennis. I can't go now. I just *can't*. I can't even cope with seeing her now. I'm a mess.

The door panel trembles. 'Lauren, open the door or tell me to piss off. Just let me know you're alive.'

'I . . . don't feel too good. I can't come to tennis.' My voice is croaky with crying.

Silence, then an anxious voice. 'OK, don't worry. Is there anything I can do?'

'No. No. Nothing.'

I want her to go away. If I have to show that video to her, knowing her reaction, I'll howl the place down.

'All righty, but I'm going to be around for the rest of the afternoon. Phone me if you can't get up, and I'll call round later.'

A few seconds later, her footsteps retreat down the

landing and I hear her door close. I lie on my bed staring at the ceiling until the sun has gone from my room and the corners grow dark. I keep replaying the video in my head, looking for some way to explain it away, but there is no mistaking that it was Alexander and Valentina in the clip. No mistaking the bed either, despite the jerky webcam footage. It's the bed at his Oxford house, the one I share most nights, the one he tied *me* to a few days ago and did those things to me.

The numbness I felt when I first viewed the clip has worn off and anger has taken its place. A wild anger with no direction that seizes me like a tornado. The questions tear at my brain with their Harpies' claws. Who sent it? Rafe must have had his email hacked – he couldn't possibly have got access to a video like this. It has to be Valentina . . . so how does she know Rafe is my tutor?

'Lauren, hun?'

The small and desperate voice outside my door is Immy's again.

I scramble my way up from my soggy pillow. 'Uh-huh.'

'Can you open the door or do you feel too sick? Shall I fetch the college nurse?'

'I'm not sick.'

A pause. 'Then, hun, why don't you let me in?'

If I stay like this any longer, Immy will either get someone to break the door down or call the porters. I've been lying down for ages and skipped lunch so I feel a little light-headed as I climb off the bed and inch open the door, knowing I'm letting in more than just Immy. Knowing I'll have to share the humiliation and shame of that fucking clip.

Her mouth opens in an 'O' of dismay as soon as she sees me.

'Oh my God, what the hell's happened? You're white as a sheet. Have you had awful news from home?'

'No.'

'Has something happened to Alexander?' She walks past me and I close the door behind her.

My anger boils over like acid. 'Yes, I think you could say that something's happened to him.'

'Jesus. What?'

I cross to the laptop and click on the link again. While Immy watches the video, I stand by, hugging myself as if I might otherwise break apart. I can't see her face but I can hear the sharp intake of breath, the 'Oh my God's and the gasps.

Afterwards, she murmurs, so quietly I can hardly hear her, 'Oh fuck.'

She turns away from the screen and already she's looking at me like I just lost someone close. Maybe I did. 'I feel sick every time I watch it.'

'I'm not surprised. It is revolting. Valentina sounds like a scalded cat. Alexander has a nice arse though.'

'Immy!'

'Sorry. Gallows humour. Oh, hun, I am *so* sorry.' She puts her arms around me and hugs me and, as I'd feared, my tears start to flow again. At this rate, I'll flood the quad and it occurs to me that I had no idea I could feel this hurt, like a knife is corkscrewing inside me. 'I'll call Skandar and tell him I can't go for dinner.'

'No! You can't ruin your evening because of this.'

'OK. OK, but you're so upset — and I don't blame you — I don't want to leave you here on your own all night.'

'I'll survive,' I say, desperate not to spoil Immy's special night. 'But what *am* I going to do about this?'

She screws up her face. 'Well, first, we need to know when this video was shot. Second, we have to find out who sent it.'

Since I don't want to face the first question, I tackle the second. 'It came from Professor Rafe's email but it must have been hacked.'

'Mmm, I agree. He is a perv and a manipulative bastard but even he wouldn't dare send this and besides, he would have no way of knowing it existed. What reason could he have?'

'I suppose he has been trying to split me up from Alexander . . .'

Immy grimaces and shakes her head. 'Then he's a wanker. Does he think you're going to run into his arms and beg him to comfort you?' She brackets her fingers around the 'comfort'. 'Even if by some miracle he had seen this clip, he wouldn't email it to you because he knows you'd go straight to the Dean.' She pats my arm.

'But . . . but you'll *have* to tell Rafe anyway, if his account has been hacked.'

'No! I'd die rather than let him know about this. He'd love it and he'd milk every last drop out of it.'

'OK, OK.' Immy picks up the box of Kleenex on my bed and grabs a bunch from the now half-empty box. 'Then we have to find out who did it, somehow.'

I wipe my eyes. 'How?'

'I'm not sure yet, but Skandar has friends in the Computer Science department. There *must* be a way; most of the engineers know how to hack an account anyway. It's not difficult to hack someone's emails . . . You're an American politician's daughter, you know that.'

She smiles but I'm too angry to laugh. 'I still don't know how to do it personally.'

'Don't worry, forward the email to me and I'll ask Skandar tonight.'

'I can't have it spread all over the university!' I sit down on the bed and blow my nose noisily. 'Please, don't stress over this tonight.'

'OK, but we must try to find out who sent it because then we'll know why they did it.' She sits on the bed next to me and hands me a fresh Kleenex. 'I'll help you find out who did this but it's up to you to find out when that video was filmed. This is absolutely the shittiest thing in the world to happen, but no matter how awful this clip is, it means nothing if it was filmed before Alexander met you.'

'I know that, but how can I find out? I've watched it until I want to vomit and there's no way of telling. That's the worst thing.'

'Then you have to ask Alexander.'

'I can't. Not now. Not until I've calmed down. If I see him now, I might kill him and I'll definitely start screaming and shouting and I *hate* being out of control.'

'I'm sure there's an explanation for this. No matter how awkward and irritating Alexander can be, I'm sure he would never cheat on you – and Valentina hasn't even seen him since the ball, so it's impossible that it was filmed recently.'

'It's *not* impossible. Valentina was at Alexander's house when he got back from Falconbury after the funeral. I found an envelope in his bin, from a card she'd taken round. He said she only dropped by to offer her condolences.'

Immy snorts in derision, which isn't helpful, but I don't blame her doubting him.

'He swore that nothing happened and that his cleaner was there but now I don't know what to think. That's his room – our room – at the Oxford house. Immy, I don't know what to believe.'

'Then you need to talk to him as soon as you can bear to, no matter how awful it is. You *have* to find out the truth.'

'There's something else . . .'

She frowns. 'What?'

'Look at this.' I cross to the laptop and open up the Facebook window.

'What are you doing now?'

'I know it's crazy but I couldn't help it.'

I open Valentina's profile page.

Immy rolls her eyes. 'Silly cow, why hasn't she got the privacy setting on?'

'Because of *this*, maybe?' I point to the part where her status says: In a Relationship. 'That only went up yesterday. Until last night, it said single.'

'You've been checking out her profile?'

'Only since I heard she'd been to Alexander's house earlier this term. I couldn't stop myself.'

'Fair enough, but changing her status means nothing. She could be referring to anyone, or it could all be bullshit. She's probably sitting over her laptop right now, cackling and muttering Italian "mwha ha ha"'s.'

I'm in no state to laugh. 'Look at these pictures. I don't think they were here when I last checked her profile.'

I click on the old albums Valentina has on her account. They chart an ultra glamorous calendar of events: Valentina and Alexander lounging by an infinity pool; next to the bride and groom at a society wedding; drinking Pimm's at a polo match; her clinging to his arm at a military function, with Alexander in full army regalia.

'Oh my God.' Immy takes over the mouse pad, clicking through the photos. 'She actually has an album called "The Proposal"? So long after he finished with her? The woman is barking mad.'

Even so, 'La Proposta' obviously happened in Paris and is backed up with dozens of photos: Valentina and her *fidanzato* in front of the Eiffel Tower; by the Arc de Triomphe; in a restaurant, where Valentina is sliding an oyster down his throat.

'I feel nauseous all over again.'

'I'm not surprised. Eww.' Immy snorts at a close-up shot of Valentina's ring finger. 'I always think a diamond that big looks cheap . . .'

I want to smile, I really do, but my lip muscles seem to have been Botoxed.

'Valentina's behind this. She has to be! Who else would be crazy enough to be so bloody obvious?' says Immy, echoing my own conclusions.

'I agree. It *has* to be her and I keep telling myself this is all a sick and malicious trick to try and split us up, but Immy, what if I'm wrong and it *isn't*?'

Immy takes me by the shoulders and looks me in the eyes. 'It *is* a trick and it's already worked. Look at the state of you! This isn't the Lauren I know. Wipe your eyes and kick some bloody arse or whatever you do in Washington. Fight back!'

'I'm not sure I want to. I'm not sure Alexander is worth it any more.'

'Crap! A, I don't believe that and B, even if he isn't, you can't let that bitch get away with this.'

Immy stayed another hour, handing over tissues, listening to me ranting and encouraging me to tackle Alexander. I've already ignored two of his calls but I know it can't be long before he comes round to find out where I've been. Eventually, Immy leaves to go to meet Skandar, promising to ask 'hypothetically' if his friends could find out who hacked Rafe's email. Barely have I watched her disappear under the Lodge archway when Alexander knocks at my door.

'Lauren. Are you in? Are you all right?'

I stand in the middle of my room, but he knocks again almost immediately. 'Your light is on so I know you're in there, and I just saw Immy come out. Why haven't you been answering your phone? What's going on? I'm worried about you.'

Worried? I snort in derision, then get up and open the door.

His face is obscured by a huge bouquet of flowers. 'I know it's a ridiculous charade and you're probably totally unimpressed but' – he pulls the bouquet aside – 'happy Valentine's Day.'

I burst into tears and his face creases with concern. 'What's the matter? Have you had bad news?'

He follows me in and shuts the door. I say nothing, just walk to the laptop and open the lid.

His brows knit in a deep frown and he abandons the flowers on the coffee table. 'What's this? Lauren, why won't you speak to me? Is this some kind of joke?'

I click the play button and I sit on the edge of the bed.

I can't see his face and I don't want to, but I can hear the groans and the dirty talk. Valentina is screaming and Alexander is telling her he loves her as he fucks her.

The clip ends abruptly; and although my eyes are shut, the frozen image of his bare butt and her gaping mouth is as clear in my mind as if it were projected on to a Cinemax screen. When I open my eyes, Alexander is still facing the laptop, silent.

'Happy Valentine's Day,' I murmur.

Chapter Ten

He turns to me, and says, coolly, 'So this was sent to you by Professor Rafe?'

'You can see that.'

He snorts in derision. 'Obviously, it's been hacked.'

'Obviously . . . It *is* you and Valentina, isn't it?'

'Yes, it's us.'

There you are then. No hesitation, no attempt to soften the blow. I feel light-headed again but I force the words from my mouth. 'And it is filmed in your bedroom here in Oxford?' This morning, I might have said 'our bedroom' but that now seems laughable.

'Yes.' He walks over to me and tries to reach for me but I push him away. I expect him to burst out angrily but he says calmly, 'You do know that this was taken before I met you?'

'Do I?'

'Come on, Lauren, you can't possibly believe that this was filmed after that?'

'I don't know. Why was it filmed at all?'

'I have no idea. Do you think that starring in a sex tape is my style?'

'I don't know what your style is. I thought I did but

now it seems to be kinky bondage sessions and sordid home porn movies!'

He bursts out laughing and I totally lose it. 'It's not fucking funny!'

The smile evaporates. 'No, I agree, but it *is* ridiculous that you would fall for this. If Valentina did film it, then I have absolutely no idea why.'

'Oh, really?'

'Yes, really. I'd no idea it existed until you just showed it to me. She must have done it for some kind of joke.'

'Well, you seemed to be enjoying the whole process.'

'Did you expect me to be screaming for mercy? I had no bloody idea I was being filmed. I'm sorry you're so upset, and I'm not trying to make light of it, but I don't want it to make any difference to us.'

I can't bring myself to reply to this, not while the images from that tape are still imprinted on my brain, not while I'm still trying to come to terms with exactly what I feel. Naive for one thing; I'd only ever slept with Todd before Alexander and I know he's way more experienced than I am. I loathe the video. All I can see is Valentina tied to that bed and I did the same only a few days ago. I feel cheapened, used ... or am I overreacting?

I don't have to speak; Alexander can read my emotions from my face. 'You still don't trust me, do you? No matter what I say?'

'I don't know. The whole disappearing-off thing you

did last term, the not telling me that you were engaged to Valentina or that she'd come to your house with that card. It doesn't exactly engender trust, does it?'

'Firstly, you know I can't tell you anything about my work with the regiment. Secondly, I thought we'd agreed long ago to put what happened at the hunt ball behind us and thirdly, I didn't try to hide the fact that Valentina turned up at my house. I was perfectly up-front, just as you were about going to see Scott.' His logic is faultless, as ever, but the calmer he sounds, the more upset I feel. Which I know is both totally illogical and completely understandable. God, I hate feeling 'managed'.

'As for this stupid video,' he goes on, 'you'll just have to take my word that it happened way before I met you and I didn't know that she was filming us, but I *am* going to find out who sent it and I'm going to deal with them.'

'Even if it *was* Valentina?'

'If emailing it from Rafe's address was her idea, which I doubt since Valentina has never had computer hacking on her list of accomplishments, then the best thing we can do is ignore it.'

He's right and I force myself to take a mental deep breath. I give a truculent nod that's worthy of Emma and that snaps me to my senses. 'Maybe you're right,' I say, and allow him to pull me into his arms. Even while he's kissing me tenderly and soothingly, I'm already holding a piece of me back from him in a way I wouldn't

186

have a few hours ago. Already, that film has eroded the fragile trust that had slowly been built between us.

'Whoever sent this clip, it can't be a coincidence that it arrived today. That must show you what a sick joke this is. He or she must have deliberately set out to ruin the day for us.'

'I didn't know you even realized it was Valentine's Day. I know you hate that sort of commercialism and public gestures of affection.'

'I do, but bringing you flowers and booking a chef to cook us a meal at the house isn't a public gesture.'

'You booked a chef?'

'Yes, and I can unbook him, if you want. It's too late to unsend the flowers.'

'They're beautiful,' I say, finally sparing a glance for the hand-tied bouquet on my table. They're my favourite: pink long-stemmed roses, perfect and dewy, their fragrance filling the air. 'But I don't think I want to have anyone else around me tonight.'

'I'll cancel then, but he can be gone as soon as the main course is served. You won't even have to see him.'

He holds me in his arms. I wonder if this is exactly what Valentina wanted. Am I being cowardly to let her affect us in this way? Probably, but I'm no saint. Who wouldn't wonder, just a little bit, if they were being taken for a ride? Let alone if they were going out with a man like Alexander, whose raison d'être is repressing his feelings, whose job is built on stealth and secrecy?

'Can I think about it?'

'Of course.' His voice is rich and soothing, balm dripping over my wounded pride and trust. I've already wasted half a day crying and stressing over the video, so when Alexander leads me to my bed and pushes me down gently, I let him. When he starts to undo the buttons of my top, I lie there and allow it to happen. My body responds, of course it does, but I find my hand closing around his fingers, without having made a conscious decision to stop him.

'I'm not sure I feel like doing this now.'

His brow creases and he drops a soft kiss on my mouth. 'OK. I understand, but if you let this ridiculous video affect us, then whoever sent it really has achieved their objective.'

'You make it sound like a war.'

'Isn't it? Someone has decided to launch an attack; they've wounded you but you have the power to respond any way you want to.'

'I can't shrug it off as easily as you.'

'You think it's easy for me? I'm fucking furious that my privacy has been invaded, and far angrier that you're hurt, but how we react is in our control. For instance,' he says, removing his hand from under my fingers and easing open another button on my top, 'if you let me undo your blouse, then their plan has failed.' His eyes glint as he throws down this sexy challenge to me. 'Prove to them that you don't care.'

'How? By letting you get inside my knickers, as you like to put it?' I say, my voice still edged with cynicism.

'Well . . .' He undoes the last button of my shirt. 'Yes.'

He circles my navel with his tongue and I suck in a breath as my bared skin dimples with pleasure, despite my misgivings.

'Alexander, that thing you were doing in the film . . .'

He shifts his attention back to my face and rests his head on his elbow next to me. 'The tying-up thing?'

'Don't you dare joke.'

'OK.' He puts on his serious face. 'You can't seriously be bothered by it?'

'I don't know.'

'Don't tell me you're shocked? I don't recall you looking outraged when I tied you up.'

Does he honestly not understand why I'm upset? Of course he doesn't; he's a *guy*. 'I'm bothered because you did exactly the same thing to me. It's made our . . . thing seem dirty and cheap.'

He looks down at me thoughtfully. 'It wasn't cheap but it *was* dirty. Sex is always dirty, and when it's other people's sex, it's usually disgusting, but you can't seriously expect me – or Valentina – to lie there fumbling under the bedclothes like some Victorian newlyweds?'

My response is a grunt, because he may have a point but I'm definitely not ready to agree with him on anything.

'The only thing you need to understand is that I never for a single second thought of anyone but you while I was doing it. The fact that we'd been experimenting in that way before you saw the clip is a horrible

189

coincidence, nothing more, and we don't have to do anything like it again or anything you don't enjoy.'

'That's not what I meant.' Because, even now, my body tells me how much I enjoyed being tied to his bed and handing over control to him.

'Then we should do something I've never done before,' he says, in between kisses on my stomach and cleavage.

'Is there anything?' I ask sarcastically.

'Hmm. You're right. It might be quite difficult to come up with something completely novel.'

'Alexander!'

'I'll think of something.'

I shake my head, unable to laugh because I can't get the image of him screwing her out of my head. It won't be driven away so easily, no matter how much he tries to reason or kiss away the hurt and disgust. I slide upwards, out of his embrace.

'Alexander, *why* has she done this?'

He looks deep into my eyes. 'We don't know "she" has yet, but you can be sure of one thing: it won't make any difference to us. We mustn't let it.'

He pushes my arms above my head, capturing my hands in his, and kisses me so deeply and for so long that it's not until he's finished that I process what he's just said. How *does* he feel about me? I certainly don't know how *I* feel about *him* right now, in this instant. I thought I'd fallen for him until today; I know for sure I fell in lust with him long ago.

Yet the way I've reacted this afternoon, the fact that the shock and the possibility of betrayal hit me so hard – that must mean I am in love with him. Otherwise, why would I be so hurt at seeing that video?

'Are you going to trust me?' Alexander says softly, his fingers resting on the bottom button of my blouse. 'Or are you going to let them win?' His eyes glitter with challenge and desire. 'You are the only woman in my life, Lauren, and the brightest, most beautiful, most maddening woman I've ever known. Please don't let a spiteful joke ruin everything.'

His hand slips inside my blouse and the roughened palm flattens over my stomach, melting my resolve with its warmth. It's me who reaches up and guides his head downwards and his mouth on to mine. It's me who pushes her tongue inside his mouth, needing to feel the heat and texture of him, wanting to be inside him somehow, the way he loves getting inside me.

I am in control here, because I choose to be. I haven't raced out of my room and run until I drop. I've chosen to stay with Alexander and enjoy the moment, because I have him in my bed and Valentina can only watch a film and remember how good he felt.

By the middle of the following week, Immy still hasn't come up with any answers about the hacked email. The Valentine's dinner was OK, considering what had happened earlier. The food, as expected, was exquisite and the chef kept discreetly out of the way, but I was so on edge that I only picked at my food. I haven't watched the clip again but I still haven't deleted it from my computer. Likewise, I haven't deleted the seed of doubt from my mind, despite Alexander's attempts to soothe me with a strategy that seems to involve logic and cunnilingus.

'"*L'opera d'arte è sempre una confessione.*"'

I glance away from the window to find Rafe peering at me, over his glasses. I've been in his tute for forty minutes and suddenly he throws in some Italian. Is he trying to hint at something? Provoke me?

'That's the theme we'll be discussing in the seminar next week. It's a quote from Umberto Eco, and means "Artwork is always a confession".' He smiles. 'I assume you've heard the phrase before or worked that out from your Italian classes.'

'Oh, yes, of course. I'm sorry. I do know the quote.'

'Good. I look forward to hearing your presentation on a work that illustrates that theme. Now, let me throw another quotation at you, one you may also recognize. '"*Bisogna fare della propria vita come si fa un'opera d'arte.*"'

'Gabriele d'Annunzio,' I say, mentally giving myself a slap. I'm studying art history, the tutors quote Italian all the time; it's merely a coincidence, not a hint or a clue that Rafe sent the clip. He obviously hasn't any idea his email was even hacked. 'One should always live one's life as though it were a work of art.'

'Bravo. Your work of art seems somewhat fractured today, Lauren. I know you've had a busy and stressful time but I must warn you that the end of term will come upon us sooner than you think and you'll be getting your take-home exam questions. I assume you won't be missing any more tutorials or making any more trips away from Oxford before the vac? I've overlooked the time you spent at the funeral but technically speaking you shouldn't leave Oxford during term.'

'No. I'm not going anywhere. In fact, I'd planned to stay on a couple of weeks to do some extra research.'

'That's not a bad idea. Can you keep your room over the Easter vac? I think we have some conferences.'

'I'll be, um . . . I've got somewhere to stay.'

'Mmm.' The way he says the 'mmm' he must have guessed I plan to stay with Alexander but he hasn't got the balls to ask me directly because what happens after the end of term is none of his business.

'Well, I'm delighted to hear you're going to spend some of the vac, at least, focusing on your work. A missed tutorial may not seem like much but I'm a very busy man and as I've said before, there are many students needing my attention. Several have already indicated that they want to stay on and do a DPhil, but obviously a doctorate takes a lot of commitment and dedication. It's not for everyone.'

'I understand that.'

He stands up. 'I'm afraid I have to cut the tutorial slightly short but I think we've covered all the important points. If there's anything you don't understand or want to discuss before we meet again, email me or call me.'

'Thanks, I will.'

Relieved to be let out of jail early, I gather up my papers and put them in my laptop bag. Rafe collects my coat from the rack by his door but instead of handing it to me, he keeps hold of it.

'Oh, there's one more thing. I may not have mentioned it but I've organized a special screening of *Il Conformista* at the Art House cinema next Sunday morning. I know it's an odd time but the cinema is doing us a special favour. I presume you can make it?'

Oh fuck. '*Us?* You mean me and you?'

He laughs. 'That would have been very stimulating for both of us, I'm sure, but alas, no. To make it worthwhile, I had to promise to gather at least a dozen people. I did post a notice in the faculty and email you. Have you not received it?'

I might have received anything, I've been so caught up in the Valentine's Day Film Massacre. For a second, I wonder if Rafe is hinting he did actually send it, then I decide I'm being ridiculous. How would he get it? Even if he had a copy, he knows Alexander – and the college authorities – would go nuts if they found out.

'Um, no, it must have been lost in cyberspace and I hadn't seen the notice in the faculty.'

'I noticed your name wasn't with the others, but if you're not too busy, I think you'd find the film of great interest. I'll see you there, shall I?'

So, there are others, and I can't really refuse and

I ought to show I am committed to my course. 'Sure. I wouldn't miss it for the world.'

'Good.' He hands me my coat. 'You know, Lauren; I meant what I said about making your life a work of art. Please, don't ruin it or waste it. You arrived here with such promise and *joie de vivre*. It would be a shame to throw that away.'

'I've no intention of wasting a moment,' I say, stung by the malicious edge to his 'advice'.

'No, but be wary. You may want to move on but some people will always try to hold you back. The world never changes for some people; they cling on to tradition and will do anything to maintain the status quo.'

The bastard, he must be referring to Alexander. Who else could he mean?

Steaming inside, I smile sweetly on my way out. '*Ciao*, Professor Rafe.'

I'm supposed to be meeting Immy after my tute but I need a few moments to calm down after this encounter. Rafe has every right to remind me that my focus should be on my work, not my love life, but his mean, manipulative way of doing it is way beyond acceptable. I walk through the cloisters on my way to the JCR, deliberately slowing my pace and my breathing and trying to calm myself. Years ago, these cloisters would have been used for quiet contemplation and study. Maybe some of that vibe will rub off on me.

My heeled boots ring out on the flagstones, which are hollowed with age. It was here that I first met Alexander and I think I knew even then that he was trouble with a capital T. Didn't stop him blowing my mind, however, with his body and face and his arrogance.

The kitchen staff have started to set up for lunch and the metallic ring of trays and glasses being transported from the kitchens to the Great Hall, next to us, shatters the peace. Before I reach the end of the cloister, my phone pings to tell me I have a text.

> Hi. Are you coming to the
> USSoc party on Friday?
> Hope so, I'm celebrating.

Judging by the row of smiley faces at the end of Scott's text, I have an idea what he may be hinting at. I text back:

> Wow. Yes. Sounds good.

He replies:

> Will Alex be with you?
> Does that bother you?

As my text flies off into the ether, I try to picture the look on Scott's face. I've reached the quad before I get a response.

> You know me.
> I love a *ménage à trois*.

Now I know he knows I was joking but I think I had him hooked on my line for a moment.

I slip my phone back in my bag. Alexander would rather wear a pink tutu than share a Fuzzy Navel and a mini-burger with Scott, I'm sure, but I'm really looking forward to it.

Immy is waiting for me outside the JCR and my face must tell a story.

'Hey, you look like you want to commit a murder. What's up?'

'Rafe is such an asshole!'

'What's he done now? If he's touched you, you have to report him, Lauren.'

'He hasn't touched me; in fact he hasn't even used an innuendo. He's just such a small, mean man under the "big, cool professor" facade. He's been hinting that I haven't been pulling my weight and that if I miss any more tutes, he might report me.'

'He's a complete shit.'

'Yes, but the worst thing is, he's right. I have missed tutes and I haven't "kept term", as he calls it, which could get me into trouble. The problem is I can't decide if he's threatening me because he's jealous of Alexander, is trying to blackmail me into sleeping with him or really is concerned for me.'

We walk up the spiral staircase to the upstairs common room. 'Probably all three. Did he give any hints that he might have sent the clip?'

'No, I don't think he has a clue he was hacked. If he

had, I'm sure he wouldn't have been able to resist tormenting me by now. Have Skandar's friends any ideas?'

'I've asked but everyone's either ignoring me or been too busy with work. I can't believe it's Fifth Week already. Time's running out.' She nibbles her lip.

Tell me about it, I think, realizing how fast the past term has flown by. 'Immy, I'm sorry, I've been so wrapped up in my own dramas that I haven't asked how your work is going . . .'

'It's all right, I suppose. My tutor says that if I work really hard and if the right questions come up on the day, I should get a 2:ii. Whatever, I've got to keep my head down for the rest of term.'

'So you can't come out at all?'

'No.'

'Not even to the USSoc party? I'm sorry, I got a reminder about it the morning I got the sex tape but I'd forgotten all about it. It's this Friday night.'

'I might, possibly, be able to sneak out in between essays. If you really, really insist.'

'I demand your attendance.'

'OK. What are you wearing?'

'Stetson, leather chaps and spurs.'

She laughs a second too late.

Chapter Eleven

What I'm actually wearing are Calvin Klein jeans, a silk shell top and spike-heeled Kate Spade boots. Immy's in a mini, her new Ghost top and ankle boots. She looks knock-out so I sure hope that Scott makes good on his promise to turn up. I'm not sure what Skandar would make of her being in pursuit of Scott, but that's none of my business.

I told Alexander I was going and he told me to 'enjoy myself' and that he was going to stay in to work. I couldn't work out whether he was being ironic or not but he's been treading very carefully since the video. The party is being held in the Hall of St Vesey's College, tucked away off the High, one of the oldest colleges in Oxford. When we walk into the medieval hall, Immy bursts out laughing.

'Oh my God. It's fiesta time . . .'

Indeed it is. The hall is smothered in papel picado, snaking through some of the lower beams and festooned around the lamps on the long tables. High Table is now a tequila bar, and college staff dressed in Mexican costume mill about serving cocktails and hors d'oeuvres. Quite a few of the guests are rocking Tex

Mex outfits so my Stetson comment wasn't that far from the truth.

Immy giggles. 'When does the mariachi band get here?'

'Behave, Imogen, this set-up must have taken our hostess most of the term to plan.'

Our hostess herself, Maisey Amster, descends on us before we make it six feet into the Hall and while Immy is still feasting on the fiesta-themed decor. 'Maisey makes Martha Stewart look like a slattern . . .' I whisper to Immy.

'Lauren, hi there!'

'Hi, Maisey.'

She's rocking a full Spanish señorita costume. 'You did know it was a costume party?'

'Sorry, I forgot.'

'And I thought you were bringing Lord Falconbury along,' she says accusingly.

'Really? No, he's working. He's been very busy.'

'Oh, yes, I heard that his father has passed but I guess it's cool being marquess.'

'I don't think he quite sees it like that . . .'

'Will he be taking up his seat in the Lords?'

I dare not even glance at Immy. 'Like I say, he's working so I brought a friend along – the invitation did say plus guest. This is Imogen Hawthorne; she's doing Geography at Wyckham. Immy, meet Maisey Amster, president of the USSoc.'

Maisey manages a smile but I can tell we're both poor substitutes for Alexander. Especially, maybe, an Alexander in a sombrero . . . 'Good to meet you, Immy. Now, Lauren, have you seen Scott around?'

'So he's *definitely* coming?' Immy is all innocence.

Maisey looks astonished. 'Of course he is. Why would he miss it? Why don't you help yourselves to a Sundowner? Or there's some Shiner Bock; I had to get it shipped specially. Must go, I have to make sure the PA is working.' With a flick of her fan, she flounces off.

'What the hell is Shiner Bock?' whispers Immy.

'A type of beer, I think.'

We check out the guests and Immy is nibbling on a canapé when I hear a 'Guess who?' behind me and turn to find Scott.

'Hi, guys.'

He kisses me – on the cheek this time – and says, 'Howdy, Imogen,' while she's otherwise occupied with a mouthful of taco. He's ditched the Blues tracksuit for jeans, a checked shirt and steel-tipped Western boots, which I suspect are an ironic touch but work well with his six-and-a-half-foot frame. I guess he'd probably look good in a trash-can liner.

Immy's eyes are popping. Poor Skandar . . .

'Go on, then, tell me your news, though I think I can tell by the entirely justifiable smug grin on your face,' I say.

'If you've heard already, why should I share it?'

'Because you want to tell me and I would love to hear you say it.'

'You are looking at one of the Blues squad rowers.'

I hug him. 'That's awesome! I knew you'd do it, but congratulations.'

'It's incredible. I mean, perfectly credible because you're very fit, obviously, but still it's awesome.' As Immy finally gets a word in, Scott's grin gets even wider until I worry his face might break apart.

'It's pretty neat. Is there a non-alcoholic option?' He takes a glass of Virgin Tequila Sunrise from the table and chinks it against our Sundowners.

'It must have been incredibly tough to get into the final sixteen,' Immy says, her eyes seemingly fascinated by his guns. 'Was the training as awful as they say?'

'Oh, it was nothing,' he says airily, then laughs. 'In truth, it was hell and I'm pretty pleased with myself for having survived this far, so you'll have to put up with the smugness.'

Immy giggles. 'I think we can live with it. Would you mind if I felt your bicep? I've always wanted to touch one and see if they're as hard as they look.'

I literally have to bite my lip at this, and after a moment of confusion, Scott laughs. 'Sure you can, but I think you'll be disappointed.'

'I doubt it.' With her free hand, Immy reaches out and squeezes Scott's bicep through his shirt as if she's testing a mango for ripeness. 'Yes, that definitely lives up to expectations.'

'I'm happy to be of service.'

Immy slurps her cocktail, then says, 'Really?'

'So does this mean you've a good chance of being in the First Eight?'

'Possibly. I'll either be in the Blues boat or the reserve boat, which I suppose I should be happy with. Some of the guys didn't make the cut and I'd hate to be in their shoes after all this training. Now at least I know I'll get to row on the tideway; whether it's in the Blues boat or *Isis*, we'll have to wait and see. I don't think I can work any harder than I am and the final eight is down to the selectors. However, while I have breath in my body, I'm going to work like fuck to get there.'

'I'm sure you'll do it,' says Immy.

'You'll make it,' I say, planting a kiss on his cheek, which may be a mistake but it's what I feel like doing and after recent events, I'm not going to let anything or anyone stop me from doing what I feel is right. 'You deserve it.'

His eyes shine with pride, lighting up his handsome face, tanned by all the hours spent on the river. His features are chiselled in the way of the super fit. Alexander has the same honed look, but definitely in the English style, leaner and not so square of jaw. Alexander has an austere handsomeness and an animal sexuality that makes him feel unpredictable and dangerous to be around. Scott makes me feel so relaxed and at ease, like I shouldn't have a care in the world.

'Uh-oh. Maisey has spotted you.'

'Oh fuck.'

She homes in on us like a heat-seeking missile and grabs his arm. 'Scott, you should have told me you were here! It's so amazing you turned up. We are all so proud of your achievements. Come here, I've got some people I want you to meet. Do you know . . .'

I don't hear the names of the lucky and important people who get to meet Scott because Maisey has whisked him off.

A few minutes later, Scott is, literally, being dragged out to the front of the Hall by Maisey, a feat I would have thought impossible. She calls for silence down the PA and regales the guests with tales of his exploits. He shoves his hands in his pockets and looks incredibly embarrassed when we all have to give him three Brit-style cheers before he's toasted in tequila. Her request for a speech, however, is met with brief yet good-humoured thanks before he escapes. I think he's trying to get to us but he's being clapped on the back and smothered with congratulations.

'Imogen? What are you doing here?'

'Oh, hello, Anna!'

Immy's attention is claimed by a girl who I think is one of the Blues women's tennis squad members, who sweeps her off to the other side of the room, just as Scott finally looks like making it back to our side. I can guess she doesn't want to be drawn away from Scott but she has no choice.

'Will you be coming to watch the race in London?' Scott asks when he finally reaches me again.

'I've no plans yet but as you're going to be one of the stars, I'll make sure I do.'

'You'd better not let Alex hear you say that.'

I laugh off the comment. 'If you're trying to provoke me, it won't work. I meant what I said, about not letting anything stop me from seeing my friends.'

Maybe I see something change in his expression at the 'friend' word but the smile is quickly back. 'You're right, I was trying to stir things. You seem a little edgy, however.'

Of course I'm edgy. The sex clip is never that far from my mind, but I know what would happen if I mentioned it to Scott. He would only use it to reinforce my doubts about Alexander, and I wouldn't blame him.

A waiter arrives with a plate piled high with appetizers and hors d'oeuvres. 'The hostess sent these over.'

'Great.'

'Mini taco? Pulled-pork slider?' My mouth waters but I'm trying to avoid the many temptations on offer in Oxford. I've had to start jogging again to keep my figure, and added an extra dance class to my schedule. Nonetheless, Scott's not about to help me resist temptation of any kind and he offers up the plate to me.

'No, I'll pass.'

'What about a stuffed jalapeño?'

'Really, I shouldn't.'

' "Really, I shouldn't." ' He mocks me in a high-pitched 'girly' voice. 'You're picking up the accent, Lauren.'

'I am *not*!'

He slips the jalapeño into my open mouth before I can stop it. Wow, that is hot. My mouth tingles like crazy and not in a good way. Scott watches, obviously relishing every moment. After I've swallowed the jalapeño, hoping my mascara isn't running, he thrusts a taco in front of my nose.

'No more. Mercy!'

The taco waggles. 'Go on, you know you want to.'

'I do want to but I daren't,' I laugh.

'And that is the story of my life.' His expression changes from teasing to serious. 'Listen, my friend, in just a few months we'll both be back in the US. How are things with Alexander?'

'I'm taking each day as it comes,' I say quietly.

'Really? I would have thought that Alexander might have longer-term plans.'

'He's in the army; he can't afford to have long-term plans, especially since his father died.'

'Yeah, I can believe that, and I'm sorry. But what about *your* long-term plans, Lauren?'

Whew. He is *not* going to let me off the hook and it's not something I can really face thinking about right now. 'I have plenty,' I lie airily, 'but none I want to discuss now. I just want to get through this term. You would not believe how much I have to do before the vac and I get my exam-essay topics at the end of term.'

'I know – still, the year will be over before we know it. I hope we'll stay friends once we're back in the US,' he says brightly.

I make my reply super casual. 'I don't know if I'll definitely be going straight back yet. I had thought of working with an art auctioneers in New York but now I think I might get a job as a curator with a museum or gallery in Europe instead. Maybe even in London.'

'So you won't stay on at Oxford to do a DPhil?'

I laugh. 'My tutor seems to want me to, but I'm not sure that's because he's interested in my intellectual skills.'

Scott pulls a face. 'And does Alex figure in any of these scenarios?'

I bat this one right back to him: 'I don't know that either.'

He gives a low whistle. 'Does he know *that*?'

'I refer you to my previous answer. Can we change the subject, please?'

'Sure. Sorry, didn't mean to put you on the spot. You are OK, aren't you?'

'Yes, I am OK. I'm fine. More than fine.'

'OK. So I take it things are going well with Alexander?' He carries on probing me.

My toes curl in embarrassment. I don't want to answer this question, even to myself, in case I decide that the answer is 'yes'.

'I plead the Fifth.'

'You've a right to but it's a legit question because,

let's face it, Lauren, you could have your pick of any guy in Oxford. Any guy in England or the States. You're smart and sexy. Your parents are practically US royalty and you blush *so* cutely.'

I blush some more at this and try to laugh off his teasing. 'I could name you plenty of guys who don't agree,' I say, thinking of Rupert, Henry Favell and a couple of guys from last term who hit on me and Immy in the pub and got punched by Alexander – not to mention a few of his relations. Since I met him, I've definitely made some enemies.

'Show me who they are and I'll show them the error of their ways.' Scott is only half serious and I relax, realizing I'm probably reading too much into what he's saying. We go back to our usual easy chat when suddenly I feel a hand rest on my back, and smell the crisp scent of Creed.

I turn to him and his hand caresses my lower back. 'Alexander? How did you get here?'

'I walked. So we meet again, Scott. Someone told me you made the Boat Race crew. May I offer my congratulations?' Alexander thrusts out his free hand while keeping the other firmly at my waist. 'I'm seriously impressed.'

I'm so surprised to see Alexander, and that he knows Scott's news and that he's shaking hands with him and sounding genuinely impressed, that I am speechless.

'Thanks, Alex.'

I wait for the bone-mashing contest to start but the

handshake is brief this time and seems almost normal. I still wouldn't want to be part of it. They drop hands and I suspect the truce is over.

'I don't think Lauren was expecting you,' says Scott mischievously.

'I know, but she did invite me and I decided I needed a break from my work.'

'She told me about your father. I'm sorry for your loss.'

'Thank you.' Alexander's facade is in place, ultra polite, but he swiftly moves on. 'So, when do you hear if you've made the final cut?'

Maisey's laser guidance system has kicked in and she rustles up while Scott is explaining the selection process, her headdress fluttering madly. 'Oh my God, you must be Lord Falconbury?' She pronounces the name as 'Falcon-berry', like it's an exotic variety of soft fruit.

'Alexander will be perfectly acceptable.'

'Are you sure?'

'Absolutely.'

Oh, I so love watching Alexander pretend to be delighted to meet someone.

Maisey simpers. 'I *told* Lauren to invite you but *she* said you were way too busy with your work. I was so sorry to hear about your father's passing, by the way. I read his obituary in *The Times*. It's always so tragic when a war hero is taken before his time.'

Ouch.

'Was he a war hero?' I ask, without thinking.

'He was awarded the DSO but he'd have despised anyone who called him a hero.'

'What's the DSO?' Maisey asks, fan fluttering, working the blushing señorita for all it's worth.

'Distinguished Service Order,' says Scott unexpectedly. 'The brother of one of the guys in the squad has one.'

'Really? Who is he?' Alexander's interest is piqued and he's clearly keen to move the focus to someone else.

Scott names a guy and a regiment and Alexander nods. 'I think I know his cousin; we were at Sandhurst together.'

'You guys are unbelievable,' Maisey purrs, wide-eyed. I smile. 'They sure are.'

One of the waiters brings a tray and Maisey pipes up, 'Lord Falconbury, can I offer you an hors d'oeuvre? A pulled-pork slider, perhaps?'

'Or a stuffed jalapeño?' Scott swipes one from the tray, and pops it whole into his mouth, with a look aimed squarely at me.

'I've eaten, actually, but thanks for the offer,' says Alexander.

A guy dressed in chaps and a Stetson hurries up to us. 'Maisey, can you come to the bathrooms? Some guy smashed a glass and there's blood all over the tiles. It looks like *Saw* in there.'

'So? Can't you deal with it? I'm *busy*.'

'I would, but the Dean just phoned. He wants to

speak to the organizer about the noise levels. People are complaining and you know what he's like.'

'Oh, screw the Dean, he's an asshole . . .' She clamps her hand over her mouth and glances at Alexander in horror. 'I am so sorry for the language, Lord Falconbury.'

'Hadn't you better go?' I butt in. 'It sounds serious.'

'I guess so, but I'll be back. Don't you dare go anywhere.' She bats Alexander on the arm with her fan just as Immy reappears.

'Hello, boys.'

Alexander's lips twist in amusement. He likes her, despite the fact I know he suspects she gossips about him behind his back, with me.

'You look very well, Immy,' says Scott.

Immy pulls a face. 'I hope that doesn't mean I look fat.'

He gives her a look up and down. 'It means you look great. I'm American, I don't do sarcasm.'

'Oh, I think you could do everything, Scott. But your glass is empty – can I get you another Sundowner? Or maybe a Margarita?'

He pulls a face. 'Unfortunately, I'm on the Virgin stuff for the time being.'

'Never mind, I can be a Virgin too, if required.'

'I had no idea about your father's war record,' I say when I'm alone with Alexander.

'Why would you?'

'I suppose it should have been obvious, yet he didn't approve of you doing the same?'

'Clearly not.'

I'm more convinced than ever now that General Hunt didn't want to lose his son as well as his wife, but had no means of expressing that beyond demanding he run the estate. Then again, he could have been punishing Alexander for what happened to Lady Hunt. Oh, screw it, I really have no idea; I'm no psychiatrist.

'I still can't believe you came along tonight,' I say.

'I decided that keeping an eye on you was more important than work.'

'You know what? I don't think it's me who needs watching.'

'Oh, I don't know. I think we both may.' We hear a giggle and spot Immy and Scott laughing over at the cocktail bar.

'Is Immy still seeing Skandar?' asks Alexander with a frown.

'When has being in a relationship stopped anyone from flirting with someone else they fancy?'

His eyes darken but I couldn't resist it, even though I know I'm stepping into dangerous territory.

'I hope that's not a hint. I've said that video was filmed before I'd even met you. How am I ever going to convince you of that?'

'I don't know but you'll have to try very hard and very often, and even then, I may never believe you. Is that why you turned up here after all? Out of guilt? To make it up to me?'

He meets the challenge of my gaze without a flicker

of emotion. 'A, I have absolutely nothing to be guilty about and B, I don't need to make anything up to you. The person who sent the film should be the one apologizing and we don't know who that is.'

'No, we don't, and maybe we never will, but I've got a little list and it starts with "V".'

'The reason I decided to come along,' he says, ignoring my unsubtle hint, 'is that I thought it might amuse you if I showed my face.'

'Oh, it has.'

'And now I've done my duty, I'd better take you home.'

'What makes you think you've done your duty, Captain Hunt? I think you still have some considerable time to serve here. I know Maisey would just love it if you asked to be introduced to the rest of the USSoc committee.'

He grimaces. 'Fuck. Do I absolutely have to?'

I smile sweetly. 'Yes, you absolutely do.'

Chapter Twelve

Whether Alexander's motives for attending the party were for my sake or his, I'm glad he did turn up. Immy stayed on until Scott left to get an early night because of his training and we all walked home together.

After we'd made love on Saturday morning, Alexander had a call from Falconbury and had to go back for a few days. Whenever he leaves, I have mixed feelings, because I obviously love the sex and I love being with him, but I also know I should use the time and space for my studies and to have a good time. It's now the following Friday and he's still at Falconbury. Technically, he could be sent down for spending so much time away from Oxford but I don't think any of the college authorities would dare do that in view of what's happened to him. Even if he hadn't lost his father, I still don't think they'd dare, just because he's Alexander.

I have to say that by this stage of the week, I'm itching to be back in his bed again and looking forward to seeing him tonight, as he's promised he'll be back.

I've just got back to my room after having lunch with some of my coursemates at the wholefoods cafe near the faculty and decide to Skype my mother, whose first reaction is to tell me it isn't her birthday again. I'm not sure if she's being ironic but I make a mental note to keep in touch more often from now on. My parents still don't know I'm seeing anyone, although I think they have their suspicions, and my lack of calls will only reinforce that impression. My moodiness over the Christmas vacation must have put them on their guard and my mother asked me more than once if I needed to 'talk'.

By now, having attended Alexander's father's funeral, you would think I might have mentioned him to them, but I'm still wary. Things are so up and down between us, and my parents will consider things 'significant' if I confess I'm dating him and then I'll *never* hear the last of it.

My mother's parting comment to me was a hint to check my mail so I skip down to the Lodge, where my favourite young porter is on duty.

'Any packages arrived for me?' I ask.

'As a matter of fact, I was going to call your room.' He pulls a white cardboard box from behind a chair and lays it on top of the counter.

'Thanks. I'm expecting something from home.'

'It's not from America. It was delivered by a courier while you were out.'

'Oh, OK, thanks.'

The moment I shut the door of my room, I open the box and tear open the tissue paper inside.

Wow!

It's a dress and heels, and not just any dress or any heels but a full-length Alexander McQueen bustier gown in a blue so pale and translucent it's like the ice of a glacier. The silk chiffon material falls from the strapless bodice like a waterfall. It has to be from Alexander but . . . wow. Where on earth can he be taking me in a gown like this?

I lay it reverently on the bed while I hold up the shoes. Oh, the *shoes*.

They're Manolo Blahniks, six-inch silver stiletto-heeled pumps. I think they may be the ones I saw in *Vogue* over the holidays. Whatever, they are more a work of art than footwear and it feels almost wrong to slip my feet into them, but of course I do. And of course they fit perfectly.

At the bottom of the box, I find a note that simply reads:

Wear this tonight. Be ready and waiting in the Lodge by 5 p.m.
Alexander x

This 'stealth date' is typical Alexander, and the extravagant gifts, like the Cartier necklace he sent after we'd almost had sex for the first time. I returned it, of course, because I'd thought he was trying to buy me. It took a lot of persuading on his part to convince me otherwise and it was the convincing rather than the necklace that finally got me into his bed.

Now I know Alexander better, I believe these grand gestures aren't about trying to buy me, they are how he shows his emotions, or rather how he avoids showing them. It's not a good thing, but I'm only human and the cryptic note has me intrigued. This may also be his way of making up for not seeing me as much as he'd like.

I slip out of my jeans and top and step into the dress. It's not only the perfect fit for my frame, it's also exactly the right length. So now I'm standing in my room, in full evening dress, with no idea where we're going to.

It kills me to take off the outfit and try to settle down to some work, but I have to. Finally, at four, I give in and grab a lightning-fast shower and start to do my hair and make-up. I go for the simple low ponytail that's worked for me before because there's no time to get my hair done professionally. Luckily, Immy and I got French manis a couple of days ago at a spa in the centre of town. At the top of my closet, I find a Kate Spade silver clutch and a cashmere pashmina that my mother gave me for Christmas. If we're going to the ballet at Covent Garden again, it's going to be freezing, even stepping from the Bentley into the opera house.

I just make it into the Lodge at one minute past five but there's no sign of Alexander. In most places, I'd attract attention dressed in evening wear at five in the after-noon, but this is Oxford and spotting people in tuxes and ballgowns is de rigueur. I am shivering, however, and the Hunts' chauffeur, Brandon, standing outside by the Bentley is a welcome sight.

'Good evening, Miss Cusack,' he says, going ahead of me to open the door as I walk towards the car.

'Hello, Brandon. Where are we going?'

'Lord Falconbury said to tell you it's a surprise.'

'Can't you even hint?'

'Lord Falconbury said you'd ask me that.'

'Oh, really, and what else did Lord Falconbury say?'

'That I'd be fired if I told you anything.'

'Really? He must have been joking.'

'His lordship rarely jokes about things like this.' Brandon looks genuinely astonished.

It's all I can do to stop myself from laughing. 'That figures. OK, I guess I'll have to be patient. I wouldn't want you to lose your job.'

He allows a smile to touch his lips. 'Oh, there's no danger of that, Miss Cusack. Would you care to get into the car? We're on a tight schedule.'

'Is that a hint as to where we're going?'

He looks pissed now, and waves his hand in the direction of the door. 'If you wouldn't mind, please?'

Though I'm half tempted to tell him I've left something I need in my room just to see his face, I really shouldn't tease him, especially when Alexander has obviously read him the riot act. I decide to obey and manage to get inside without putting my heel through the skirt. The Bentley purrs away from the kerb and twenty minutes later we're in the middle of nowhere. I don't recognize any of the place names in the twilight; they all have Middle Earth-type names like Piddlehinton-by-Tew and Footminster-on-Stour. The sun is just disappearing below the horizon as the car turns off the main road and along a drive to a checkpoint in a wire fence.

Then I see the sign by the gate.

'This is an airfield, Brandon.'

He glances in his mirror. 'It looks that way, miss.'

'Are we going to Scotland or some offshore island?'

'I really couldn't say, miss.'

My mind works overtime but whatever I'd expected, it wasn't *this*. After a brief word with the security guy on the gate, Brandon drives on to the tarmac and stops the car beside a private Gulfstream jet. I know it's a Gulfstream because I've waved my father off in one, but I've never been in one. Alexander emerges on to the steps as Brandon opens the door for me. The wind knifes through my silk dress as I climb out of the car and my wrap threatens to fly away, not to mention my gown, which pastes itself to my bare legs.

'Here, let me help.'

Dashing forward, Alexander rescues my wrap before it sails off to wherever we're headed.

'You look out of this world,' he murmurs, before shouting thanks to Brandon and taking my hand.

'And you're driving me crazy.'

'In a good way?'

He looks so hot in his beautifully tailored tux he could scorch the tarmac all on his own, but I think he knows that so I'm not telling him.

'I'll let you know.'

Before the wind steals my wrap, Alexander helps me

up the steps. I'm intrigued – I love the mystery – but I'm also wary. There's still a part of me I've held back since the sex tape. I may pretend that nothing has changed between us yet something *has*. No private jet or designer gown is going to alter that, *but* . . .

The howl and slice of the wind dies away instantly the moment I step inside the totally clichéd and totally wonderful haven of luxury that is the Gulfstream. It's a big jet for a private charter, with enough headroom for even Alexander to stand up in. It has a dozen seats, all clad in hand-stitched creamy leather, including a triple sofa-style bank, which I suspect may be about to see some action.

'Wow. James Bond meets Rihanna.'

'So you approve?'

'Who wouldn't? Are you going to tell me where we're going?'

'Can you be patient a moment longer? I'm waiting for someone.'

'Not really.'

A man appears at the cabin door and Alexander smiles. 'Ah, that must be Passport Control.'

The guy steps inside, smiling. 'Miss Cusack, Lord Falconbury, good evening.'

I'm about to protest that I don't have my passport when Alexander pulls his and mine from a drawer. The guy glances at them, smiles again and says, 'That's fine. Have a good trip.'

As soon as he's gone, and the cabin steps are secure, the wind noise is replaced by the heightened note of the engines. Slightly poleaxed – make that totally poleaxed – I'm grateful to sit down on the leather sofa. 'Wow. I think I'm being kidnapped.'

Alexander sits next to me. 'In a manner of speaking.'

'I don't know what to say.'

'That'll be a first.'

'You . . .' The engine note rises and the pilot's voice comes over the intercom. 'Miss Cusack, Lord Falconbury, do you mind fastening your seat belts for takeoff? Once we get airborne and over this storm, you can relax because the weather looks fine all the way to Rome.'

My mouth opens in shock. 'Did he just say what I *thought* he said?'

Alexander's face is the picture of innocence. 'What did you think he said?'

'That we're going to Rome?'

'Yes, he did.'

'Rome as in Rome, Italy? How can I? I don't have any luggage – or have you thought of that too?'

'I packed a bag from the clothes you keep at my house, of course.'

'Oh, of *course*.'

'We'll be back tomorrow, Saturday evening. I've booked a hotel and I have a few surprises in store for you. But first, this evening, we're going to the Teatro dell'Opera to see a ballet. Have you been to Italy before?'

'My father took us to Milan for a few days, as part of one of his trade visits to Europe, but that was when I was very young. Actually, he did once plan a trip to Rome, when I was little, but we never made it.' I'm still too shell-shocked to answer properly.

'Why not?'

'It was just before my father was attacked.'

My whole body tenses at the memory of that horrible time. My father had driven to the drugstore to get some medication for my mother, but he never even made it inside. Some maniac in the parking lot decided it would be fun to beat him over the head with a baseball bat. For a while, we thought Daddy might not make it, but he recovered, although the brain injury destroyed part of his sight. It didn't stop him getting re-elected to the Senate.

'Then I'm even happier that I can finally take you to Italy. I'd assumed you'd already been, so the fact you're a virgin to the city is a bonus.'

'How did you get my passport?'

He taps the side of his nose. 'You really ought to be more careful, you know. The desk drawer isn't the safest place to keep it. There are some bad people about.'

'I agree. Some very bad people. Wicked, in fact.'

His eyes gleam. 'I do hope so. Now buckle up so we can get on our way.'

He clips my belt in place, then his own, and kisses

me while we start to taxi to the runway. The plane accelerates and is up like a rocket, while I'm still processing the fact that I am going to Rome for the evening and that Alexander has gone to all this trouble to arrange it. He knows I adore ballet, and although he's wealthy enough to have 'people' to organize a trip such as this, I'm genuinely touched at the attention to detail, even at a time when he's weighed down with work and worries about the estate and his family. He must still be grieving the loss of his father, too. The thought of Emma creeps into the corner of my mind but I dismiss it. Alexander hasn't mentioned her so I'll run with the idea that 'no news is good news'.

As the plane climbs steeply, the lights of the airfield are quickly obscured by clouds and the sky is a sharp indigo blue. Over to the west, the horizon is tinged with pink, which disappears very fast as we bank towards the south and east.

My ears pop and Alexander squeezes my hand. 'OK?'

'I still can't believe you did this,' I say, slowly coming to terms with the fact that I'm dressed for the red carpet and on my way to Italy.

'Good. I'm happy to know I can still surprise you. I hope it's only the first of many surprises this evening.' He pauses, then says, 'I wanted to make up for that video, and the fact that it ruined my Valentine's surprise, and to say thanks for all the support you've given me and Emma over the past few weeks. When I landed outside your door at the start of term, you could have simply left me outside or refused to come to the funeral with me.'

'I could,' I reply, enjoying having him grovel – or as close as Alexander comes to grovelling . . .

'I also wanted to make up for the fact I had to spend more time at Falconbury.'

'I guess you were busy, but I think I can stand getting this trip by way of an apology.'

He shakes his head at my remark, but the smile is there. Seeing him like this – relaxed, enjoying himself and looking super sexy – reminds me of just why I fell for him in the first place. My skin tingles in anticipation of what might be to come.

The pilot announces that we can unfasten our belts and the engine note lowers a little.

'Champagne?' Alexander asks me.

'I think I definitely need something.'

Alexander retrieves a bottle of Cristal from a fridge concealed behind a wood panel. He pours the straw-coloured liquid into two flutes and the froth almost spills over the rim.

'To tonight.'

We chink glasses and I take a large gulp, bubbles bursting on my tongue. Butterflies stir my stomach, like on our first few dates, and yet I don't know why.

Alexander sips his wine carefully. 'Even if this is your first visit to Rome, you must have been on a private jet before.'

'Oh, all the time.' I shake my head. 'As a matter of fact, I'm not in the habit of travelling by private charter. My father uses them for business and my mother occasionally travels with him, but we're not the Clintons. Not yet anyway.' I smile. 'Daddy has been on Air Force One, however.'

He lets out a low whistle. 'Now, I have to admit I'm impressed.'

'That makes a change. I thought Alexander Hunt wasn't impressed by anything.'

He gives me a look that I fear may cause the airplane fuel to ignite. 'I wouldn't say that. When I saw you climb out of the Bentley, you took my breath away.'

'No, I didn't. Nobody does that to you.' I blush but I am also incredibly turned on.

'Yes, you did.' He doesn't take his eyes off mine.

My God, he really means it – and the temperature in the cabin just went up another ten degrees. There is something in that glance that's more than lust, an intensity that's scrambled my brain. My cheeks heat up and I resort to a large gulp of champagne.

'Oh, look, isn't that the coast already?'

I twist around and press my face closer to the cabin window. Through a gap in the clouds, orange lights fringe the coast like beaded trim on a black cloth. On the other side of the Channel, the lights of the Continent beckon and we speculate on the towns and cities thousands of feet below.

'How long is the flight?'

'A couple of hours. I wonder what we can do to pass the time.'

'Yes, I wonder . . .' My body shimmers with desire under that intense gaze. I don't really want to let him know the effect he's having on me tonight, so I resort to my Cristal again.

'Have I ever told you that you're the sexiest girl on the planet?'

'So I've been promoted from being merely the sexiest girl in the county? I think that was your last assessment of me.'

'I've revised my opinion of late and I'm willing to promote you.'

'If we weren't twenty thousand feet up, I might have to hit you, Alexander Hunt.'

His response is to take my empty glass from me and slide his hand under the silk of my dress and up my shinbone. Every inch of skin tingles where his fingers rest on my knee.

'The dress is beautiful,' I say.

'I hoped you'd like it. You looked amazing in the one you wore to the ball so I knew you liked the designer. I was a little worried that the shoes might not fit, even though I checked your collection thoroughly.'

'I've noticed you seem to have some kind of shoe fetish.'

'Is it a crime?' he says, doing one of his terrible impressions of my East Coast accent.

'No, but this . . . ah . . .' I catch my breath as he

removes his hand from my knee and slips off one of my shoes. I point my toe as he holds my foot in his hand and lifts it up. Leaning down he kisses it, right in the centre. It's intensely erotic, like being worshipped.

'You were saying?'

I can hardly breathe, let alone reply, as he balances my foot in his palm and runs his tongue from my ankle and over the blade of my foot, ending with a kiss on the top of my toe. 'I was . . . going to ask . . . if checking out women's closets was part of special forces training.'

'No, but stealing passports is.'

Gently, he lowers my foot and starts to draw down the zip at the side of my dress. 'We can't do this up here,' I say.

'Can't do what?'

'Join the Mile High Club.'

'Oh, we're well over a mile high now. Probably four or five.'

He pulls down the zip and tugs the silk away from my chest. The bodice parts company with my skin and I catch my breath sharply at being bared.

'What's the matter?' he asks, in between planting butterfly-soft kisses on my bare shoulder.

'Nothing, other than it feels a little weird, knowing the pilot's on the other side of the door. He must know what we're doing.'

'I'm sure he does but he's hardly going to leave the controls to come back here and serve peanuts, is he?'

'Alexander, you've never been on any airplane where they serve peanuts.'

He laughs. 'True, but I've been on plenty where I've been shot at.'

'Really?'

'Many times, but I'm hoping the Romans are going to be happier to see us than most of the people on the receiving end of my visits. More importantly, I'd hate you to crease this beautiful dress.'

With both hands, he pulls the bustier completely down so that I'm topless. 'Personally,' he says, 'I love the idea that I have you captive up here and I'm about to do filthy things to you.'

My throat dries and I am instantly creamy. 'Just how filthy are we talking?'

'Extremely filthy. You'd be shocked if I told you.'

'Try me,' I say breathily.

'Well, I'd probably break you in gently with something mild like this.' He dips his head and closes his mouth around my left nipple, which is hard as a pebble and red as a cherry. He sucks, gently at first but then harder. My head drifts back and I moan, unable to decide if the tingling in my nipples is pleasure or pain or a little of both. He stops, but only to transfer his mouth to the other nipple, giving it the same treatment. His teeth graze the tip softly, drawing a squeal of delight and pain from me. When I look down, my nipples are deepest crimson, aching and ready to pop.

'Shocked yet?' he murmurs.

'No.'

'Good. Then I'll move on to the next stage.'

'Which is?'

'I'll show you in a moment but let's get you out of this beautiful dress.'

He takes my hand in his and helps me to my feet, before tugging the side zip down the last few inches. The gown slithers over my hips and settles around my knees. So now I'm standing in the middle of a jet, with a three-thousand-dollar gown round my ankles and only an itsy-bitsy lacy thong to cover my modesty. Not, I might add, that I have any modesty left.

His eyes are molten with desire for me and he shakes his head and tuts. 'Now *I'm* shocked. You look fucking incredible.'

'The underwear isn't too much, then? It's La Perla. I was saving it for a special occasion.'

'Too much? I love it. I especially love the lack of it.'

He sinks to his knees in front of me, running his palms up my calves and the backs of my thighs and resting them on the bare cheeks of my ass. He presses his face to my mound and pushes his tongue through the sliver of silk over my sex. I was wet already and now I'm soaked, as his tongue pushes the fabric between my lips. His fingers tighten on my butt cheeks and he pulls me against his face and inhales. 'You smell incredible too.'

Even the roar of the Gulfstream's engines can't dull my whimper of delight when he pulls aside my thong and slips his forefinger inside me. I moan, grasping his shoulders for support while he eases his finger deeper inside me. He hooks his fingers either side of the lace string and pulls it sharply over my hips and down my thighs. Just as I try to wiggle out of it, the plane drops.

'Oh God!' I make a grab for the back of a seat and half fall on to the flat bed. 'Shouldn't we be buckled up?'

'Probably, but we'd better get on with this, just in case.'

He unbuttons his fly, strips off his tux trousers and black silk socks revealing a massive erection only restrained by a pair of brief black boxer shorts. He climbs on to the leather flat bed above me.

Something cold and hard touches my bare butt and I let out a squeak.

'What?' he says, pulling off his jacket.

'Seat-belt buckle.'

He raises his eyebrows. 'Ouch.'

Then he returns to my body, laying a trail of hot, wet kisses around my navel, and below it, over my pubic bone.

'How appropriate, a landing strip . . .' he says, glancing up at me from between my legs.

No matter that I'm naked with a hot man between my legs, this comment makes my cheeks burn. 'Pure coincidence,' I say, before my ability to speak is snatched away by the soft pressure of his thumb on my clit. His sensual assault is relentless; he thumbs me and circles the nub, varying the pressure, soft and firm, until I cry out, and my climax begins to take hold.

His erection brushes against the inside of my thigh, as he kisses his way back up my stomach and between my breasts, ending with a long, deep, wet kiss on my mouth that tastes of *me*.

Loving the weight of his body on me, I slip my hands down the back of his boxers, kneading his glutes in my fingers. I tug at the side of his shorts, pulling them over his behind so I can grind my bared pussy against his cock. He takes the hint and shifts his weight off me, pulling down his shorts. His cock springs out, thick and hard, and I close my fingers round it, loving the smooth feel of his skin and the weight of it in my hand.

'Fuck, I love this.' Alexander has ecstasy in his eyes when I slide the circle of my fingers up and down his length. When I tighten the circle, he groans in sheer pleasure and I feel all-powerful.

In a second, he's on top of me again, pushing inside me. I claw at his back, clutching the thick cotton of his dress shirt. He drives into me, the pressure of him deep inside combining with the friction of his pelvis against my clit. It's a frantic fuck, against the clock, as we both grapple for our climaxes. I think I feel the plane jink again but it's too late to do anything because my body tenses in that taut-sinewed, high-tension way as my orgasm spirals through me.

When I open my eyes, Alexander is slumped on top of me, coming down from his own climax.

'Oh!' I grab him as the plane suddenly drops again and the pilot's voice crackles into life.

'Sorry for the bumpy ride; we should be out of it very soon but it may be a good idea to fasten your seat belts.'

'How does he know we're out of them?' I say, in between gasps.

Alexander climbs off me, still naked except for his dress shirt. I manage to slide into my seat and fasten the belt, worried we'll end up tossed around the cabin like bubbles in the champagne bottle.

Alexander buckles up next to me as the jet seems to hop across the sky. My fingers tighten around his in a death grip.

'Not scared, are you?'

'Of course not, but this *is* a little disconcerting.'

He gives a knowing smile. 'We're absolutely fine.'

'I suppose you're going to tell me this is nothing for someone used to abseiling from helicopter skids.'

He laughs. 'Well . . .'

'Look at us. Imagine if we did crash and by some miracle they found us both, buckled up next to each other like *this*.'

We stare at each other and burst out laughing. I'm completely naked; he has only his dress shirt on. He slips his arm around me and manages to kiss me, despite the plane bumping along.

'Apologies again for the rough ride. I've re-routed to go around the storm so we should be fine from now on.'

'I hope so!' A few minutes later, we get the all clear,

so Alexander unbuckles his belt and rescues his boxer shorts from the carpet.

'I'm staying where I am,' I say while he dresses. 'But I'd appreciate some help with my underwear.'

He retrieves my thong from the top of the cupboard containing the fridge. How the hell did it get there?

I hold out my hand but Alexander loops the thong over his finger and holds it up in front of my eyes.

'Sorry, but I don't put knickers back *on*.'

'Give it back!' I try to snatch the thong but he waggles it tantalizingly just out of reach. 'You bastard!'

'Shh. Our captain will hear you.'

'I don't care!'

'If you want your knickers, you'll have to come and get them.'

I undo my belt and stand up, just as the plane decides to have one last hurrah. The drop is tiny but it overbalances me and I tumble against Alexander. He catches me, of course, and I find myself pressed against his chest, with his arms around me.

'Please, Alexander, may I have my underwear back?' I ask sweetly.

'With a very sexy and very naked girl in his arms, what do you expect a man to say to that?'

Chapter Thirteen

We managed to get our clothes back on; after all, it wouldn't have been great to greet the Italian customs officer naked. Once the formalities are over, Alexander helps me down the steps to where an Italian version of Brandon, in a sharp suit like a Mafia boss, stands by a Mercedes.

Italian Brandon – who turns out to be called Antonio – whisks us straight to the Teatro dell'Opera. Lights glitter in the river as we cross the Tiber, towards the city. As Alexander helps me out on to the sidewalk in front of the Teatro, and takes my arm, Rome makes an assault on all my senses at once. The night is milder than in Oxford, but it's still cool and I tug my wrap tighter as we walk up the steps. Sirens blare and horns toot and tubs of spring flowers perfume the air. Couples in tuxes and full evening dress sashay along the red carpet to the foyer, diamonds glittering in the lamplight. I could claim that I'm not seduced by the glamour, but I'd be lying.

'Wow, I had worried we might be a little overdressed,' I say as we're handed a programme.

'It's a Gala Night in aid of a charity,' Alexander explains while the concierge shows us to our front-row seats. 'And we've only just started. Tomorrow, I have some surprises that will make an art historian orgasmic.'

'Orgasmic, huh? I can't wait.'

Four hours later, Alexander and I are sitting in an elegant restaurant tucked away in a corner of a piazza. A succession of waiters bring tiny mouthfuls of Italian delicacies from the tasting menu until I have to beg for mercy. Alexander confesses to knowing very little about ballet, but seems willing to listen to me telling him about the story and giving my opinion on the choreography and performances. He did take me to Covent Garden last term, when he'd come back from an op with his regiment. That was a surprise, but this trip is on another level. I'm still buzzing from the ballet, and the fact I've just had dinner in Rome, when Antonio finally delivers us to our hotel. It's situated next to the Spanish Steps, and the white marble is lit softly by lamplight. There are still some couples around, walking hand in hand, even though it's the small hours now. When I get out of the car, I hear the water in the fountain at the bottom of the steps tinkle softly.

Alexander takes my arm while Antonio hands the luggage to a uniformed bellboy. 'I hope this is OK. It isn't the grandest hotel in Rome but I think it's the most beautiful, and it was a favourite of Picasso so I thought it was appropriate.'

'It's gorgeous,' I breathe.

The faded stucco exterior of the boutique hotel

looks divine to me, and it occurs to me how much effort Alexander has put into arranging this trip.

We're greeted by the concierge and shown to a suite on the top floor.

'Would you like me to unpack your bags, *signore*?'

'No, thanks. We're fine.'

Taking the hint, the concierge leaves us alone. OK, I've stayed in some nice hotels with my parents but this is sensational. The decor and furnishings are contemporary yet perfectly in keeping with the hotel's historic charm. There's a king-size bed and a dressing room that leads to an opulent marble and mosaic bathroom, with a huge sunken tub.

'This is the best part.' Alexander opens the windows on to a private roof terrace, where dozens of tea lights are arranged on the deck and the tables, casting flickering shadows over the flower tubs. I cross to the rim of the balcony and lean on the wall, transfixed by the Roman skyline, the domes and the church towers, temples and tiled rooftops. The flowers fill my nose with scent.

'Wow. Just *wow*.'

'Is it what you expected from Rome?'

'It's beyond anything I ever imagined. I think I'm in love.'

I can't see his face but his breath is warm on the back of my neck. 'With Rome, of course . . .'

'Of course.'

His answer is to slip his arm around me and to point out some of the cityscape twinkling ahead and below us. 'That's the Villa Borghese and the Pincio. You might just be able to glimpse the Colosseum and the Palatine Hill, but we'll get a better look tomorrow.'

'What *have* you got planned for tomorrow?'

'After we've checked out that bathtub? You'll see.'

Of course, I'm aching to see the finest art treasures of Rome, but I'm afraid they aren't foremost on my mind when his fingers rest lightly on the soft flesh of my shoulder. Maybe it's his touch, maybe the cool night air, but goose bumps prickle my skin and I shiver.

'You're cold,' he says simply.

'I'm fine.'

Too late – he is already slipping off his tux jacket and drapes it around my shoulders. His arm is tighter around me now as we drink in the view. I can't believe we're here, and I feel shivery inside and out. How can I distrust him at a time like this? How can I not love being here with him and being part of this world? It's not the money and the lavish gifts that impress me, it's the way he's planned this whole thing so carefully to make me happy. I *suppose* it could all be an elaborate apology to make up for the sex tape, but I genuinely don't think that's Alexander's style.

I kiss him softly on the lips. 'This is a wonderful surprise. I don't know what to say . . .'

'Then don't say anything. There are other uses for your mouth.'

'That's outrageous.'

He folds me in his arms and looks so handsome in

the light from the flickering candles that my knees feel wobbly.

'If I had my way,' he says, 'I would lock the door to this suite right now, forget the art and keep you here until you passed out from being shagged by me.'

'How do you know you wouldn't crumble first?' I tease, tracing a line along his jaw with my finger.

'That sounds like a challenge.' The gleam in his eyes is wicked, and I realize again that issuing any kind of challenge to Alexander is quite literally asking for trouble.

'I think we should go to bed,' he murmurs. 'We've got an early start and a lot of things to see and do.'

'Of the orgasmic variety?'

'Those start now. I believe you offered to put your tongue to good use earlier?'

'No, I believe *you* made the suggestion first.'

In the end, both our mouths were put to very good use – or should that be very bad use? – and neither of us has had a great deal of sleep. Yet, he shows me no mercy and it's not quite light outside when I wake to the sound of water splashing into the huge tub. I'm still rubbing sleep from my eyes when Alexander crosses to the bed, naked, and says, 'We have an early start but first it's bath time.'

I blink, taking in the sight of his naked torso and burgeoning erection. 'But I'm not dirty, Alexander.'

He grins. 'Don't worry, I'll soon put that right.'

The mosaic tub is set into a recessed platform in the centre of the bathroom. Alexander turns off the tap and the torrent is replaced by the gentle swish of bath oil being swirled into the water. The scent is divine – orange blossom, I think – and wisps of fragrant steam rise from the surface. With a naked and fully ripped Alexander standing by, I feel like some Roman goddess about to be bathed by her warrior slave.

'What's so funny?' he asks.

I try to look innocent. 'Nothing whatsoever.'

My slave steps into the bathtub first and sits down, and I get in after him, sinking down into the warm water, which laps at my breasts and licks my nipples. His chest is a solid wall behind my shoulder blades and his erection juts very satisfyingly against my butt cheeks.

'You see, you *are* dirty, Lauren . . . filthy, in fact, and I'm going to have to clean you very thoroughly,' he says.

When he picks up a bar of soap and starts to rub it gently over my damp skin, I am in no state to contradict him. I rest my head on his shoulder and close my eyes as he soaps my breasts and slides his fingers over my nipples. Tendrils of steam rise around us and the fragrance of the oil is intoxicating. The whole sensory experience is so hedonistic and sensual, I can't help wriggling back against his cock, over-eager to be satisfied.

'Good?' he whispers, rubbing my chest with the soap bar.

'Mmm.'

When I've been thoroughly laved, he puts the soap

bar back in the tray and dips his hand below the water, down between my thighs. He plays with me, gently teasing and stroking me. The warmth of the scented oil and the incredible sensation building in my core lulls me into a kind of erotic daze.

'Bad, dirty girl,' he murmurs. 'You are in so much trouble.'

'Am I?'

'A bath won't be enough to cleanse those filthy thoughts.'

'You think . . .'

'I *know*.' Gently, he scoops his hands under my butt and lifts it up a little. I know what he wants and I wriggle back, feeling for the tip of his penis under me. Water splashes over the edge of the tub and I giggle, then cry out as he spears me on his cock in one fell swoop. It's not the easiest position to make love in, but it's wonderful trying. Our bodies are slippery slick with soap, and I'm writhing and wriggling against the mosaic base of the tub but the sheer wantonness of the whole experience is enough to drive me insane. He keeps up the pressure on my nub while I rock back and forth on his penis.

'Fuck, that is so good. You are so good . . .'

His voice is full of wonder, just like a slave worshipping me. I know I feel like a goddess, lying in the tub. If he knew what I was thinking, what I want him to do to me . . . what I want to do to him after this. My orgasm ripples through me, in wave after wave, and the tightening of my muscles is his cue to let go and thrust up and into me until he comes himself with a groan of agonized release.

Our early-morning 'bath' meant we had to pass on the hotel's breakfast, and instead we snatched pastries and cappuccinos standing at the bar with the real Romans at a tiny cafe. As for the Colosseum and the ruins of the Forum, they will have to wait for another visit because Antonio whisked us to the Pantheon to see Raphael's tomb and then to the Villa Borghese to view Bernini's sculptures and the Caravaggios and Titians.

Now, eight hours later, I have run out of superlatives. I have indeed experienced more cultural orgasms than one Art History student can handle in a day. After a panini on the hoof, we moved on to St Peter's and the Vatican, where a feast of incredible art treasures was laid out in front of me. I'd heard the collection was astonishing, but to see in the flesh the pieces I've read about and studied blows my mind. We walk through gallery after gallery, marvelling at Renaissance paintings, Roman mosaics, Flemish tapestries, and Greek and Egyptian sculptures.

We stop in front of a huge marble torso of Hercules by Belvedere that has caught Alexander's eye.

'You do know that this is meant to be the most perfect six-pack in the world,' I say.

Alexander looks doubtful. 'Really? Are you quite sure of that?'

'Well, maybe I need to make a further comparison later.'

'I highly recommend it,' he says, his arm shifting below my spine.

I lean up and whisper in his ear, 'Are you sure you should have your hand on my butt in the Vatican? We must be breaking some laws.'

Finally, we reach the Sistine Chapel itself, and when we walk inside, I can't even speak.

We sit together on a bench at the fringe of the chapel, gazing upwards at Michelangelo's frescoes. There are scores of people around us, all doing the same, and I guess it's incredibly 'touristy' but I don't care.

When I get my voice back, Alexander listens patiently as I tell him the story of each of the panels.

'I'm not boring you, am I?' I ask, suddenly conscious that I've been babbling for the past few hours.

He laughs. 'Lauren, the one thing you could never do is bore me. Though I can't claim to have your knowledge and enthusiasm for art, I do appreciate beautiful things.'

I glance at him. 'But do you enjoy collecting them?'

'If you mean do I see you as some kind of acquisition, then you couldn't be further from the truth.' He looks down at his watch. 'I'm afraid we need to go if we're to have dinner before we fly home. I booked a table at a trattoria in the Trastevere.'

I shift my focus back to the magnificent ceiling. 'Do we have to leave now?'

'I'd love to stay another night, but I need to get back to Oxford. I've *got* to spend some time preparing for my next tutorial. The Real World awaits, unfortunately.' A momentary trace of bitterness tinges his voice, but it's soon gone and he kisses me, a deep, hot kiss that sucks away thoughts and words. It goes on and on and on and finally, when he breaks contact and leaves my mouth tingling with the aftershock, I realize that right now I could forgive him almost anything.

Antonio is waiting at the edge of St Peter's Square and drives us into the Trastevere district, where Alexander leads the way through the maze of cobbled streets lined by medieval houses. With the metal braziers burning on the covered terrace, it's just warm enough to eat our pizza outside the little trattoria on the Piazza di San Callisto. The restaurant and the food are nothing fancy, but the aromas wafting from the doorway make my mouth water. Actually, I think I like it even more than the elegant restaurant we visited last night and after a day wandering the galleries, I could eat a horse.

Alexander bites into his pizza slice with relish.

'I didn't have you down as a pizza kind of guy,' I say with a smile.

'You're talking to a man who's eaten live grubs and live ants. Pizza is one of my favourites,' he quips.

'You're kidding me. People' – I lower my voice – 'like *you*, don't really do that stuff, do they?'

'If Bear Grylls does it, it must be true,' he says before popping a shrimp from the pizza into his mouth.

'The guy on the Discovery Channel? You're putting me off my margherita.'

When I shudder, he laughs and sips his wine. Lamps throw soft light and shade on the faded ochres, pinks and blues of the stucco fronts of the houses and shops. There's a realism to the place, an earthy vibrancy, a determination to enjoy life that I adore. I can hardly believe Valentina shares the same heritage as the people we met and saw today.

'You love Roma, then?' he says when I tear my eyes from the architecture and back to him.

'I do. I could spend a lifetime here, studying the artworks, maybe working in a gallery or curating a museum. You have *no* idea what you've started.'

'Is that what you want . . . after your master's?' He sips his Chianti and watches me thoughtfully. 'To stay in Europe, and not go back to the States?' Is that hope I see in his eyes?

'Maybe. Today has made me realize how much I need to see and do and experience. There are some wonderful galleries in the US, of course, but now I'm here, I want to explore Europe, Russia, the Middle East . . .'

'That sounds like a plan.'

'I wouldn't say it's a plan, yet. I need to finish my master's first, and you know I've been somewhat distracted from that.'

'I hope not all of the distractions have been so terrible.' He strokes the back of my hand with his fingers, an innocent gesture that's still intensely erotic.

'Not *all* . . .'

'Good. I wish I had any kind of plan for the future but I can't see a solution that doesn't involve me giving up the army. I certainly can't run the estate and carry on with my military career. I knew that one day I'd have to leave and take over from my father, but I never dreamed it would be so soon.'

'No, and I'm very sorry. It's been a huge shock.' It's the first time we've really talked about this stuff for ages and I'm relieved that we can.

'It isn't just that I lost my father before we had any chance to resolve our differences. I deeply regret the rows we had and the animosity, but how could either of us ever have known what was around the corner?'

'You couldn't possibly . . .'

He traces a circle on my hand. 'Of course, it's a huge responsibility running the estate . . . and anyone who decided to tie themselves to that life would have to know what they were getting into. The house, the people, the land, they aren't something you can run away from once you decide to commit to them.' He looks serious as he talks and I find myself already mourning our carefree time in Rome.

'No, I can see that.' I'm struggling here, wondering if what he's not saying is far more important than what he actually *is*.

He glances up at me. 'And, of course, there's Emma to consider too. Even when she turns eighteen and goes off to uni, she's still going to need to know that the only person she has left isn't going to go off and get themselves killed.'

'I'm sure that won't happen,' I say, trying to soothe him. I don't like the idea of him having to give up his military career, even though I clearly see his dilemma.

'No, I'm pretty good at staying out of trouble. Usually.' He grins.

'Although, the first time I saw you in the pub, you got involved in a fight with two idiots. That's not staying out of trouble.'

'True, but by now I think you know that anything involving the Hunts isn't going to be an easy ride, is it?'

What is he trying to say here? Against my better judgement, I find myself hoping the ride is a long one, even if it will never be easy.

'I never asked for an easy ride, Alexander,' I say, voicing one small part of my thoughts.

'Perhaps you didn't realize what you were getting into?'

'Perhaps I knew full well?' I keep my tone light and teasing.

'Then you won't be surprised to know that it may not get any easier in the foreseeable future. I wish it weren't that way,' he says, seeming distracted again.

'No one can foresee the future, can they?' I dance around his words, parrying question with question, but all the while his eyes are intent on me, leaving me no hiding place. My stomach flutters, my appetite temporarily gone.

'That's true.' Suddenly he smiles and lets both of us off the hook, whatever the hook was. 'Shall we have dessert?'

'I'm not sure I can manage one.'

'Oh, I'm sure you can squeeze something else in. You always do.'

While we wait for our orders, the conversation is Rome again, Alexander the guide this time, telling me a little of its political history. The waiter has just brought my tiramisu and Alexander's *affogato* when his mobile rings. He pulls it from his jacket pocket and frowns at the screen.

'Work?' I ask.

The line between his brows deepens. 'No. It's Emma's school. I'm sorry but I *have* to answer this.'

You know those moments when so many conflicting emotions hit you at once that you can't process them? This is one of them. Emma's school would not call this late on a Saturday evening unless something was ser-iously wrong.

His *affogato* abandoned, Alexander is already striding back into the restaurant towards the restrooms, phone clamped to his ear. People around us glance at me as I sit, suddenly bereft, at the table. I push my own dessert away from me. I hope she's OK. I hope there hasn't been an accident, because Alexander could not survive another family tragedy.

Even if she is OK – physically – what the hell can have happened?

247

Is it selfish of me to hope that this is *anything* that doesn't involve Henry Favell?

The minutes pass until I half worry that Alexander won't come back at all. I sip my iced water, now wishing we weren't so far away from home.

'Is everything all right? Can I get you anything?' the waiter asks me. 'Did the *signore* not enjoy his *affogato*?' He looks at the puddle of muddy cream in Alexander's dessert dish.

'No, *grazie*, but could we have the check?'

'Of course, *signorina*.'

A few minutes later, I see Alexander threading his way through the tables. By the set of his jaw, I know there's something seriously wrong and the dessert I ate feels like it's lead in my mouth.

'I'm sorry but we need to leave now. I've called the driver, and he should be here in a few minutes. Can you wait here while I pay the bill?'

'I already asked for the check.'

'Thank you.'

'Is Emma OK?'

'She will be,' he says grimly, 'but only by a bloody miracle.'

'Oh God, what's happened?'

'She's in A&E. The paramedics found her passed out outside some nightclub, out of her skull on booze. That was her housemistress on the phone.'

The conversation halts while the waiter arrives with

the check and our coats and Alexander hands over a wad of euros.

'Who was she with?' I ask nervously as he opens the door for me to walk outside.

'Not sure. It seems like she'd sneaked out with a couple of girls from her house; the police think they may have called an ambulance and then made their own way back to school once she'd been picked up. The nurses found her ID in her handbag and phoned the school.'

'Will she be OK?'

'They've got her on a drip now, which is standard procedure, and she's unhurt. She's been vomiting, of course, but there won't be any lasting damage. Oh fuck, I hope she manages to finish school without dying of alcohol poisoning, being attacked or raped. Jesus!' He paces the street. 'Where *is* that fucking driver?'

The fucking driver sweeps up a few minutes later, just as Alexander has his mobile out to read the guy the riot act. I don't think I've ever seen him so upset, and by that I mean not in control of his emotions. Normally, his anger takes the opposite form: he's ultra in control; in fact, he's so cold and collected that it scares me, like when he broke up a fight in a pub out of a (misguided) need to protect me. Like when he saw Scott and me kissing in the street.

But this is different; it's Emma in trouble and he has no clue how to deal with it. Neither do I, but I do know that shouting won't help.

With a growl at Antonio, he opens the door for me and climbs in after.

'Do you want another tour of the sights, *signore*?'

'No, I want to get to the bloody airfield as fast as possible.'

'*Si, signore* . . .' The driver's face is impassive in the mirror. I guess he's used to rude clients, then Alexander mutters a 'fuck' under his breath and says, 'I apologize for that, but we're in a hurry so if you could get us to the airfield quickly, I'd appreciate it.'

That's pretty much the last I hear from him before we reach the airfield, where the limo takes us right up to the plane again. The immigration official is already waiting at the bottom of the steps and barely even glances at our passports before Alexander helps me up the steps with a gruff 'be careful' and the door is shut. There's no champagne now, of course, and we buckle up in silence before we take off once more. It's only when the pilot tells us we can unfasten our seat belts that he slips his hand over mine and squeezes it briefly.

'I know it doesn't seem like it now, but I'm sure she'll be OK,' I say, and he mutters, 'I hope you're right,' before telling me he wants to make some more calls. Somehow, the twelve-seater cabin now seems faintly ridiculous, rather like the huge dining table at Falconbury when the four of us ate dinner before the ball. There's no consolation outside the window, because all I can see is a few dark clouds against an even darker sky.

Chapter Fourteen

'Lauren, we're here.'

I wake with a start to see Alexander's face looming above my seat in the cabin. He touches my arm. 'We've landed.'

'Uh?' I glance down to find I'm covered in a blanket.

'I fastened your seat belt for landing. You were completely out of it.'

'What time is it?' I mumble.

'One a.m. local time. Two in Rome.'

'Oh God.' I get up, a little shaky from sleep, while the engine dies. Alexander hands me his jacket.

'You'll need this. It'll be freezing outside.'

'What about you?'

'I'll manage, thanks.'

Minutes later, the cabin door opens and he hands me down the steps. The frosty night air pinches at my face. Rome was hardly warm but it's ten degrees colder in Oxford and, having just woken from sleep, I instantly start to shiver.

'Let's get you into the car.' Alexander strides ahead and opens the door. He says something to the driver, then gets in the back, next to me.

'Do you mind coming to the hospital? I don't want to waste time going back to Oxford now. You can sleep in the car if you want to.'

'It's fine. I'm wide awake now.'

'Thanks. I need to call Emma's housemistress to see how she is and tell her we're on our way.'

What I'm not telling him is that I should be going to the showing of *Il Conformista* this morning. I'll have to email Professor Rafe as soon as I can and tell him I'm sorry, and that it was a study trip. Right now, I don't want to complicate things for Alexander, and I'm just as anxious as he is to see Emma.

Half an hour later, we arrive at the hospital and Alexander opens the door almost before the car stops.

'Brandon needs to move the car. Do you want to wait here?' he asks as he gets out.

'No, I'll come in with you.'

'I really don't want you dragged into this bloody mess any more than you have been. I'm sorry I've ruined your evening.'

'You haven't. We've had an amazing time, and now Emma needs us,' I say softly.

He squeezes my hand but grimaces. 'A&E isn't a particularly pleasant place at this time of day.'

'I'm not expecting it to be. I don't need to be wrapped in cotton wool.'

'Come on then,' he says before speaking to Brandon through the window. 'Can you wait for us, please.'

Even though it's the middle of the night, and the

hospital cafe and shops are all shuttered up, there are still plenty of people slumped on chairs in the waiting room outside the ER, in various states of disrepair, inebriation and boredom. My heels click-clack on the tiles while I find a chair and he announces his arrival at the nurses' station. A bald guy with no discernible neck and dried vomit down his shirt leers at me from the chair opposite.

When I tear my eyes away from a skinny youth with a bloody nose, Alexander is just disappearing behind a curtain, which, I assume, conceals Emma.

I pull the jacket tighter around me and disappear behind a tattered copy of UK *Glamour* magazine, which probably contains enough germs to infect the entire population of Oxfordshire. I don't take in the words, however, because my mind is full of Emma. Two machine cups of tea later, my butt is almost numb and the clock above the nurses' station shows it's well past four.

Alexander finally emerges, his face set in a mask of tension and restraint.

I stand up and walk towards him. 'How is she?'

'Still on the IV but she's stopped throwing up. They did some blood tests to check for any other substances, as they put it, but she's clear, so I suppose I should be grateful for that. I've told Miss Fisher to go home.'

A reed-thin woman with long red hair who looks not that much older than Alexander approaches. He takes her aside and says something about 'not being able to thank her enough' and 'making sure it won't happen again'. Miss Fisher nods and seems relieved to be off to her bed.

'Can she go home yet?' I ask after the teacher has left us.

'Soon, I hope. The doctors just want to make sure she gets all the fluids into her before she can leave. Why don't I call you a cab to take you back to Oxford while Emma and I go home with Brandon?'

'I don't mind staying, but if you want some privacy . . . ?'

'It's not that . . . After your evening has been ruined, I can hardly ask you to get involved in our problems again. You ought to be in bed.'

'We both ought to be in bed.'

That comment raises a smile for about a nanosecond before he says, 'I think Emma might like someone neutral in the car, and she does like you. What about work? Can you spare the time?'

'Yes, I have work but nothing that won't wait.' I don't tell him that I desperately need to stay as I'm so worried this episode with Emma has something to do with Henry.

Alexander doesn't bother to hide his relief that I'm staying, so I know he must be at the end of his tether.

It's still dark by the time we turn off the main road on to the lane that leads to Falconbury. I'm sitting in the front seat next to Brandon, while Emma dozes in the back seat, her head resting on Alexander's shoulder. A glance in the vanity mirror shows Alexander staring into the darkness outside and Emma, pale but tranquil as a baby, covered in a tartan car rug. She was still groggy when we helped her into the car and didn't have much to say for herself, partly, I think, from awe of Alexander. When we arrive at the house, Robert and Helen immediately hurry down the steps, their breath misting the air. Benny shoots out from behind them, barking joyously, and launches himself at me.

'Down, boy!' At Alexander's command, Benny drops to his haunches. I feel sorry for the poor dog; he must be completely confused at finding his master home unexpectedly yet in no mood to play.

Helen wraps the rug around Emma's shoulders and puts her arm around her. 'Lady Emma, let's get you out of this cold and up to your room.' Still out of it, Emma allows herself to be ushered up the steps and into the house.

Robert approaches. 'Lord Falconbury, Miss Cusack, I'll have some refreshments brought to the library. I've already laid a fire.'

'Thanks, Robert.'

I ruffle Benny's ears and Alexander turns to me. 'Would you rather go to bed?'

Though we've been up all night and I feel shattered, I'm also feeling too nervy to sleep. 'I think I'll have some tea first and wait until Emma's settled.'

In the library, there's a cafetière of coffee, a pot of

tea and cookies. Even at this hour, nothing escapes Robert's notice: it's the exact brand of Earl Grey that he knows I prefer, which I find a little bizarre. I've no appetite but I pour a cup. Alexander stands with his back to me, staring into the fire, too stressed to sit.

'Want a coffee?' I ask.

'No, thanks.' He wheels round. 'Yes, go on then. Fuck this, why did she have to do it? Why tonight, when we were a thousand bloody miles away?'

'She had too much to drink, she made a mistake, and she didn't know we were in Rome. It's just bad timing.'

'Is there ever a good time to get so paralytically drunk that you pass out in the bloody street?' He rounds on me but I try not to snap back.

I pour coffee from the cafetière into a cup. He looks exhausted and incredibly stressed. 'Obviously not, but she didn't do it deliberately to haul us back from Rome.'

'Are you sure? She definitely wanted someone's attention.'

'Are you sure she wasn't simply being a teenager? Have you never done anything like that?'

'A couple of times, of course I have, but I waited until I was a student or in the army.'

'What did her housemistress say?'

'That she should come home for now and they'll decide what to do on Monday. I've been warned she may be suspended for a short time.'

'Ouch. She won't get thrown out?'

'Not this time, but they won't put up with this happening too many times. Dad would have gone ballistic. I'm glad he's not here to see this, even if it would have been his problem. Jesus, I don't need this, not now.' Rarely do I ever hear him make an admission that he's finding things overwhelming.

I hand him the cup. 'Why don't you sit down and have this?'

Even deciding whether or not to take a seat seems to be too much for him, but suddenly he nods. 'Thanks. I apologize for shouting at you. None of this is your fault. I should have made you go back to Oxford.'

'No one makes me do anything, Alexander.'

He looks at me. 'No, I should know that by now . . . Lauren, I know this wasn't how you wanted to spend your evening but I'm glad you stayed, no matter what I just said. Maybe you could talk to Emma tomorrow, when she surfaces. She likes you and I'm sure if I wade in like a bull in a china shop, it'll only end up in another blazing row. It's a lot to ask, but do you mind?'

It's not just the lack of sleep and the night spent in an ER waiting room that makes my stomach unsettled, it's my guilty conscience and the fact Alexander clearly thinks I'm some sort of good influence on his sister. The last thing I want to do is to act like some kind of counsellor to her.

'I don't know if I can give her any advice. I don't know that I can say the right thing to her,' I say, trying to be honest in this respect at least.

'Neither do I, that's the problem. I have no idea how to deal with this.'

'Then we're even.'

'But you will speak to her? Even if she won't tell you anything, at least will you try? If you can find out anything at all about how she's feeling, or if there's anything specific that made her sneak out of school and get so pissed, it would be a huge help.'

'OK, I'll try, but I can't make any promises. I guess people don't need a reason to get smashed once in a while.'

He downs the coffee and gets up again. I stand up too, light-headed with tiredness. 'Thank you for this. I won't forget it.'

Sheer exhaustion overcame my guilty conscience last night and when I wake, Alexander's side of the bed is cold and I remember him telling me that he wanted to see how Emma was before he got some rest. I'm not sure he's even been to bed at all. When I get up, I find him sitting at his desk in the library, flicking through documents, a fountain pen in one hand.

'How is she?'

'Still sleeping it off.' He puts down the pen, screws up his eyes and rubs the bridge of his nose.

'Did you stay with her the whole night?'

'I tried, but I fell asleep in the chair so Helen woke me and made me come to bed.'

'I don't remember you coming to bed.'

He treats me to a weary smile and gets out of his chair. 'You were out of it too. Have you had any breakfast?'

'Not yet. What time is it?'

'Almost eleven.' He looks hard at me. 'Why, are you missing something?'

'Nothing important.'

'Are you sure? Do you need to get back to Oxford?'

'No, it's OK. My next tute is tomorrow. It's just that Professor Rafe asked me to go to a movie with him but I've obviously missed that.'

He looks incredulous. 'He asked you to go and see a film with him on a Sunday morning?'

'Not only me. It was a faculty trip, and the cinema had arranged a special screening. It doesn't matter.' I don't tell him that Rafe did try to persuade me to go on a date.

He sighs. 'I'm sorry this business has fucked up your morning.'

'I'm not sorry, I didn't want to go that much but I felt I ought to show willing, and I'd much rather have actually been in Rome than watching a movie about it.'

He kisses me. 'Thanks. I'll have Robert lay out some brunch.'

We've just finished eating in the morning room when the door opens and a little ghost-like face appears.

He stands up and drops his napkin on the table. 'Good morning, Emma.'

She manages a grunt in return and inches her way to the table.

'Do you want some tea or orange juice?' I ask, feeling sorry for her but probably not as sorry as she feels for herself.

She shakes her head, then closes her eyes as if even that was too much for her.

'The hospital said you should keep drinking to replace your lost fluids,' says Alexander.

'Don'wan'anything.'

'Tough.' He walks over to the side table and grabs a jug of iced water. He pours a full tumbler and hands it to her. 'Drink this.'

'I might be sick.'

'Drink it,' he barks.

'I'm not in the fucking army,' Emma growls but sips the water anyway. 'God, that's rank.'

'Not enough vodka in it for you?'

I wince and Emma glares at him. I don't really blame her. 'Maybe mix it with some juice or have some chamomile tea?' I suggest, expecting to have my head bitten off.

'S'pose I could try.'

'The water's not that hot now but it'll do.' I pop a teabag in a cup and pour the water on it while Emma rests her head on her arms on the table. Alexander clearly can't bear to watch and is taking a great interest in the gardens. He's so used to controlling and hiding his emotions but he has totally lost it with Emma and probably doesn't want us to see how worried and over-whelmed he is. I know he's worried about her, and I'm no expert but even I can see that being angry with her won't help. On the other hand, she's not my sister; if she was, I think we'd have come to blows.

I offer the cup. 'Here. It's lukewarm but it'll be gentle on your stomach.'

After staring at the tea like it might bite her, she picks up the cup and takes a few sips.

'OK?'

She nods and mutters a word I think is: 'Thanks.'

Alexander turns around. 'At last.'

I try to telegraph a 'shut up' to him but it's no good.

'Why do you have to get on my back?' Emma wails.

'Because I care about you. Why do you think?'

'You're a hypocrite; you were off your face after the funeral.'

'That's different. I wasn't lying in the road at the time.'

'It wasn't the road, it was the High Street and I would have been OK.'

He clearly can't bring himself to speak for a moment, then shakes his head. 'Oh, really? You were uncon-scious, for God's sake! Did you expect people to just leave you lying there? I don't want to see you end up raped or dead in some alley. Where were your friends?'

'They stayed until they knew I was OK. I'm glad they left. They'd only have got into trouble.'

261

'They already are. Miss Fisher said she knows who was there. They've been suspended too.'

'I don't care if I'm suspended. It's a study week this week anyway.'

'Luckily for you, otherwise you'd be out of school for a week.'

'Well you needn't worry about staying here with me. I can stay with Allegra.'

Oh fuck. Allegra was her alibi when she last saw Henry. The last time I know about, anyway. What do I do now?

Alexander jumps in for me and I have to say I'm relieved. 'No, you're not staying with Allegra. You're coming to Oxford with me.'

She slams the cup into the saucer. 'You can't do that, Alex! I don't want to live with you for a week.'

'Sorry, no choice. I can't stay here at Falconbury or I'll get kicked off my course, and nothing's going to stop me finishing it.'

'No!'

'It's decided. No negotiation.'

She rounds on him. 'I may not go back to school at all, you know. I might pack in my A levels and go travelling or off to London. Why should I bother doing my exams anyway? I've got Mummy's money; I've got friends I can stay with or I can rent a flat. I don't need my inheritance.'

'Don't start this, Emma. You know how much you want to do that course.'

'I'm not sure now.' She folds her arms. 'I'm not sure about anything.'

'Grow up. You fought hard enough to be allowed to go there.'

Her eyes flash in triumph. 'What do you care? You just want me to go to Oxford, like Daddy. You want me to be a clone of you.'

'A clone of me?' he laughs. 'Actually, you couldn't be more wrong. I was the one who told him that you should be allowed to go your own way and if you must know, he agreed in the end.'

I really think I should take cover under the table.

She's momentarily silenced before she laughs at him. 'I don't believe you. He never said that to me.'

'He was going to.'

'How do you know that? When did he say it?'

The struggle to keep his cool is stamped all over Alexander's face. 'He said so the last time I saw him. He told me that you should do what you were passionate about. He was going to tell you . . .'

Emma gulps in air. 'You bastard! Why haven't you said this before?'

'I didn't want to upset you. Like this.' He looks anguished, seeing her real distress.

'Oh, I wish Mummy was here. I miss her so much, and I even miss Daddy.' Emma crumples and suddenly she looks much younger than her seventeen years.

He stares at her gently and lowers his voice. 'So do

I, but I'm afraid I'm all you've got.' He walks over to her and to his relief she accepts his hug.

Tears pour down her cheeks now and she gulps back a sob. They are both so distressed and I wonder if I should leave them to it. I am just beginning to creep to the door when I spot Emma looking at me pleadingly. Seeing the look too, Alexander pulls away, ruffles Emma's hair and walks slowly towards the door.

'I think I might go for a ride,' he mutters shakily. 'I need some air.'

Emma and I look at one another and as soon as he's gone, Emma starts to cry again, leaving me to pick up the pieces. I'm wrung out myself by lack of sleep and the sheer drama of the night, and I simply don't know what to do.

I cringe as Emma blows her nose on one of the white table napkins. 'What do I do now?' she wails. 'Alex is furious with me.'

'He's upset.'

She snorts. 'Alex? Upset? He doesn't do "upset". He's like Daddy, a robot.'

'I wouldn't say a robot . . . and he does love you.'

'Yeah?' she sneers.

'He has a strange way of showing how he feels at times, I'll admit.'

'*Very* strange. My God, how do you put up with him?'

'Sometimes I ask myself the same thing,' I murmur.

'I suppose you're in love with him?' Emma throws down the challenge, so she can't be too hungover.

'I think that's between us.'

'Hmm. That means mind your own fucking business, doesn't it?'

I smile. 'It means what I said.'

'OK, I suppose I don't actually *hate* him. I suppose I love him, really, and I even loved Daddy, though I would never have said so to him. He didn't say it to me very often; I had to guess and hope and assume.' She sniffs. 'I can hardly remember Mummy. Do you know how horrible that feels, having her fade away a little more every day? Even the memories I do have I think I might have dreamed or I've heard them second-hand from Alex.'

I'd have to be made of stone not to be moved by this comment. 'I am truly sorry for what's happened to you and Alexander and that I can't do more to help you.'

'You listen. That's something.' She toys with a spoon. 'Do you want to know the real reason I got so pissed last night?'

My mind cartwheels over and over. Yes and no and no and yes because I have a horrible feeling that the answer is going to involve Henry.

She taps the spoon against the cup, faster and faster, and then says into her tea, 'I think I might be pregnant.'

Chapter Fifteen

'Oh my God!'

She drops her spoon on the table with a clatter. 'Oh fuck. If you're so shocked, imagine what Alex will do. Not that he's going to find out!'

'Is it Henry?'

'Of course! I'm not a complete tart.'

'I didn't mean that.'

Her eyes plead with me. 'I know, sorry. Oh, Lauren, what am I going to do?' she wails.

She asks me? 'First of all, I guess, you need to find out if you actually *are* pregnant. Why do you think you might be?'

'I'm ten days late.' She pulls a face. 'I'm pretty regular usually. I keep a diary.'

'Even so, aren't you on the pill?' I ask, horribly out of my depth.

'Well, Henry thought I was, but it gave me massive headaches so I stopped.'

I manage to bite back an 'oh fuck'. 'Have you done a test yet?'

'No. I'm too scared.'

'You have to before you can decide what to do.'

'I can't have a baby,' she wails.

'Then the sooner you find out for sure, the better.'

'I don't want Alex to know.'

'Right then, we'll go get a test now.'

'How? I can't drive and anyway Alex will want to know why I've been out when I should be resting. Brandon will definitely tell him.'

'I don't have a licence to drive here, even if I dared take the Range Rover out. What about if I have Brandon take me to the drugstore? Where's the nearest?'

'At the Waitrose on the bypass.'

'OK, I'll go now and hopefully I'll be back before Alexander's finished his ride.'

'Won't he find out you've taken the Bentley?'

'Sure, but I'll tell him I needed some Tampax or something, not that it's really any of his business.' I give her a confident smile. 'Stop panicking, it may well all be OK.'

'Oh, I hope so. Lauren, thanks for this.' She throws her arms around me.

'It's OK,' I say, 'but when we've got this over with, we need to have a talk.' And boy, have I heard that before. My mother would be laughing her cashmere socks off.

The one thing about Brandon that I do like is that he's obviously skilled in the art of not asking too many questions, and my request to be taken to Waitrose is met with: 'Of course, Miss Cusack.' Half an hour later, I'm being let into the front door of the house by Robert, a pharmacy bag inside my tote, feeling like some kind of Cold War spy.

'Um, is Alexander back from his ride?'

'Not yet, Miss Cusack.'

'OK. Thanks, Robert.'

I slip upstairs to Emma's room and knock softly. 'It's Lauren.'

There's a thud and she opens the door. 'You got it?'

'I got two.' I pat my bag.

'Good. I am so grateful.' I'm thinking she should wait until she has the result but then she starts crying and I put my arm around her.

'I can't do this.'

'Yes, you can. If it's negative, you can relax, and if not, then you can make a decision.'

'I already know what that'll be.'

'Then let's get this over with.' I hand over the packet.

'You won't tell Alex, whatever happens?'

With a great effort of will, I answer, 'It's your business. I'd prefer to tell him but I won't if you really don't want me to.'

'Thanks.'

'Do you want me to leave you or wait while you do the test?'

'Would you stay?'

'Sure.'

She goes into the bathroom while I wander to the window, looking out over the stables. My nerves are on a knife edge so God knows how Emma must be feeling, but I'm certainly not going to wait there in the bathroom while she pees on the stick. My heart rate ramps up a little when I spot a rider trotting along the path that leads out of the woods before I realize it's only one of the grooms. I'd laugh at myself, if Emma wasn't so worried. All this secrecy is ridiculous.

'Are you OK?' I call through the door.

My answer is the sound of the toilet flushing so I head back to the window. Talia is chatting to the groom I mistook for Alexander, which is crazy because the groom is a foot shorter and forty pounds lighter. Talia pats the horse's muzzle before leading him off to the stable.

The door to the bathroom opens and Emma emerges. I hadn't thought she could look any paler or sicker than she did last night but her whey-face comes pretty close.

'What?' I blurt out, dreading the answer.

'Nothing yet. I've peed on the stick and I've put it on the window ledge. I can't bear to look . . . I think I'm going to be sick. You don't think that's a sign, do you?'

Only of a raging hangover and major stress, I think. 'Sit down and take some deep breaths. You need to wait a couple of minutes.'

She lies back on the bed and closes her eyes while I check my watch, pacing the room like it's me who's waiting for the result. Instantly, I wish I hadn't empathized with Emma because a baby is the last thing on my mind right now – I've not even begun my career – and yet it *can* happen. I know my parents didn't plan me; in fact my mother had only just graduated from Sarah Lawrence and she's quite upfront about the timing. 'Condom fail, honey, just so you're aware,' she told me as soon as I started dating Todd, while telling me in the same breath that I was '*the* best thing that ever happened' to her and Daddy. I winced when she mentioned it – wayyy too much information – but I think she was trying to be helpful. And yes, there would be 'options' if I did get pregnant, but the idea of having to take one of them isn't the happiest thought.

Screwing up my courage on Emma's behalf, I walk to the bed and touch her arm. 'I think we could look now.'

Her eyes stay shut. 'I can't.'

'You have to. Alexander could be back any time.'

She stares back at me and sits up. 'Fuck.'

'You don't want him coming in here when you've just found out the result, do you? Whatever it is.'

'I don't want to be on my own!'

'Then you have to check the test *right now*. You might be worrying for nothing.'

Muttering a string of 'fuck's, she marches into the bathroom. Seconds later, I hear a shriek and an 'Oh my God!'

Now it's me who closes my eyes, wondering how the hell I'm going to advise a pregnant and hysterical teenager on her life choices, but then she rushes out of the bathroom and launches herself at me.

'It's negative. I'm not pregnant!'

Once I can breathe again, I heave a huge sigh of relief. 'Fantastic.'

'I must have been late.'

'You've had a really rough time; maybe it messed up

your cycle – and worrying about being pregnant won't have helped.'

'Maybe. Oh, Lauren, I am *so* happy.'

She virtually dances around the room. I guess the hangover has worn off, so that's one good thing.

'That's great. Emma . . . It's really none of my business who you see or what you do, and it's none of Alexander's either, but I still don't feel comfortable with lying to him.'

She stops jigging and frowns. 'I don't know what you mean. What lies have you told him?'

'None . . . yet, but I have let him assume things that I know to be untrue, which is the same thing. When we dropped you off at Allegra's house, he told me he was glad you were safe. Imagine how I felt, knowing you were spending the night with Henry.'

'Of course I was safe. I was with Henry.' She sighs dreamily.

I fear there is no hope of her dropping him yet but realize there's no point in persuading her otherwise. 'That's up to you, but I'd be a lot happier if I didn't have to be in this position.'

'You mean don't tell you any more about my private life?' she says warily.

Oh shit, am I doing the right thing? Am I cutting off her only source of advice; am I leaving her with no one in the world to talk to? What kind of person does that make me?

'If you need to talk, then I'm here, but try and look at things from my point of view.'

She hugs me again. 'I'm sorry, I do appreciate you helping me and listening to all my dramas. It must be difficult being torn between me and my brother but he is *so* unreasonable.'

'In some ways, maybe, but that's because he *does* love you.'

She smiles. 'I know that and I will try to be nicer to him from now on. I'm sorry I spoiled your trip to Rome, by the way. Bad timing.'

I give a weak smile. 'The trip was almost over,' I say, thinking back to Alexander's words at the trattoria last night. 'I *really* have to go now. I need to do some work.'

'I won't forget this, Lauren.'

I just smile again, knowing she probably will and wishing I hadn't become a player in her drama.

There's a knock on the door.

'Emma? It's Alex. Can I come in?'

Alex? He must really want to mollify her, but hearing his deep and serious voice has the opposite effect on her.

She mouths 'help' and throws up her hands in panic.

I spot the crumpled test packet and cellophane on the bed.

'Emma? Are you OK?' asks Alexander again.

Emma snatches it from me and bundles it under her duvet cover. 'Er . . . hang on a minute. I was just getting dressed.'

'I should have told him to go away!' she hisses as we hear impatient footsteps outside the door.

'Too late now.'

'Emma, can you open the door, please?'

She flies to the door and pulls it wide open. 'Sorry about that.'

Alexander's face registers total confusion, firstly at spotting me and secondly because I suspect our smiles are way too wide. He must have headed straight up here from the stables because he's still in dark-navy jodhpurs and riding boots.

'Hello . . . Lauren . . .'

'Lauren and I were just having a girly chat, weren't we?'

'We were. How was your ride?' I ask as he looks at each of us, in turn. The chances of fooling Alexander are slim but thankfully I don't think even he is telepathic.

'It was good . . .' he says, and I have to admit he does look more relaxed. His thick brown hair is ruffled from the wind, his face is spattered with mud and he looks super hot in the jodhpurs. Is that a wicked thing to think at a time like this?

'I wanted to talk to you but I can come back later if you two are busy,' he says, addressing Emma.

Hearing this, I decide there is *no way* I'm letting either of them off the hook this time. 'No, we're done here and I need to do some work.'

'You don't have to go.' Emma throws a pleading glance at me.

'I do. I really must. I'm glad you're feeling better. Hope the Advil helped the headache.'

'Thanks,' she mutters.

'I won't be long,' Alexander says to me.

'It's fine. Take all the time you want.'

I pick up my bag and leave before I end up playing umpire again, while also keeping my fingers crossed that peace might break out between them. When I don't hear the sound of vases being smashed against the walls, I take it as a good sign and manage to settle down to an essay outline.

It's a while before Alexander returns and my pulse flutters at the soft click of his bedroom door opening. For all I know, in her wild state of mind Emma might have decided to go all confessional. Maybe, I reason, that would be a good thing, as long as I'm not part of it.

'Hello.' He sits on the edge of the bed next to me and starts to pull off his boots. I notice a trail of dried mud from the door to the bed and wonder if Helen will have a fit, or if she's used to the Hunts' quirks by now. Muddy floor aside, he looks calmer and more at ease than I've seen him since Rome.

'How did that go?' I ask.

Once one boot is off, he tugs at the other one, so I can't see his face for a few seconds. 'I suppose it could have gone a lot worse. In fact, it was better than I'd hoped. I explained why I didn't tell her about my father giving his blessing to her going to Saint Martins.' He glances up at me. 'I admitted that I'd been scared of upsetting her even more than she already was by talking about what happened the day he died. I know it was cowardly of me not to have told her sooner.'

'I wouldn't say cowardly.'

'Maybe, but I misjudged her reaction. I thought she'd be devastated that my father didn't live to tell her himself, but in hindsight I should have given her more credit. And I also admitted that I probably shouldn't have been so hard on her this morning.'

'How did she take it?'

Before replying, he stands his boots upright, next to each other, perfectly aligned. So it's OK to leave a trail of mud but not to have his boots out of line. Finally he meets my eye. 'She was upset that my father never told her himself but she seems to understand why I didn't say anything sooner. Thanks for keeping her company earlier, and I'm sorry I walked out but I needed to take some time to calm down. What were you two talking about while I was out?'

'This and that.' At this statement I have visions of myself at the end of a pitchfork, like in Dante's *Inferno*.

'Did she say anything about why she got so pissed last night? I called the school when I got back from my ride and they said she'd seemed upset in her lessons last week. The housemistress thought it was delayed grief and tried to talk to her, but she didn't want to say anything.'

Oh fuck, I can't tell him an outright lie. 'She didn't say much about your father. Did she get into trouble at school last year?'

'Yes. Dad was called in a couple of times about her being involved in late-night parties, and once or twice I think she was rude to the staff. The only reason they're willing to have her back in school is because of all the upheaval she's been through, though the headmistress thinks she'd benefit from another week at home. But they've made it clear they want her to settle down to her A levels when she does get back. She's so fucking bright, the problem is she doesn't need to work as hard as some of the girls; it's like it comes too easily to her.'

'I guess it's a very difficult time for her.'

He sighs. 'Thanks for trying, anyway. I'm afraid I'll have to have her to stay with us in Oxford for most of the week. I need to spend some time with her.'

'Are you sure that's a good idea?'

He frowns. 'Taking her to Oxford? I've no choice.'

I can see he thinks I don't want Emma with us, which is the last thing on my mind. 'I meant, is it a good idea to let her go to her friend's house?'

'I can't keep her in the whole time. She could tell me to piss off now if she really wanted to. All I can do is my best. How many people have lost both their parents at her age and have a brother who's never around?' He rakes his hands through his hair.

'I suppose you're right,' I reply, reminding myself that I can't police Emma's movements every minute of the day, even if I wanted to.

He pulls me to him suddenly and kisses me. He smells of exertion and earthiness, of clean sweat and cold, damp air, and this turns me on more than the two-hundred-dollar aftershave. 'Look, Lauren, I know you've done far more than anyone could expect you to for Emma and you're busy, but I am grateful.'

'You *really* don't have to be.'

'I think I do. In fact, I owe you a special treat, but first I ought to shower.' I should feel bad that he wants to 'treat' me for something I probably shouldn't have done, but honestly? I'm too relieved that the conversation has moved on from Emma.

I lick the tip of my finger and dab at a speck of mud on his cheek. 'Don't bother on my account.'

He raises an eyebrow. 'I forgot you like me fresh from the field.'

Sparks fire at this reminder of when we had sex after he'd been hunting last year. I should hate myself for loving the whole red-coat thing, but I couldn't wait to rip his clothes off then and I can't now. I want to lose myself in wild passionate sex.

'It's only the jodhpurs . . .' I say.

'Oh, really? As long as they have the desired effect, that's fine by me.'

'Is this the kind of treat I've had before?'

'Possibly, but with a twist.'

Very shortly afterwards, I'm lying on my back, minus my clothes, with Alexander between my legs. He makes slow circles with his tongue around the rim of my clit, first one way, then another, teasing me. Wow . . .

'Good?'

'Mmmmm.'

'I'm going to make you come like this, however long it takes.'

'Even if your tongue gets tired?'

'I have plenty of stamina. Now, be quiet.'

He resumes the circling, then reverses it and then, God knows what he's doing with his tongue, but I'm fisting the bedcover and trying not to knock him out while I'm bucking my hips. It goes on and on and every time I open my eyes, his dark head is between my legs, his hands keeping my thighs apart. Part of me wants to hold on, to defeat him and not to come . . .

'Sometimes it's good to lose,' he says, a while later, as he unbuckles the strap of his watch. I'm lying face-up on the bed, my thigh muscles aching and wrung out.

'Alexander, I've no idea what you're talking about.'

He bends down to plant a soft kiss on my lips. 'Have it your way.'

'Oh, I did.'

He lays his watch on the nightstand and I shuffle up the bed, watching his shirt tauten over his shoulder muscles while he unfastens his cuffs. He's still wearing the soft check shirt he went riding in. He turns around and starts to unbutton it, slowly, keeping his eyes on me the whole time.

I don't think I've ever had the pleasure of watching him undress especially for me before. Usually he insists on stripping me or that I undress for him. The role reversal – him in a position of vulnerability, with me watching — is a massive turn-on that makes me feel powerful and in control.

The shirt is undone, his broad chest bared and the ripped abs I love are exposed. I want to run my tongue over the ridge of muscles and circle his nipples with my tongue but I know I have to stay where I am. Maybe he *is* in control, after all.

The shirt is off, tossed on to the bedroom chair. Socks next, and he stands up again, bare-footed and bare-chested on the carpet.

Cleanly, smoothly, he slides the zip of his jodhpurs down and pushes them down his thighs. His growing erection strains against the cotton of his black briefs. So what if I only came ten minutes ago? It's not a crime to want to touch myself, is it? Or to want him inside me?

'Tut tut. I obviously didn't do a good enough job.'

I whip my hands from my between my legs. 'You did but I want to do it again to check.'

'Patience is a virtue.'

He shoves his hands down the sides of his briefs, pulls them down, taking his jodhpurs with them. Hell, I want to worship his penis, not that I would ever tell him. Not in a million years. I want to get on my knees right now and bury my face against the soft hair that surrounds it and take him in my mouth, feel the girth and taste him.

He picks up his shirt from the pad of the chair and tosses it on to the dressing stool. Then he lifts the chair and moves it to the centre of the rug so it's facing me.

I'm on fire with anticipation, and my ought-to-be-sated clit is a knot of nerves again.

What the hell is he going to do? Take me over it? Bend me over it?

My mind spirals into a cocktail of lust and panic.

Alexander crooks his finger. 'Come here, Ms Cusack, and don't look so scared.'

I laugh in his face. 'Scared? Of you? Don't be ridiculous.'

He pats the seat of the chair. 'Then get yourself over here.'

He smiles in that way and I almost think of folding my arms and telling him to go screw himself, yet I won't, because I want to taste what's on offer, and he knows it. He sits down on the seat, his legs a little way apart, soles planted squarely on the rug. I notice his feet for some reason, like I never saw them before. They're big, of course – he's six foot three – and his toes are long with pale square nails. Then my gaze travels up his muscular calves to the powerful thighs and his erection, jutting out of the dark soft hair.

'Lauren?'

His voice is softer now, and I think he realizes I'm genuinely hesitant, which makes me even more determined to play it cool. If he could see inside me, he'd see mush, a mass of lust and wantonness. I scramble off the bed and stand in front of him. His thighs are closed now, his cock signposting where he wants me. Where I want to be.

'Face the bed, away from me.'

So now I see. From behind, his fingers slide between my legs and gently part my lips, spreading my juices around my entrance, smoothing the way for him.

His voice is husky. 'Sit down.'

I sit down, in a manner of speaking, because it's more of a wiggle in which he nudges into me and I slide down on top of him.

'Oh my.'

'You feel amazing. You look amazing,' he breathes, holding my waist and burying his face into my hair, his intake of breath long and languorous as he savours me. I give a little wiggle against his thighs, and feel the blunt tip of his shaft deep inside me. He palms my breast, capturing my nipple between his thumb and forefingers, rolling it gently, but in my super-sensitive state, the lightest pinch makes me wriggle and writhe in his lap.

'Fuck, but this feels good.'

My eyes are shut, revelling in the heat of his palm over my breast. 'Oh yes.'

'You'll need to touch yourself while I hold you.'

I reach between my legs and stroke myself. It's only been a short time since I came but I'm still slick and ready to go again. His teeth graze my shoulder, softly, and I moan in pleasure. When I'm getting close, he holds on to my waist while I slide up and down, rocking in ecstasy. He groans. 'Lauren, fuck, I can't hold on much longer, if you do that. Are you close?'

My answer is to touch myself again until I feel my climax build and then focus begins to splinter and shatter.

Alexander must sense me losing control and he starts to circle his hips and lift me up a little with each thrust. His grip is tight on my hips, the fingers dig into my flesh. Then his fingers are pressing down on mine, circling my clit, a surprise I didn't expect that finally tips me over the edge. My orgasm stutters, fails, then rips through me. Alexander takes it as a signal to go for it, using the seat for leverage, lifting me up and down until his body stiffens and his eyes close in a shuddering climax.

The next morning, while I'm doing my make-up at the dressing table, Alexander emerges from the bathroom, a towel slung around his hips, though I have no idea why he feels the need for modesty when I got closely acquainted with every inch of him last night. In the end, I stayed overnight. I have a tute today, but not until the afternoon so I can still get back to Oxford in plenty of time. I'm glad I did stay because it would have been a shame to miss the sight that greets me now. He's been for an early-morning run and his hair is still damp from the shower. Beads of water dot his torso and glisten on his pecs. The woody scent of Creed shower gel hangs around his lean, honed body.

'Lauren?' He crosses to the dressing table and stands behind me, hands on hips.

I put down my mascara wand. 'Uh-huh.'

'Are you feeling all right?'

I see his face in the mirror, watching me. 'Yes. Great. Why?'

'Because I saw Brandon this morning and he told me he'd taken you to the pharmacy while I went for my ride yesterday.'

Screw Brandon, the snitch! My pulse rate speeds a little, even though I'm well prepared for this eventuality. 'I needed some women's stuff,' I say, picking up the wand and rubbing the excess off against the bottle.

'Really? You seemed OK, earlier.'

'False alarm.'

He studies me intently while I kick myself for my choice of words. 'I thought I was due but I wasn't.'

'Should I be worried?' he says.

'No. I'm sure it'll happen soon enough.'

'Good.' He moves right behind me and skims my shoulder blades with the back of his hand, almost idly, yet I know that nothing he does or says is ever idle. 'If you were worried about something, anything at all, you would tell me, wouldn't you?'

I laugh, though inside I shiver. 'I'm not worried and anyway, some things are private, even from you.'

'But not if they involve me.'

I put the mascara wand down and turn to him. 'What does that mean?'

'This, perhaps?'

He holds up the drugstore receipt for the test kits and my heart skips a beat.

'What's that?' I make light of it.

'I dropped my razor and I found it on the floor behind the bin.'

283

'So you're in the habit of reading my receipts?'

'I couldn't help but see it and after Brandon told me about your trip to the pharmacy I did put two and two together. Imagine what you would have thought, if you were in my shoes.'

'That's hardly likely.'

His mouth hardens in a line. 'If you're pregnant, I'd appreciate it if you shared the information with me.'

'I'm not pregnant, Alexander, so you can relax.' I pick up the wand again and lean forward to the mirror.

'But you thought you might be?'

'It's always better to be safe than sorry.'

'So you're late with your period?'

I cover my annoyance – and a little panic – at being interrogated in this way with a casual shrug. 'It happens.'

Which is different from saying: 'It happened.' Isn't it? A little white lie to protect Emma is justifiable, surely?

To signal the conversation is over, I apply the mascara to my upper lashes, hoping my unsteady fingers won't give me a poke in the eye. When I've done one eye, Alexander has moved out of view.

'I'm sorry for giving you the third degree,' he says from somewhere behind me. 'I've not had much sleep over the past few days and I've been worrying about Emma.'

'No problem,' I say, not daring to do my other lashes yet. 'Like I said, it was a false alarm.'

And it was. Just not mine.

Chapter Sixteen

The shops are full of tea dresses, beachwear and picnic sets and I can't believe that it's already Seventh Week. Emma has been staying over at the Oxford house, but I decided to give her and Alexander some time together and take the chance to catch up with my work and friends. After finally seeing a late-night showing of *Shame*, earlier this week, Immy and I went to a club last night with Chun, Isla and a few more of the gang. I also managed to fit in my dance classes and today we've squeezed in a lunchtime game of tennis.

The yellow heads of the daffodils nod in the spring breeze next to the clubhouse.

'So, how's the babysitting going? Any more dramas?' Immy asks as we walk off the tennis courts. 'Is Emma still behaving herself?'

I've told Immy about the trip to the ER, and it's been on the tip of my tongue many times to confide in her about the pregnancy scare, but I can't bring myself to do it. I do trust her to keep the secret but telling Immy, and not Alexander, feels like a double breach of trust.

We grab Diet Cokes from the drinks machine. 'I haven't seen so much of them, partly because I wanted to give them some time together and also because it seems inappropriate to be shagging his brains out with his sister in the next room. But did I tell you we went up to London on Wednesday night to see *Billy Elliot*?'

'And?'

'Musicals aren't normally my thing, but I have to admit it was brilliant.'

'I know. I saw it last year. Do you fancy going up to town to a club at the end of term, now that you're staying on? I need a treat and we could stay over in my parents' flat for the night and hit the shops too, if you can bear to leave Alexander for that long.'

I know she's teasing me but I still rise to the challenge. 'Sure, that would be fun, if you can bear to be parted from Skandar.'

'How long have you got your college room for?' Immy asks as we find a sunny spot on the clubhouse porch to sit with our drinks.

'Same as you, an extra week, but if I want to stay any longer, it'll have to be with Alexander. The rooms are needed for conferences.'

'We could go up to London then for the Boat Race. Jocasta's family have a house by the river and she always has a massive party. If you're still here, you have to come. Alexander too, if it's his thing. You're not going to miss Scott's moment of glory, are you? Some of the Blues rowers sometimes turn up later in the night. Jocasta's parties are legendary.'

'Yes, the masked ball she gave us tickets to was pretty

memorable.' I think back to Alexander almost getting my panties off and having sex with me on a billiard table that night. 'Alexander's not into rowing but I'm sure he can suffer it for one day, as long as Emma's OK. He might want to see her that weekend if she's not busy at school.'

Immy winces. 'Looking after Emma in the vacs must be a nightmare on top of all the other stuff he has to deal with.'

'At times, but there's nothing he can do about it. She is his sister.'

'True and I'd do the same for George, I suppose, if anything happened to my parents, but it would be tough. Do you mind babysitting her?'

'Ouch, she'd go batshit insane if she heard you call it that. It's not ideal having to keep an eye on her but she's – um – entertaining to be around and she's had a shitty time.'

'*But?*'

I tap the toe of my tennis shoe on the deck. 'She can be a little challenging at times.'

Immy laughs, then covers up a tiny hiccup. 'She sounds like tackling an army assault course.'

'Oh, no, I'd have said more of a scaling-Everest level of challenge. And then some.'

'Then it sounds as if you're totally justified in having a night off and coming to the party, with or without Alexander.'

'It's a deal. It sounds great and I haven't booked my flight home yet. I learned my lesson after what happened last term.'

We finish the Cokes while quietly laughing at a quartet of middle-aged Fellows attempting to play doubles, very badly, on the court in front of us.

'Have your contacts still no clue who sent that sex tape?' I ask, after a while.

'Sorry, none. I did ask but Skandar's been stressing over his Finals, so I haven't wanted to push it.'

'Thanks for trying. Alexander hasn't mentioned it again either, and I'm sure he wants to forget it. He also has a lot on his mind.'

'I'll bet. Are you OK, Lauren? You've been quiet the past few days.'

'I'm fine. A little apprehensive over the take-home exam we get at the end of term. "Take-home" sounds so casual and tempting, like you're going to get a delicious Chinese meal. In reality, we get three short essays to write and they're expected to be fantastic.'

'Yuk. I have a dissertation too, but the main marks are made up by the whole horrible round of Finals. It'll probably coincide with the only heatwave of the year, prime hay-fever period and we have to wear stupid subfusc.'

'I remember the subfusc from my matriculation ceremony at the start of last term. We all had to get dressed in gowns and attend a ceremony at the Sheldonian Theatre. It seemed like fun then, but doing exams in the whole outfit must be a pain.'

Immy throws her empty bottle at the trash can and misses. 'Fuck.' She picks up the bottle and sighs. 'Even if they didn't make me wear a Hallowe'en outfit, I'd still be stressing that I haven't put in enough work.'

'I need to make up for what I missed earlier this term. Professor Rafe still hasn't forgiven me for skipping his *Il Conformista* party, even if I did go to Rome itself rather than watching it in a movie.'

'Are you sure it's a good idea to spend your study time with Alexander?' She brackets the words 'study time' with her fingers.

I smile. 'I think it's a very bad idea but that won't stop me.'

She bites her lip. 'I have to admit that Alexander – any guy – is a major distraction. Alexander more than most. It must be hard not to get swept along by all the glamour . . .'

'Believe me, I have no intention of being swept away.'

'You said that before. Last term and at the start of this one, and guess what happened to us both?'

Immy laughs and I think she's joking or maybe she's telling herself not to get too hooked up on Skandar. The thing is, I am worried that I spent half the term in bed and much of it caught up in the drama of Alexander's life and now the term has whizzed past in the blink of an eye.

'Is everything OK between you and Skandar?'

She laughs but I think there's a touch of nervousness

behind her smile. 'More than OK, and now the Unthinkable has happened to me. I'm wondering what happens after my Finals. I don't know what I'm going to do, whether to get a job in London or go travelling. I've certainly no idea what Skandar might do; he mentioned coaching tennis in the States or Oz for a year.'

'And you want to go out there with him?'

She shrugs. 'You know me, I'm the good-time girl. We haven't talked about what happens next and I've obviously no intention of settling down.' She brackets 'settling down' and rolls her eyes.

'So does that mean you really like him?' I bracket 'really'.

'Hmm. I have a horrible feeling I probably do. Shall we cycle back to college now? I don't know about you, but I'm getting cold now the sun's gone in.'

A week or so later, I can't believe I'm walking up the steps to the Hall on the final Friday of term. The time has raced by, or it seems like it because I've finally managed to get my head down (not a term I'd use to Professor Rafe) and get some serious work done. Alexander has been back to Falconbury twice, if only for the night, and he's also been to London a couple of times, once to see his lawyers and the second time, from what I can gather, on military business. Even Immy has been in the library, working on her dissertation, and she crammed in as many lectures as she could before her Finals term, which starts when we get back after Easter.

I'm staying on for a couple of weeks to work and go to the Boat Race – an excuse my parents accepted readily enough. But tonight, I'm going to forget work and enjoy Wyckham's end-of-term Formal Night, for which everyone has broken out the suits, ties and academic dress. Miraculously, the sun is out again, the evening rays mellowing the golden stone of the Front Quad.

My gown stirs in the breeze when I reach the top of the Hall steps and pause to look back over the lawn, now bright with new spring growth. There's something different about the light these days, and this evening, I cycled back from the faculty without my lights. They're small details that tell me that a new season is definitely here, but I'm still glad of the extra layer of the grad gown over my dress as the breeze freshens and tugs at a stray strand of hair.

Alexander has gone to a drinks reception with his tutor in the minstrels' gallery above the Hall and said he'd meet me inside, which I'm looking forward to. I want to make the most of our final weeks together before I fly home.

Just when I'm thinking that life is pretty good, I find that every silver lining has a cloud, and in this case it's a big black one in the shape of Rupert de Courcey. He saunters up the steps behind me, a smirk on his face. He follows me into the Hall and plonks himself next to me on the bench seat.

'Lauren. Nice of you to grace us with your presence at college dinner. How's Alexander?'

'Why don't you ask him yourself? He'll be down any minute.' I glance up at the gallery, where Alexander is nodding at his tutor, champagne in his hand.

'I don't need to; you're so close to him now that you can tell me what he's thinking and how he's feeling, can't you? When can we expect you to announce the engagement?'

I put my hand over my mouth, stifling a mock yawn. 'Change the music, Rupert; hearing the same old song is getting very boring.'

'Make a joke of it, but you know how much you'd like to be Marchioness of Falconbury.'

'Actually, I don't think I could get that on my business card and I have no ambitions to be lady of the manor. I've got plans and ambitions of my own.'

'Oh dear. Does Alexander know yet? The poor boy seems smitten and much as it pains me to say it, it's going to hurt him when you fly off.'

'Get a life.' I glance up at the gallery again where, much to my relief, Alexander can no longer be seen, which means he'll be down here very soon. Even better, Oscar, one of the few friends that Rupert and I have in common, sits opposite. He's a cox and is as close to an elf as a man can be. He puts his hand over his glass when the waiting staff arrive with the wine.

'Still on a diet?' I ask.

He pours water into his glass. 'Sadly, yes, but I've been training with the Blues squad.'

'I thought I hadn't seen much of you this term. How's it going?'

His face lights up. 'Not too bad. I'm the reserve cox for *Isis*, the reserve boat, so if someone drops out, I'll be in charge of *Isis* for the Boat Race.'

'Wow. Congratulations, that's awesome.'

He pushes his specs up the bridge of his nose, like the compliment was too much for him. 'Well, not *that* awesome because it needs something terrible to happen to one of the other coxes before I would get my chance.'

'Still, you never know. I could sort out one of the other coxes if you wanted, Oscar?' I grin at him.

'Nice thought, Lauren, but I think someone would suspect.'

'I could be discreet.' I persist, laughing now.

Alexander arrives, catching the last part of our conversation, and squeezes into the space next to me. He rests his hand on my thigh and I try not to smile too widely, but I half wish Rupert could see what was going on under the table.

'So,' says Rupert, watching Oscar chase a few vegetables around his plate, 'being in the Blues squad, you must know a friend of Lauren's.'

Oscar frowns. 'I don't think so.'

My antennae twitch and not in a good way. It was Rupert who told Alexander I'd been for a drink with Scott last term. I just know what's coming. 'I think his name is Scott. American. Big friend of Lauren's, isn't he?'

Alexander is intent on cutting up his steak.

'Oh, yes, I do know him,' says Oscar. 'Excellent rower and a nice bloke. I'm not surprised he made the First Eight. I didn't know he was a friend of yours, Lauren.'

'Yes, he is.' Scott called me last week to tell me he'd made the First Eight, but I'm not revealing that over the dinner table.

Rupert smirks. 'I guessed you two were close when I saw you in the pub.'

'He's my ex-boyfriend's cousin, actually. I've known him for years.' So screw you, Rupert. I glance at him in triumph as Alexander pops a forkful of steak into his mouth.

Rupert seems momentarily silenced by my honesty and Alexander's lack of reaction and to show how little I care, I re-start the conversation with Oscar about his training. I knew it couldn't last long however, and once the dessert arrives, Rupert starts on another topic.

'How's Emma?' he asks. My hackles rise and I wonder if Alexander has told him about Emma's night in the ER. He may have done because he did get Rupert to warn off Henry. Even though they don't seem to like each other much, they are cousins and his father is an executor of the Falconbury estate. I go for a neutral answer, hoping to take my cue from Alexander.

'Fine, as far as I know. As a matter of fact, she's coming up to Oxford this weekend.'

'Best to keep an eye on her,' Rupert says, milking his role as the concerned relative. He reaches for the wine bottle. As he does so, his thigh brushes against mine under the table. I try to inch closer to Alexander, who's deep in conversation with the guy next to him, but there's barely any room.

'So will you be going to Jocasta's Boat Race party?' he asks me.

Is he going? Damn. 'Maybe. Immy said it's a lot of fun.'

'Oh, it is. One of *the* nights of the year.'

'So you'll definitely be there?'

'I don't know yet. I may be otherwise engaged, so it's possible you and Alexander might be deprived of my company.'

I put on a mock pout. 'That would be *such* a shame, Rupert.'

His beady little eyes bore into me. 'I'll see what I can do. I'd hate you to be disappointed.'

'I shouldn't try too hard; you always live down to my expectations.'

On Saturday morning, I wake up in Alexander's bed to find him sitting next to me and watching me thoughtfully.

I rub sleep from my eyes. 'Hiya. Anything wrong?'

He slants me a sexy smile. 'Should there be?'

'I hope not but you seem to be scrutinizing me.'

'*Scrutinizing?*' He shakes his head.

'Wrong choice of words. It's early, but how long have

you been watching me? Have I been talking in my sleep?'

'Do you have a guilty conscience?'

'Now, why would you think that?' I laugh. He glances down at his hands, toying with the signet ring on his little finger. You know, I think I still haven't actually lied about keeping Emma's secret. I've decided no news is good news as far as Henry is concerned, and if she's coming to spend the weekend with us, at least there won't be any problem from that direction, but Alexander is acting strangely this morning.

'Lauren . . .'

I slide up the pillows, instantly put on the alert by the tone of his voice. 'What?'

'I have to go away for a few days.'

I knew something was coming. 'Uh-huh. This is not a trip to the seaside, I guess.'

'There may be sand involved.'

It's meant to be a dark joke. 'But you won't be sitting on a lounger with a Mojito?'

'Unfortunately not.' He plays with the ribbon of my cami idly but I think he doesn't want to look me in the face.

'When do you leave?'

'Thursday, and it means I won't be able to come to the Boat Race party.'

I try not to show my disappointment. 'Hey, I knew you'd do anything to get out of watching the rowing.'

'Of course. I can't face seeing Brett's moment of triumph.'

I roll my eyes. 'This is a little OTT, however, even for you.'

'Like you say, I'd do anything to avoid a party.'

'I understand that you have to go sometimes but I thought they didn't need you at the moment, I thought they were leaving you alone to get on with your master's?'

He glances up at me. 'They were, but I volunteered.'

I sit up straight. 'You did *what*?'

'One of the guys . . . he's a good friend of mine and he was injured on a training exercise. They needed someone with his special skills to step in and there was only me.'

'Special skills? You mean a foreign language? Dress-making?' I say, trying to make light of this news, while shocked at his revelation. I don't know which is worse, that he's going or that he volunteered.

Impatience and, perhaps, guilt break out in his voice. 'Not exactly. Look, Lauren, I knew you wouldn't like it and I'm sorry about not being able to make the party, but I have to go.'

'Where are you going? Helmand? The Middle East? North Africa?'

'You know I can't tell you and it wouldn't help, even if I did, but there's no need to worry about me.'

'I'm not worried, just furious.'

He smiles at my joke, or maybe because he knows

297

I'm only half joking. 'It's only a short op so I promise I'll be back before you fly home to Washington.'

I know better than to rely on his promises by now but I let this pass. 'What about Emma? What will you tell her?'

'I'll tell Emma I'm on a training exercise, like I always do. If she asks for any details, that's what I've told you too.' His lips graze mine in a casual kiss that's meant to disarm my frustration and worries. My skin prickles with unease, despite his reassurances. This, I remind myself, is because I was looking forward to the party and to making the most of every moment with him until I go back to Washington, not because I am worried about him.

He lies down and pulls me down next to him. 'I'll be back. You know you can't get away from me,' he says, his eyes full of amusement. I sense a distraction tactic incoming at any moment . . .

'You think?'

'Oh, I *know*, Lauren.'

I ought to challenge him but he captures my mouth in a kiss so long and deep I truly think it may go on for ever. I *want* it to go on for ever.

He lowers his head and slides his tongue between my lips for another delicious French kiss. When it ends, he skims the back of his hand, with agonizing slowness, between my breasts, down my stomach, until his fingers pause at my mound, gently tapping it until I ache for him to push his fingers inside me.

'I'm sorry,' he says. He must know I'm in no position to complain now, with his fingers holding me to ransom.

'It's OK, I understand.' I push my pelvis against his hand and manage a strangled, 'Hey, I never expected to compete with world peace.'

He smiles, circling me with his fingertips, so lightly and tantalizingly that I want to scream. 'I'm not sure that peacekeeping will play much part in the proceedings.'

I know I'm being teased and I can't stand it any longer. 'And I'm not sure your mind's completely on the task in hand.'

He looks into my face. 'I must try harder then.' Ah, finally. He slides his fingertip inside me and I moan in sheer relief. I'm already creamy and whimper in delight as he uses my own juices to lubricate my clit and my entrance. When he slips another finger inside me, then another, and presses on my G-spot, I could take right off from the bed.

I'm writhing now, arching my pelvis towards him like a desperate woman as he pushes his fingers in and out of me, driving me wild.

'Hold that thought,' he murmurs.

While I keep up the pressure on my clit myself, he gets off the bed and pulls his top over his head. His jeans are down and off in no time, showing me he's just as ready for me as I am for him. Then he's back on the bed beside me, so we're face to face, with no hiding place from each other.

'Who's going to come first this morning?' he says, his steely erection butting my entrance.

'I don't care.'

He enters me, slowly, carefully, and then rolls me gently back on to my side, straddling my hip with his thigh. We have to wrap our arms around each other, and we're still face to face while he moves gently in and out of me. My thighs are pressed together which intensifies the snug fit of him.

'You are so tight like this. I love it.'

'Me too.'

It's super intimate and leaves no hiding place. With each slow, careful thrust into me, he never takes his eyes from me. I flatten my palms over his butt and wriggle around his shaft.

'Fuck, I can't hold on,' he says, his voice ragged.

'Don't. Enjoy. Permission to come, Captain Hunt.'

So he goes for it, rolling over and shifting his weight on to his elbows so he can drive into me without restraint. The mattress complains and the headboard bangs against the wall. I dig my nails into his back and his buttocks, knowing he won't even notice, he's so intent on screwing me. I feel him tauten and his whole body seems to let out a massive cry of relief when he comes, pumping into me. I'm on the edge myself, not quite there, but I don't care. I love doing this to him, making him lose control completely.

Carefully, he pulls out of me and lies back, exhausted.

I prop myself up on one elbow, watching him come down and he opens his eyes lazily. 'Come here,' he commands.

After he's gone down on me and brought me to a shameful mess of writhing and begging, we lie together in a tangle of sheets.

'That wasn't bad,' he says and I shake my head at his understatement.

'You know damn well it was amazing, Captain Hunt.'

'Mmm, on this occasion, I'll probably have to agree.' He robs any protest from my lips with a kiss. I close my eyes at the soft pressure of his mouth on mine and the gentle sweep of his tongue on the roof of my mouth that leaves my palate tingling.

'I'd like to stay in bed all day. In fact, I'd like to stay here for the rest of the year,' he whispers.

'We could be found dead of exhaustion but with smiles on our faces. Imagine being found by Robert. I can see him now.' I mimic Robert's deferential voice: 'I'm so sorry, my lord, I didn't realize I was interrupting something.'

Alexander joins in. 'Shall I come back when Miss Cusack has finished giving you a blow job?' Then he shakes his head. 'I shouldn't take the piss. Robert is a loyal and invaluable member of staff and I wouldn't blame him if he and Helen told us all to fuck off after all the shit that's been going on. It can't have been easy living with the Hunts, any of us.'

'Tell me about it,' I say, totally joking but Alexander shoots me a look; he's not offended but there's something else there.

'No, I don't think I could expect many people to put up with it . . .'

He has the same expression I saw in Rome before Emma's teacher phoned. The flicker of doubt and uncertainty. Alexander is unsure of himself. I do the mental equivalent of holding my breath. I think we both do, because a second or two later, we both laugh in unison.

We're both cowards.

Alexander breaks eye contact first. 'I'd better get up. I need to do some work before Emma gets here.' He gets off the bed swiftly, turning his back on me while I lie there.

'Do you want a shower first?' he says.

My answer is interrupted by his phone ringing. I can tell how on edge he is by the way he snatches it off the dresser and answers: 'Hunt.'

From the way he keeps his back to me, and his clipped responses, he's definitely not comfortable with me being in the room.

'I'll go take a shower,' I murmur but I don't think he even hears me.

Chapter Seventeen

Brandon delivered Emma to the house after lunch and we went to see the shrunken heads at the Pitt Rivers Museum – her choice, but hey, each to their own – while Alexander met his tutor. Then we all went to dinner at Jamie's – also Emma's choice – before coming back to the house.

Now, Emma's Skyping her friends, and I'm curled up on the sofa with Alexander. He's drinking a beer from the bottle and watching the flames flicker in the hearth. I feel his fingers idly playing with my hair.

'I have to go to a regimental dinner tomorrow evening,' he says over the top of my head.

'OK. This is out of the blue.'

'I didn't know my presence was required until earlier today but I can't miss it. If it's any consolation, it won't be all pleasure because there are some people I need to meet while I'm there before I leave on Thursday. I won't be late but do you mind keeping Emma company?'

I squash down my disappointment at this. 'No, but she might mind it a lot.'

'I doubt it. She likes you, which, believe me, is a great honour, if not a privilege.'

I laugh and twist around so I can see his face. 'I do

appreciate what you've done for her this term. She can be difficult to handle, but I can tell how much she trusts you. You get on better with her than I do.'

He kisses me and I summon up a smile. 'I suppose we could get in a pizza and watch DVDs. How girly is that?'

He laughs softly, and there's definitely a touch of relief there. 'I'm almost glad I have to go to the dinner.'

On Sunday night, at seven, Alexander goes off in his mess dress, looking so handsome and sexy I want to screw him right there and then in the hallway. He leaves, with a kiss for us both that Emma pretends to hate, and I close the door, wishing he didn't have to go on this 'op', whatever it is. I don't totally mind hanging out with Emma, but it wasn't how I planned to spend my Sunday evening.

'So, do you want Chinese, Indian or a pizza?' I ask, following Emma into the sitting room. 'And for dessert, do you fancy Max Irons, Channing Tatum or Tom Hiddleston?'

She hesitates. 'Actually, I was thinking of going out.'

'Do you want to eat out, then? We could go to one of the places in Little Clarendon Street and into G&Ds after we've had dinner.'

She looks sheepish. 'I meant, out on my own. Well, not *literally* on my own but I've arranged to meet some friends from school.'

This statement fills me with a sense of foreboding to rival a horror movie.

'I don't think that's a great idea. Oxford can be a little lively.'

'On a Sunday night?' She giggles.

'Well, Alexander may not agree, and he's expecting me to keep you company this evening. How will he feel if he knows you've gone out alone?'

'You mean he's expecting you to keep an eye on me. Oh come on, Lauren. You're not much older than me. You must have hated it when your parents went all over-protective. You've told me you had a hell of a job getting them to accept that you wanted to study here.'

Now, this is sneaky, I think, and I'm not going to be a pushover. 'No, I'm not that much older but twenty-one is way different to seventeen, in all kinds of ways, and this situation is different. If you go out on your own, I'll never forgive myself if something happens.' I smile at her and try to keep my tone light, while seething inside. 'You wouldn't want me to worry any more than I already do, would you?'

She sighs and shakes her head, as if I'm the kid. I have a horrible feeling I'm losing the battle and I feel a stir of panic.

'Stop stressing,' she says. 'We'll be perfectly safe, because I've arranged to meet my mates at a pub out in the country.'

'What mates?' I shoot back.

'Allegra and Rachel and a couple of boys.'

Hearing Allegra's name does not fill me with confidence. 'At the pub? Remember, you're not eighteen yet;

you can't drink alcohol.' Oh fuck, is there nothing I can say that won't make me sound exactly like my mother? But I don't care. I smell bullshit.

'Don't worry, I'm not going to disgrace myself again, and the boys are in the Upper Sixth at their school so they're mostly over eighteen. I'll stick to Coke, I promise, and I've already booked a cab so there's no need to ask Brandon to take me.'

Don't worry, I had no intention, I think, knowing Emma's real reason for not using Brandon is that she's terrified Alexander will find out.

'When will you be back?' I ask sharply.

'Oh, by eleven at the latest, well before Alex gets back. Will you be OK here on your own without me? And you won't let on to Alex, of course . . . You know he's paranoid.'

I am momentarily speechless at this comment but I honestly don't know what more I can do, short of barricading the front door or calling Alexander back from his dinner. 'I'd like to know the name of the pub.'

She sighs. 'The White Hart at Woodstock. I'll text you when I get there.' I must still look worried because she hugs me. 'Please don't worry. I'll be fine and I'm desperate for an evening out after the past term. I promise I won't get into any trouble.'

'You don't have to make me any promises you can't keep.' I'm only half joking and still wondering if I should call Alexander after all, or threaten to do so.

'I don't *have* to do anything but since Alex decided to cast you in the role of jailer, I swear I'll behave.' She crosses her fingers over her chest. 'Cross my heart and hope to die.'

'And this is meant to reassure me?'

She laughs but I almost feel sick. 'You are funny, and cool. Alex should marry you.'

'What if I don't want to marry him?'

She laughs. 'Every girl does, don't they? Though God knows why; he's just plain *weird* at times.'

'Would it stop you if I stand in front of the door?' I say a short time later, watching her apply a last coat of lip gloss in the hall mirror before shrugging on her velvet Goth coat.

She gives me a quick hug and trills, 'Not one bit. Now please, stop stressing. I'll be back in no time.'

'Make sure it's well before eleven or I'm not refereeing the bout between you and Alexander.'

She giggles. 'There will be no need to referee anything. I'll be tucked up in bed before he gets in, if he even notices. He'll probably be pissed anyway and way later than he said. Have a good evening.'

Like it's going to be a blast. I grab some granola, yoghurt and fresh pineapple from the fridge, as if eating healthily will make up for the unease I feel at letting Emma out 'on licence' and being put in this position by Alexander. I pour myself a large glass of chilled Sauvignon and read through my take-home exam questions again to try to distract myself from worrying about Emma. Man, they really *are* as horrible as I remembered.

'Lauren?'

Alexander shakes my shoulder. His breath is warm and smells of whisky but he has a sexy smile on his face.

'Uh . . . hi. What time is it?' I blink in the lamplight and push myself up the sofa. Alexander perches on the edge of it next to me.

'About half past twelve. Sorry I'm so late. Did you two have a good evening?'

Oh hell, *why* have they both done this to me? Why have I allowed myself to get in this situation? Fortunately, Alexander takes my garbled grunt for sleepiness. It's then I realize that I haven't heard Emma come in, but that's hardly surprising.

'The last thing I remember is abandoning my exam essay and trying to get into some French crime series on BBC4.'

'And?'

'Everyone was hot in it and there was a lot of shooting, and I now know how to say "fuck" in French. I fell asleep before the end.'

'*Putain* . . .'

'Yeah, that would be it.'

He starts to unbutton my shirt and mutters something that sounds like '*couchez avec moi ce soir*', and I'm trying not to laugh while debating if he's in a fit state to *coucher* at all.

308

'We can't shag each other down here. Emma might wake up.'

'No, we can't . . . Screw these tiny buttons.'

I close my hand over his. 'Alexander . . .'

'What's wrong?'

'You're a little pissed and I need the bathroom.'

'You'll be back?'

'Of course.'

I could use the guest cloakroom off the hall but instead I go upstairs. Call it a sixth sense, but I can't help stopping outside Emma's bedroom door. It's closed and the light is off, which means nothing – or everything. I knock softly and there's no answer. She's probably asleep . . .

Except: she isn't asleep, is she? And I should have known that from the moment Alexander woke me. I should have known she wouldn't be in her bed from the moment she told me she was going out, 'on her own'.

I push open the door and the light from the landing shows me Emma's bed. It's rumpled like someone has slept in it and covered by her laptop, clothes, make-up, books – everything except a sleeping seventeen-year-old. My heart starts to pound, my mouth is dry and I have absolutely no idea what the hell I'm going to say to Alexander. I walk into the room, as if I might find her hiding in the wardrobe or under the bed. I feel cold, and it's not because I just woke up.

'She's not here, is she?' Alexander's voice, so teasing and sexy a few minutes ago, is cold and hard behind me.

'No.'

I turn to see him framed in the doorway. He flicks on the light and Emma's absence becomes almost palpable. He walks into the room and stands beside me.

'Fuck. She must have walked out while you were asleep,' he says, glancing around him, shaking his head.

'No, she didn't.'

'How do you know? Lauren, it's not your fault, it's mine. I should have been here; I should have refused to go to the dinner.'

'She didn't go out while I was asleep, she went out long before then.'

With my arms wrapped around my body, I can't and don't want to look at his face.

'What?'

'She said she'd arranged to meet some friends at a pub; I tried to persuade her to stay but she'd made up her mind. I'm sorry. I tried to stop her but short of locking the door and calling you back, what could I do?'

He pushes the laptop out of the way and sits down on Emma's bed, staring into space. 'What could you have done? You could have called me for one thing.'

'I did consider it but I didn't want to ruin your evening. You said you had people to meet and I honestly couldn't do anything once she'd made her mind up.'

He turns his eyes on me, his gaze icy. 'You should have phoned me, Lauren.'

I start to feel angry. 'I told you I thought about it and made the decision not to. I'm genuinely sorry, Alexander, but I couldn't barricade the door!'

'No, I suppose not.' He stands up. 'However, I did think that you might, possibly, have realized that once she had left it would be a good idea to call me so I could do something about it. Now, God knows where she's gone or what's happened to her.' His voice grows louder and I can see he's about to explode. 'If I'd known that this would happen, I would never have set foot outside the fucking house!' He shoves his hands savagely through his hair.

I am desperately trying to keep a hold on my own anger. 'Now just wait a moment, Alexander. I'm sorry you're upset but there's no point hitting the roof or lay-ing blame. Emma may well be back any minute. She told me who she was meeting and where. I know it's way after closing time but she's bound to have gone on to her friend's house. If we call Allegra, I'll bet she's there.'

'That's forty miles away from here! How the hell would she get there?'

'She left in a cab, but she did say the boys they were meeting were eighteen, so they probably all have cars.'

'Boys? Oh fuck. I hope she's OK.'

'You could also try phoning her?'

He gets up suddenly and thumps downstairs. When I enter the sitting room, he's on his mobile and I can hear it ringing out.

He stabs the off button. 'Bloody answerphone. I'm going to phone Allegra's mother, even if it is almost one a.m.'

I hover nearby while he calls, hearing the house

phone at their comfortable manor house ring out, imagining Allegra's mother or father waking and probably thinking something dire has happened.

'Hello, this is Alexander Hunt here, Emma's brother. Firstly, I must apologize for calling so late but is Emma with you?' His voice is clipped, ultra polite.

I rub my hands up and down my jeans while he speaks, hoping for the right answer, but then I hear him say, 'OK, I'm sorry to have disturbed you. Maybe you're right and she's with one of her other friends. I'll try them.'

He switches off the phone and, without speaking, dials another number and goes through the same routine.

While he does, I try Emma's phone again from my own cell, but I get the answerphone too.

After Alexander has hauled three different families out of bed, he throws his phone on the sofa and sits down, with his head in his hands.

'I know it's worrying, but she is seventeen; she may have gone on to a club here in Oxford or to another friend's house.'

'I hope so. I wish I'd bloody stayed here.'

'You can't keep her in all the time. It's her life.'

'I should have been here. This is my fault.'

That makes a change from it being my fault, I think, but it's no consolation to me and not helping his mood. I've heard him blame himself before, in his nightmares.

'Fuck it.' He walks to the fireplace and leans on it, his head bowed. 'I'm going to have to leave the army.' Then he snaps to attention. 'I'm going to call Brandon and go out looking for her. If I hadn't been drinking, I'd drive myself.'

'I only had a glass of wine much earlier, but I'm not insured for your car or I'd take you. But what if she comes back here while we're out? Surely it would be better to wait a while, at least until the clubs close in Oxford?'

He paces the room. 'I can't let anything happen to her, Lauren. I've got to keep her safe.'

I put my arms around him and, to my relief, he doesn't push me away. 'You won't. It's only one a.m. She's probably having a fantastic time in some club or at a friend's house and has lost track of the time.' That sounds lame, even to me, but I carry on. 'She'll be back soon, I'm sure.'

Hours later, Alexander is slumped in the chair opposite me, staring at his mobile. Like me, I think he's willing it to ring. Yet it hasn't, nor has Emma answered any of our calls. I've managed to persuade him not to call the hospitals or police so far, because I know they won't take it seriously at this stage.

The chimes of the clock in the hallway cut through the silence of the house, one, two, three, and Alexander jumps up. 'That's it, I'm calling Brandon and I'm going to look for her. Can you wait up and call me if she comes home?'

Without waiting for a reply, he dials Brandon's number and has just started talking to him when I hear the key scrape in the lock and the door open.

'That must be her!' I fly to the hallway and with a quick word to Brandon, Alexander is out of his seat after me.

Emma is framed in the doorway, her long hair plastered to her head, her velvet coat soaked. Her face is wet and, instinctively, I know that the moisture is not just raindrops.

Behind me, Alexander hasn't noticed she's crying and snaps, 'Where the fuck have you been? I've been out of my mind with worry.'

'Emma, what's the matter?' I ask and reach out to her, but she pushes past me to Alexander. He folds her in his arms and holds her while she heaves in great shuddering breaths. After a minute or two, he gently tilts her chin up to him and lifts the strands of wet hair from her face.

I'm only a spectator now and I can almost feel the strain in every syllable when he asks her, 'Has someone hurt you?'

Emma lets out a strangled howl. My heart is in my mouth.

'It's Henry-y-y,' she says with a gargling sob. 'He's d-d-dumped me.'

The clock ticks on, while Alexander struggles to process what she just said.

'You mean Henry Favell?'

'Yes.' Emma mumbles now, perhaps already wishing the name unsaid. I don't know what to do or say.

'*Has* he hurt you?'

314

'N-no. Not in *that* way.'

'So, that's where you were tonight? With him?'

She hesitates. 'Yes.'

Alexander lets his arms fall from her body and walks into the sitting room like we don't exist. Emma is left forlorn in the middle of the hall. I stay where I am, trying not to think of the fall-out which is about to follow.

Emma sniffs loudly, then says in a tiny voice, 'Oh fuck.'

She looks at me, I look at her, and then she dashes into the sitting room after him. When I walk in, Alexander is standing in front of the mantelpiece, leaning on it with both hands, but I can see his expression in the mirror. It's tight with fury and disappointment.

'Why do you hate him so much?' Emma's voice rises to a shriek.

He doesn't turn round, either because he doesn't trust himself to or because he knows we can see him.

'Look at the state of you now. Do I need another reason? Why do you think he's after you anyway?'

'He said he loved me. Why, do you think no one could love me?'

He bursts out laughing and whips round to face us both. 'Of course I do, but not that bastard. He's not fit to lick your fucking boots.'

'This is not helpful . . .' I have to stand up for Emma even if she has dropped me in deep shit.

'It's also none of your business.' Alexander doesn't even look at me as he says it but keeps his eyes on Emma.

'I could rip his balls off for hurting you but I'm not sorry it's over between you.'

Emma looks at him, distraught.

'Listen, I care about you and I don't want to see you like this. *Why* have you started seeing him again? You know he's a devious piece of shit.'

Her voice rises in pitch. 'I've already told you, I loved him. He said he loved me. I know you hate him so why would I tell you I was going out with him? I know you got Rupert to warn him off last year; you had no right to do that.'

'I have every right. You're sixteen.'

'Seventeen. I can shag who I like. You do.'

I wince.

Alexander speaks slowly, every syllable enunciated in his cut-glass accent. 'I'm responsible for you, and Henry Favell is a lying bastard.'

'You were engaged to Valentina and she's an evil bitch, so now we're even. Thank fuck you dumped her and found someone normal, like Lauren. At least I can fucking talk to her! At least she listens to me when no one else will. She understands how I feel, don't you, Lauren? What I felt for Henry?'

Emma is staring at me, pleading with her eyes and her voice.

I've never been in an auto accident but I've heard people say that just before the moment of impact, their brain slows everything down and they see the inevitable happen, but they're powerless to do a thing to stop it.

Alexander is that truck approaching, a massive object sliding towards me.

He looks at me questioningly and I try to keep my face impassive as I see his eyes widen in shock, and something else I can't quite detect. 'You knew,' he says.

Bang. I fly up into the air, tumbling over and over.

'*You knew she was still seeing him.*' He repeats the words.

'She was only trying to help.' Emma's voice is a tiny squeak, mouse-like, and my first instinct is to laugh at them both. It's really no big deal, I want to say, look at yourselves. She's young and finding her way; you're acting like some Victorian father. You're way out of your depth here, with all that's happened, and you won't admit it.

'I'm sorry, Lauren,' says Emma, touching my arm.

'Hey, it doesn't matter.' The words come out of my mouth but I hadn't actually thought of them. I certainly don't mean them.

'No, of course it doesn't matter,' says Alexander so carefully I'm shaking inside. I'm also mad as hell at him, but me shouting won't help anyone now, least of all Emma, who has crossed to Alexander and put her arms around him.

'You're angry. I'm sorry. I thought he loved me,' she says intent on her brother's face. I have the feeling that I've suddenly turned into the villain, that I've been shut out by the Hunts.

Alexander holds her. 'I'm sure he was very convincing. Did he give any reason why he decided to upset you like this?'

'He . . . he said . . . I was too young and it was too much hassle sneaking around behind people's backs. He said he wasn't prepared to act like a guilty schoolboy and that maybe you were right; he was too old for me. So, you see, you got your way in the end. You win, Alex, like you always do.'

'Winning was never the aim, Emma. Protecting you was.'

'But I don't need protecting and please, don't blame Lauren. She tried to tell me not to see him; she said you'd be like this.'

'Did she really? What a shame she didn't think it would be a good idea to share her thoughts and opinions with me.'

Emma lets go of him and scoots backwards. 'Because you'd kick off like this, just like Daddy. I bet Mummy would have let me see him; I know she'd have been more reasonable.'

'I can see you're upset and, despite what you may think, I do have some sympathy with you. I'm not some robot who has no feelings, but you have no idea what our mother would have thought or done. I can tell you now she'd have been fucking horrified to see you wasting your life on Favell and being found drunk in the street.'

'Maybe she would be here now if you hadn't been screaming at me in the back of the car. I do remember that bit!' Emma shrieks. 'She told you to stop teasing me and act your age. She looked round at us to shout at you and that's why she hit the tree. It *was* your fault. Daddy said it and he was right.'

Alexander's face is stony and I can't bear to watch them throwing accusations like this at each other. It's like a shutter has come down in Alexander and he can't be reached, even if either of us wanted to. 'Go to bed, if you like,' he says coldly. 'Go back out on the streets if you want. Do whatever you like.'

She rushes out of the room, crying. I have seen Alexander close to tears once this year and now I see it again. No matter how angry I am at being blamed for this mess, I also feel sorry for him. Sorry for them all, and glad I was born where I was, to my parents, not theirs. I stay, knowing there's nothing I can, should or want to do, but I try. I reach out to touch his arm, knowing I'm approaching a wounded tiger.

'Alexander . . .'

'Just leave me alone.'

I did leave him alone. I went up to bed but I can't say I slept much, with Emma crying down the hallway and Alexander pacing about downstairs. I feel as if I've been awake all night but each time I checked the clock at the side of the bed, the hands had leaped forward a little more, so I guess I have dozed, or dreamed or something. What I do know is that Alexander hasn't joined me and that the first light of dawn is starting to wash the wall with a blue light.

I pull on a robe and make my way downstairs. There's no sign of life so I make a pot of coffee and sit at the table. A while later, I hear the front door open and someone – it must be Alexander – walks into the kitchen. His T-shirt has an upturned 'V' of perspiration and he's breathing heavily. He walks right past me without sparing me a glance, takes a glass from the cupboard and fills it with water. He drinks it straight down and then refills it, all as if I am invisible.

I knew it would be bad, but not like this. He has wiped me from the face of the earth.

'You're going to have to talk to me some time,' I say as he wipes the back of his mouth with his hand.

He rinses out the glass and places it upturned on the drainer.

'I'm sorry, Alexander. I really struggled with not telling you and perhaps I made the wrong call, but at the time I thought it was more important that she had one person she could be honest with, and who she could turn to. I hoped it would blow over and you would never need to know,' I add, feebly, desperately hoping for any kind of reaction from him.

He stands at the sink, gripping the edge of the countertop either side. Anger bubbles up inside me and I abandon my coffee mug on the table.

'That time I found the receipt for the pregnancy test at Falconbury. That wasn't your test, was it?' He directs this question to the window above the sink. The sun has started to creep above the garden wall. It's a glorious spring morning, dew sparkling on the bushes and cobwebs. *Perfect.*

My palms are moist, my pulse spikes but the one thing I cannot do is lie. 'No.'

His face is like stone, and his eyes are twin ice chips. 'I see.' He turns away from the sink and starts to walk towards the kitchen door. Whatever I expected when he found out, it wasn't this: I have been blanked, wiped from his radar, shut out.

'I don't think you see quite how impossible a position I was in,' I plead.

He stops and, finally, he faces me, although I may as well not be in his sightline. He has already worked out his response to last night's events and his strategy is to refuse to engage. There will be no negotiation, but I won't stand for it.

'On the contrary, I see it all. You knew Emma was sleeping with a man ten years older, who actually went to her school to shag her, and who is a gold-digging piece of shit. And yet you decided not to inform me of this fact.'

'It's not that simple, and you know it.'

'It looks simple to me. You're the one who's keeping secrets now. And now I have to go away when I really don't feel comfortable leaving either of you. You knew she was – and probably still is – seeing this bastard and yet you didn't tell me. Why?'

'Because you would have killed him, because Emma begged me not to because of your reaction, because she *trusted* me and she clearly thinks she has no one else to trust.'

'That all sounds so reasonable, Lauren, except for one thing. *I* trusted you, more than anyone else. Clearly, I was deluded.'

Deluded? I'm not taking that. I've tried to apologize and explain but he won't listen to any kind of reason. 'This isn't about Emma, is it? It's about you and . . . the pressure you have on your shoulders, the invincible Alexander Hunt. I risked my studies for you, I gave you my time and my nights and my sympathy and my body. I tried to protect your sister and help her when no one else would and you seem to think I've betrayed you. Well, you know what? I want to live my life. I want to spend what's left of my time here enjoying myself, living my own life, dealing with my own screw-ups, not trying to solve yours.'

He watches me while I rant at him, without registering any emotion himself. He has pulled down the shutters again and I think it's final this time. Well, so be it.

'If that's how you feel, I'll take Emma back to Falconbury and you can stay here until your flight to Washington,' he says.

'I don't need your charity. I'm going back to college.' I hold my head up high, trying to control the tears that threaten.

'Whatever you like. The last thing I want to do is hold you back,' he spits out bitterly, and I turn and leave the room to gather my things.

Chapter Eighteen

From the Front Quad, the statues stare back at me, and their puritanical stone faces seem to say 'I told you so'. I've been back in my room a while now, convincing myself I'm working on my exam essays but largely staring out of the window and trying not to flick through my Facebook albums. I haven't cried yet; I still feel numb at what's happened, even though, looking back now, the whole mess was inevitable. When someone knocks at my door, I've half a mind to get into bed and pull the comforter over me and never come out, but then I hear Immy's voice. 'Lauren.'

When I open the door, in place of the smile, I get a face of doom and raw, red eyes.

'Skandar and I broke up,' she says.

'Oh shit. Come here.' There's a group hug and I know she's trying not to cry so I let her go and say, 'Come in. I'll get the vodka.'

I sit her in my office chair and find the bottle, some orange juice and some glasses. I could say, 'Join the club,' and tell her about Alexander but that can wait. She needs me to listen now; she needs me to be the shoulder to cry on and the maker of large vodkas, the finder of secret stashes of Hotel Chocolat.

'What happened? You seemed so happy last time you saw him.'

'I was. I thought he was too but he said it was better to do this now than wait until next term, when we have exams. He said he wants to go off to the States to coach tennis and just bum around, as he put it, and that it was better to make a clean break now. A clean break? What's that?'

She blows her nose noisily. I sit by her, helpless to do anything other than listen.

'Maybe he really thought it was best, but that doesn't help. I do know how you feel.' So much more than you think.

'Things turned out OK in the end though, didn't they? You got back with Alexander, not that I want Skandar back, the shit. I could never trust him again. You and Alexander got through so much, with Scott, and Alexander's vile relations and the whole sex tape thing, and anyone who can drive away that witch Valentina must mean a lot to him.'

'You think?' I swallow the lump in my throat, which has grown to brick-sized proportions. I can't keep this facade up. So is now the time to tell her? Really, there is no point going through the whole 'men are bastards' scenario. They are, of course – that's a given today – but in my case, I shoulder half the blame for even hoping that things might have run smoothly between Alexander and me. Whoever said marriage was the tri- umph of hope over experience must have had dating

Alexander in mind too. Or maybe that should be the triumph of lust over experience.

Instead of whining, I nod and agree while we drink the vodka. I also fetch a new box of Kleenex and feel guilty because Immy deserves my undivided attention yet inside my own heart slowly cracks in two. The shock of the anaesthetic is wearing off: finally the pain starts to hit, sharp and unrelenting. Alexander and I are over.

'What am I going to do, Lauren?' Immy winds a Kleenex round her finger.

'I can't give advice. I wish I could, but I'm the queen of fuck-ups myself.'

'What do you mean?'

I wish I could keep up the facade a while longer but I can't, and maybe it will help Immy to know she's not the only one feeling like shit. Or maybe I need a hug so badly that I don't care how selfish I have to be.

'I've had a huge row with Alexander, I'm really not sure we can come back from this one,' I manage, as the sadness hits me.

'*What?*'

'Yep, this row was terrible; he wouldn't listen to anything I said and honestly, Immy, I think I've had enough. I didn't come here for this kind of shit.'

'But what was the row about?' asks Immy, eyes widening in shock.

'Well . . . he blames me for something that wasn't really my fault, and whatever the rights and wrongs, I felt I was in the middle of an impossible situation. I guess I should have known it was going to end like this, but that doesn't make things any easier.'

The whole break-up story pours out and when I finally draw breath, Immy gives her verdict.

'Jesus Christ. That's *so* fucking unfair. Emma should never have put you in that position and Alexander shouldn't have blamed you for it!'

Well, at least I've taken Immy's mind off her own love life for a little while.

'I guess I have to take some of the blame. Henry is a piece of shit and I knew it and that he would hurt Emma and I should have told Alexander.'

'But she trusted *you*, and surely it was better to have one person she could open up to than keep everything secret!'

'They both trusted me, so I suppose I couldn't win. I still don't know what I ought to have done. Emma's had a crappy time, and a shitty childhood for all her privilege. She did try to tell Alexander it was her fault.'

'And he didn't listen?'

'Of course not, but I don't think he could cope with anything right now. I think he wants life to be black and white at the moment. He wants to keep Emma safe, but I think he maybe wants to control her a bit too much and that's backfired. I don't want to walk away from the Hunts, because I really care for Emma, let alone Alexander, but this latest row might just have pushed me too far. I can't be the punchbag for ever . . .' I stop talking, feeling utterly washed out. Pouring out the latest saga to Immy has made me feel worse, not better.

'Those two must be so fucked up,' Immy says. 'Is there a chance they just need some time to sort themselves out?' she offers hopefully.

'You told me the very first time we saw him to steer clear. You told me to keep well away and that he was a load of trouble yet I ignored you. I went looking for trouble and I got addicted to it, the danger, the drama, the rollercoaster, but now the Hunt grenade has exploded in my face – twice, in fact – and I've finally learned my lesson.'

'Oh, Lauren, I am so sorry.' Immy's face is full of sympathy.

'Don't be.' I try a weak smile. 'I had the ride of my life, but I wish I hadn't wasted two terms taking it.'

'What a mess,' she agrees, then her face brightens. 'I know this isn't the greatest time to ask, but you will still come to the Boat Race party? It'll be fun, packed with Blues rowers looking for a good time. We can get pissed, hit the clubs and shops.' She looks at me pleadingly and I realize she needs cheering up as much as I do.

I summon up a smile. It's all bravado, of course; what I actually feel like doing is lying down and howling, but that would be letting Alexander win, letting him and his troubled, screwed-up life damage me even more. I won't let it and if I have to pretend I want to go to this party and dance and drink and laugh, I'll do it.

I force a bigger smile on to my face, even though it physically hurts. 'Try stopping me.'

So the term has come to a close, not in the way I expected and not that different from the way the last one ended. I had a final meeting with Professor Rafe after the weekend, at which he said he was 'pleased with how I'd worked despite the circumstances' and told me to keep up the standard of the final pieces of work I handed in. He also said that Trinity term – the summer one – would be a huge challenge that would demand my total commitment. I assured him that I was going to be completely focused on my work from now on. I've no intention of telling him why but he's bound to find out that Alexander and I are history at some point.

But now work is over for a while and I've needed the distraction of a week away from Alexander and my worries so badly.

For the past few days, we've been staying at Immy's parents' flat in Chelsea, trying to console each other with a round of shopping, cocktails, dinner and clubbing. Hey, we even managed to get some work done, and I hit the Wallace Collection, the National Portrait Gallery and the Tate Modern. I guess we've had a good time, and Immy has shown remarkable powers of recovery. Yet even while I was dancing, I had the strangest sense of not quite being part of my surroundings, like I was watching myself dance and laugh from outside myself. Then again, that could have been the Manhattans.

I've had a couple of texts from Emma, saying she's sorry for causing so much trouble, but I haven't heard from Alexander. Did I expect him to come after me? Did I even want him to?

And by now, I guess he's infiltrating some desert outpost or tracking insurgents. I don't even want to think about it or him, because every time I do, I get angry with myself. But it would be good to know when he gets back, though what right or reason do I have now to ask? Maybe I can text Emma on Sunday, to see how she is? There has to be some way of working in his name.

Then again, if I don't hear from her, I have no need to ask. I shake my head, laughing at myself. I won't text, because Alexander will be back on Sunday, screwing up Emma's life and his own, no doubt.

This morning, we surfaced late after another night out and Immy took me for brunch at a little Russian deli across the street from her flat. We got changed for the party and now I'm watching cherry blossom drift on to the black cab crawling through the traffic to Jocasta's riverside house in south London. We had a few days of glorious sun that brought people out in shorts and T-shirts in the parks, although the rain has started again now. Immy is next to me, scrolling through her emails. I think she's secretly hoping to hear from Skandar too, although she seems breezy enough. She glances up from the screen, rubs condensation from the window and says, 'Oh, we're here.'

The cab stops and we climb out. Behind the

wrought-iron railings, the brick house is what you might call 'handsome', with rows of sash windows and a portico with stone pillars. It reminds me, just a little, of our house in Washington, which is modelled in the English style, and suddenly I want to forget trying to salvage what's left of my term and be there right now.

'Not a bad party house, eh?' Immy pays the driver and we stand on the sidewalk, admiring the house, while he pulls into the traffic again.

'So this belongs to Jocasta's family?' I say, forcing myself to man up.

'Her granny owns it but she's moved into a retirement place now. Jocasta's parents keep meaning to sell it for her, but the family is making so much from renting it that they can't bear to get rid of it yet. Of course, it's perfect for watching the Boat Race. The Thames is literally at the end of the garden.'

Immy had said the house was nice but it defies all my expectations. The moment we arrive under the portico, the door opens.

'You made it, then.'

Jocasta air-kisses us both and gives Immy a hug. She's blonde, like me, but there the similarity ends. Jocasta is barely five feet tall, I'd say, and coxes the Wyckham Women's First Eight. Uniformed staff arrive to whisk away our coats.

'You might need them later. It's bloody freezing out by the river. Do you want a drink or a quick tour?'

'Both,' says Immy with a grin.

330

Jocasta laughs. 'OK. There's Pimm's or you can have a beer. I know it's not technically Pimm's season, but who cares?'

A waiter arrives on cue with a tray of Pimm's and we follow Jocasta through the hall and into a sitting room with high ceilings and plasterwork. The building may be Edwardian but the furniture is ultra contemporary, with metal tables, black leather sofas and bare-wood flooring. A huge flat-screen TV dominates one wall and is already showing the build-up to the race. A dozen or so people are chatting and drinking in front of the TV and there are more milling about on the other side of a wall of glass doors.

'Let's go out on to the deck.'

Jocasta leads us out on to a wide wooden deck which has steps leading down into a lawned garden. The river laps a muddy shoreline directly below it. We're elevated above the water and I immediately regret handing over my coat so soon because the wind blowing off the river cuts through my dress. Little white horses flick up on the brown surface and iron-grey clouds scud across the dirty white sky.

'I am *so* glad it's not me out there today,' I say, trying not to shiver.

Jocasta laughs. 'Mmm. It is a bit choppy but maybe it will settle down when the tide turns. Immy says you know one of the Blues rowers? The big blond American, Scott Schulze?'

'Yes, I do. He's a good friend,' I say warmly, realizing

331

that I mean it, and that I've missed Scott's uncomplicated company.

'Lucky you! He's gorgeous. I've invited him over later, along with a couple of the other boys from the Blue and *Isis* crews. I don't expect they'll arrive until very late because they'll probably go to the Blues Ball first, and God knows what state they'll be in by then. They may also decide to drown their sorrows, of course, if they lose.'

'Do you think Oxford will win?' Immy asks me, as if I have insider information.

I shrug. 'Cambridge are slight favourites, aren't they?'

Jocasta snorts. 'They must be *so* pissed off after last year's thrashing and out to get revenge, but who knows? Anything can happen. Remember that guy who jumped in front of the boats a couple of years ago? I can't remember his name now.'

'Twat,' says Immy with a vicious slurp of her Pimm's. 'We lost that race because of him.'

'What time is the start?' I ask.

'It's scheduled for half past three. Most people should be here by then, although some of them like to watch the race from the pub or one of the bridges. Of course, quite a few aren't interested in the race at all, so the real party won't get going until late.'

Immy's teeth start to chatter and my fingers are numb. Jocasta takes pity on us.

'Shall we go back inside for now?'

*

My throat is hoarse from shouting, my hands are numb from the cold and my hair is blown around like a wild thing, but Oxford have won. We're all gathered in front of the TV now, about thirty of us squeezed into the sitting room, watching the Oxford squad throwing their cox into the river. Cambridge have a look of sheer devastation, standing to one side, with no purpose any more after all the months of training. Despite the gleeful jibes from some of the guests, some of whom have friends in the Dark Blue boat, I actually feel sorry for the defeated Cambridge team.

Corks pop as magnums of Moët are opened and the waiting staff hand round flutes of champagne.

Jocasta has climbed on to a sofa. 'To us!' she shouts and everyone cheers.

'There's Scott again!' Immy says, and Scott's face flashes up on the screen. He's being interviewed by a woman from the BBC. I don't think I have ever seen him, or anyone, look so happy. I want to cry for him but I hold back the tears, because it most definitely wouldn't be the done thing. I wonder if he will come along tonight. It would be nice to congratulate him. I haven't seen him for ages, what with all the dramas in my life. I must get my priorities right from now on.

Even though I'm determined to enjoy myself, I can't help feeling down; the way I parted from Alexander was so cold and bitter. The unfairness of his comments still stabs at me, even though he was upset and felt betrayed. He had the same look about him as when

I confronted him about the nightmare. It's like he has some kind of emergency switch inside that he activates when he feels threatened. I guess it's a survival instinct he's developed to protect himself but it leaves the people around him cut off. I don't know how I lived on that knife edge now, no matter how glorious the sex, and how exhilarating the whole Hunt cocktail of glamour and excitement.

I must admit I felt alive every day I was with him and, yes, I wonder where he is now, even though I hate myself for allowing him to occupy my thoughts.

'Are you OK?' Immy gives my arm a little squeeze.

'I was wondering if I should phone Emma. She was incredibly upset when Alexander and I had the row. She's texted me a few times, saying she blames herself for splitting us up.'

'Good. It was her fault.'

'I replied a couple of times telling her not to stress about it, but I still feel sorry for her. She's had such a horrible time.'

'Does she know where Alexander's gone?'

'I think he told her it's a training exercise in Wales, but I know it isn't.'

'Are *you* worried about him?'

'No ...' I say. I've always worried before when Alexander has gone away but this time, I realize, there's been so much going on, I haven't really had time to think about that side of things.

Immy raises her eyebrows. 'Have another Pimm's?'

'Maybe I ought to pace myself,' I say ruefully, though the Pimm's does look very tempting.

She smiles. 'Yes, maybe we both should. I've got a feeling tonight's going to be quite lively. I do hope Scott turns up.'

By the time Immy's wish is finally granted, it's well past midnight. Despite the effort of the race, and the fact I suspect he's been drinking most of the evening, Scott looks fresh as a daisy and incredibly handsome in his tux. No wonder every female head turns to look at him. The guys slap him on the back, congratulating him, and one guy even kisses him smack on the mouth.

Scott pulls a face and makes a barfing noise but his mile-wide grin is soon in place again; I guess nothing can ever wipe it away now that he's achieved his dream. I hang back, feeling awkward, with so much I want to say to him that I don't say anything at all. I also feel slightly not myself, and this time it has everything to do with the Pimm's, Moët and vodka cocktails I've been drinking since we arrived, despite my attempts to go slow on this.

I hesitate, watching him have his moment in the sun, and when I do eventually reach him, I have a lump in my throat. He greets me with a kiss, this time on my cheek, and a great big hug.

'Hey, well done! Let me be the first one to say "I told you so".'

'Not the first. Those were my mother's exact words

when I called her after the race. Also my grandmother's.' He grins, clearly feeling on top of the world.

'It may not be original but I still stick by it. You're amazing.' I smile at him, feeling truly happy for him and able, at least for now, to put my own problems to one side.

'You know, at the risk of sounding too American, I think I am,' he says, with a twinkle in his eye. 'Where's Alex?' He looks around, searching for him.

Oh fuck. I shrug my shoulders and answer honestly. 'I have no idea, Scott.'

'Really?'

'Uh-huh. He went on some mission and couldn't tell me where.' I giggle after making this statement. 'The name's Hunt, Alexander Hunt.'

Scott seems a little taken aback by my flippancy and I have to admit my wit isn't too sparkling or sharp by this stage of the evening.

'Wow. OK, well, I'm sure he'll be back soon enough. I have the feeling the guy will never go away.' He looks at me very directly and I'm struck once again by how easy everything feels in his company.

'I guess not . . .' He looks so happy, I decide now that I'm not going to burst his massive bubble. I raise my champagne glass to him and my voice. 'Forget Alexander. This is your night. To Scott Schulze, who single-handedly won the Boat Race for Oxford!'

So what if a few heads turn in my direction and laugh or roll their eyes? So what if I just pissed off half the

Boat Race crew? So what if Scott takes my elbow when I teeter against him and says, 'Whoa, there, steady,'?

'So what the fuck do I care what anyone thinks? I'm celebrating with a friend, a very good friend,' I add defiantly.

'Are you feeling OK, Lauren?' he asks, laughing, but there is concern in his eyes too.

'Ab:sholutely fine. Superrr,' I assure him, giving him my best dazzling smile.

'Hey, Scott.' A girl appears and threads her arm through Scott's. She's a couple of inches taller than I am and super fit by the look of her sculpted cheekbones.

He kisses her on the lips and says, 'Lauren, this is Lia. She's in the Women's Lightweight crew. Lia, meet Lauren, who's a very good friend of mine.'

'Hello, Lauren. Scott's told me all about you, really good to meet you.' Lia's accent is Northern Irish, I think, and I watch as Scott drapes an arm over her shoulder, giving her another, longer kiss.

'Has he?' My voice doesn't feel like it belongs to me any more. That feeling of being operated by another being, rather than being me, has taken over. I've had way too much to drink – why else would I feel like crying?

While some guy claps Scott on the back and drunkenly starts to tell him he wants to have his babies, Lia talks to me.

'Scott told me you used to date his cousin?' She is so

friendly, and so pretty, I just want to run away, yet I have no right to feel peeved.

'Um, for a while, yes, that's right.'

'And now you're going out with Alexander Hunt?'

I don't know how to reply, so I say, 'Uh-huh. Congratulations on winning your race too. I'm really pleased for you both,' I manage, feeling strangely empty.

'Thank you,' she grins, radiating happiness. 'We were massive underdogs but Scott gave me a pep talk a few weeks ago and I tried to focus on that. He's so bloody talented it's not fair.' She sighs, looking over at him adoringly.

'He is pretty amazing,' I agree. 'Have you known him long?'

'I've known *of* him since the start of Michaelmas; who could fail to miss him?' She laughs. 'Obviously we've both been too busy to see much of each other, although I finally got to talk to him at a party for the Blues squads a few weeks ago. Tonight, at the ball, we finally sort of got together. We're not going out or anything.' She smiles and holds up her crossed fingers. 'Yet.'

'Good luck,' I say, and I mean it, or at least I do my best to mean it.

'To be honest, I'm absolutely knackered but Scott wanted to come to the party. I don't think we'll stay long. We should both be in bed.' I have no idea how to reply to this and I genuinely don't think Lia realized what she said because she suddenly puts her hand over her mouth and goes red to the roots of her auburn hair. 'My God, I didn't mean . . .'

I dredge up a smile.

'Actually, I probably *did* mean . . .' She laughs out loud and Scott turns away from the guy he's been talking to and puts his arm around her. 'What are you guys up to? Should my ears be burning?'

'Yes.' I force a laugh. 'Hey, I see Immy over there. Catch you later.'

I have as much intention of catching Scott and Lia later as I do of making Valentina my BFF, but I do know that Immy is somewhere amid a knot of godlike Blues rowers out on the deck, mainlining pints and cigarettes like they've been in jail for a year.

The wind seems to slice through me and the blast of oxygen isn't helping my inebriated state, but I don't care. I have to get away from Scott and Lia.

'Are you OK? You look a little queasy,' says Immy.

'I feel it,' I admit shakily.

'Too much Pimm's?' she quizzes.

'No, just irrational jealousy.' I try to make a joke of it.

'What's wrong, hun?' Immy looks concerned now.

'Scott's here,' I mutter.

'Yes. And that's a bad thing?'

'He's with a girl.' I look down, biting my lip.

'Oh dear. I see,' says Immy, clearly not sure what to say now. 'Horrible, is she?'

'No, she's very pretty, and fit and nice and she has a sense of humour.'

339

Immy rolls her eyes. 'What a total bitch.'

'I wish she *was* a bitch because that would make things easier. You know that feeling when someone you know likes you and is attracted to you, and then they go off with someone else – and you feel pissed about it even if you didn't really want them in that way?'

'Not that often, but I'll try to imagine,' Immy grins, squeezing my arm. 'What's her name?'

'Lia.'

Immy nods. 'Hmm, I think I know her. Long red hair, about six feet tall?'

'That's her.'

'Oh fuck. I can't even hate her either, because she *is* nice, and she's just spent a year volunteering in a refugee camp in Africa before she completes her medical studies. That's if she doesn't decide to try for the Olympic rowing team in Rio.'

I have to smile at this. 'Lia is so perfect for Scott; in fact they're both perfect human beings. I'm really happy that Scott's found someone he likes.'

'Of *course* you are. Does he know that you're having problems with Alexander?'

'No way. I didn't want to spoil the evening by telling him.'

'Maybe the news would have made his evening.'

'I doubt it, judging by how happy he and Lia seem. No matter how irrationally jealous I feel, I'm really glad I didn't tell him that Alexander and I are history. It would have looked as if I was angling for a comfort shag.'

'He would have been one hell of a comfort shag. He's absolutely divine.'

'Yes, he's gorgeous, and he's a hero.'

'So's Alexander.'

I snort. 'I know that, but he's also a screwed-up, frustrating, awkward, repressed bastard.'

'Who you wish would walk through the door right this minute and drag you off to one of the bedrooms?'

'No, because I don't want to see him again.' I realize as I say this that I really do mean that – I need some simplicity in my life after the last few weeks. It's all really been too much.

Immy looks at me carefully and then takes my arm. 'In that case, come and introduce yourself to some rowers. I've been dying to know if it's true they don't wear anything under the Lycra.'

It is true, apparently, and within a short time Immy has also discovered that waxing goes on. Truly, I suppose, we're living every girl's dream, the centre of attention of half a dozen rowers. One minute we're laughing as Immy confesses to having watched some of them training from her friend's narrowboat opposite their Boat House, the next she's being hauled off in the direction of the hallway – and the stairs to the bedrooms, I presume – by some guy whose dress shirt is already open to the waist, showing off abs to die for.

A few minutes later, I feel a hand as broad as a shovel

curl around my bottom and a voice that could grace the RSC slurs, 'D'you fancy a shag?'

The hotty next to me is like something from a Hollister ad; he also reeks like a brewery and a couple of minutes ago was making jokes about lighting his own farts. However, somebody told me earlier that he's got a DPhil in Molecular Biology and has just discovered a test for some kind of cancer so I decide to cut him some slack. But I'm still not going to take up his offer.

'It's tempting, Olly, but I think I'll pass on this occasion,' I say lightly.

'Shame, you're the sexshiest girl in the room and the classhiest.' He lets his hand drop from my butt. 'But probably just as well because I'm not entirely shure I could finish the job. It's been a busy day.'

He sways a little and I would steady him with my hand on his arm if I didn't think he might crash on top of me and squash me flat.

'I may be a teeny bit neinbriated . . . brineanted . . . wankered.'

'I'd say that was an accurate description.'

Two of his friends catch him just as he's about to fell a lamp and possibly smash a glass table in two.

'Goodnight, Olly,' I murmur as he lies spread-eagled over a sofa, his mouth open, snoring.

I think it's time for me to call it a night too but there's no way I'm interrupting Immy. I find my bag stuffed behind the TV cupboard and dig out my phone.

Immy, gone back to apartment.
Have fun with your rower xxx

At this hour, there's no way I'm going to wander out to the street to hail a cab. The staff have left now, and won't be back until morning to clear up the mess, so I decide to find Jocasta and ask her to give me a number. I hear her voice coming from a room off the hallway and walk inside.

'Jocasta, thanks for a great party but –'

Two faces glance up at me from the sofa. One is hers and the other is Rupert's.

'Oh, hello, Lauren. I've got a friend of yours here.'

'Good evening, Lauren, or perhaps I should say good morning now.'

That lazy, sneering voice could have been designed to bring me crashing down to earth. He lounges on the sofa, smoking a cigar. He's dressed in white tie and tails with a garish waistcoat, now stained with something yellow, and he reminds me of Mr Toad. My first thought is to wonder if Alexander has told him about our row. Then I remind myself that Rupert can't hurt me now. Nothing can.

Jocasta smiles benignly – obviously she has no idea of the animosity between Rupert and me. 'Oh, of course, I forgot you two know each other through Alexander. What a shame he couldn't make it, but duty calls. My father's a lieutenant colonel in the Guards so I know what it's like when you've someone close on active service.'

343

'Lauren must be out of her mind with worry but she's trying to soldier on and be brave, aren't you?' *So, he doesn't know . . .*

He crosses one leg over the other and the smoke from his cigar wreathes through the air, catching at my throat. I come close to hating him.

'Alexander would hate anyone moping and worrying over him, and I'm not the hand-wringing type.' I turn to Jocasta. 'Jocasta, thanks for a lovely party but I'm off now. Do you have the number of a cab company?'

'You'll have a wait, at this hour.'

'That's fine.'

'I'll go and find one. I think there's a card in the kitchen drawer. Hang on.'

I decide to hang on elsewhere but before I can leave the room, Rupert speaks. 'I know you and Alexander are history.'

You know that thing about not being able to be hurt any more? I lied. But I toss his barb back at him. 'And?'

'I knew it would happen sooner or later. It was inevitable.'

'You know fuck all about me, and I don't care what you think about Alexander.' I hate myself for rising to his bait but I'm tired and screwed over and sick to death of his sneering.

He brushes ash from his thigh. 'Nice try but I can see you're trying not to cry even now. I know you've had a major row and I know why. No one crosses the Hunts, I warned you way back. They band together when they're threatened. I guessed it wouldn't be too long before Alexander came to his senses.'

'You're sick.'

'No, I'm only looking out for my family.'

'*Your* family! You're not part of Alexander and Emma's lives. You're out to destroy him because you know you'll never have what he has.'

'Meaning you?' he sneers. 'You're a very beautiful girl, Lauren, bright, classy, but you're not One of Us. Not quite the thing, as my grandfather liked to say. Incidentally, he was Alexander's grandfather too.'

'Isn't nature cruel?' I say, trembling with anger inside. 'You appear to have got all the asshole genes.'

He laughs and exhales smoke, which stings my eyes and makes me want to cough.

'I offered you plenty of chances to jump ship, so to speak. You and I could have had a good time, but you're not the one for Alexander and everyone can see it. You should have told him about Emma and Henry Favell. Bad, bad decision, but I'm not surprised you tried to go all big sister on her. The thing is, you'll never be Emma's big sister, and when Alexander told me that you knew she was seeing Favell and lied to him about it, I wasn't surprised.'

I feel physically sick when he says this and the fact that Alexander has related the whole thing to him – and blamed me – makes me sick with anger and disappointment. While I struggle to reply, Rupert flows on, spewing out more bile.

345

'Did you enjoy the tape, by the way?'

I stare at him, anger building. '*You* sent it.' Instantly, I think I already knew. It had to be.

'Don't you want to know why?'

I smile at him icily. 'No.'

As his face falls in surprise and disappointment, I fight against every urge to engage with him and tell myself not to give him one ounce of satisfaction. I turn towards the hallway and my intake of breath is audible because the woman blocking the doorway is Valentina.

Chapter Nineteen

'*Ciao*, Lauren.'

She towers over me, in stiletto-heeled boots and a black leather mini dress that must have been sprayed on to her.

'What are you doing here?' I manage.

'Rupert invited me. I am sooo sorry to hear that you're having more problems with Alexander.'

'No, you're not,' I spit, cross with myself for rising to her bait.

She reaches out to touch me but I shrink back.

'If you think he's going to rush back into your arms, you're even more deluded than I thought you were.'

'I don't *think* he's going to rush back to me, he already has.' She smiles. 'I think you have seen the tape by now?'

'Yes I have, and we both ignored it.' This is a slight twisting of the facts but I'm in no mood for semantics by now.

'That wasn't what I heard.' Rupert smirks at me from the sofa.

'How do you even know what happened? I didn't tell anyone about it except Immy and Alexander and they wouldn't have told you.'

He sniggers. 'Oh come on, I can picture the scene.

I really thought you deserved a Valentine's Day surprise.'

He's unbelievable, but I don't need to ask him why he wants to split us up so badly. He's envious of what Alexander has and jealous of anyone trying to enter his world.

'So what? That clip could have been filmed years ago.'

Valentina sniggers. 'No, it was filmed the day I went to Oxford to comfort Alexander and we ended up in bed. I hear Alexander entertained you too later, and I can't say I'm happy about that, but you know Alexander, always doing his duty. You're just a toy for him.'

I can't speak. She's just tapped into my deepest fears and suspicions.

'Poor Lauren. The whole time you and Alexander have been seeing each other, I've been sleeping with him. While you think he has been training' – she brackets her long red nails around the word 'training' – 'and taking care of things at Falconbury, he has been screwing me.'

'You're lying, Valentina, and I refuse to listen to any more.' I begin to walk off, deciding I'll find a taxi elsewhere.

'No, it is you who is deluding yourself. Alexander has told me that I'm the only one for him, and we'll get married when you've gone back to Washington. When he comes back from this place he has gone, I'll be waiting.'

'Then you'll be waiting a very long time, but I don't care what you or Alexander do, not that I believe a single word you've said. You're desperate and, in my humble opinion, completely out of your mind. And as for you, Rupert, when Alexander finds out you sent that clip, he'll cut off your tiny dick. It's a shame I won't be here because I'd have enjoyed watching that. Now, get out of my way, I'm leaving. I don't like the class of people at this party any more.'

Barging past Valentina, with Rupert's sneering laughter ringing in my ears, I march out of the room and straight out of the front door of the house. I don't believe her for a moment. She's deranged and outrageous and I shouldn't even care now that Alexander and I are over, yet even the minuscule possibility that he may have been taking me for a ride all along stabs me like a knife.

The moment I step out of the shelter of the portico, my hair and coat are drenched, but I don't care. I stumble down the street in the dark and rain, tears pouring down my face. I've had far too much booze or I wouldn't waste a tear on any of them, Rupert, Valentina, or even Alexander. Eventually, I see a black cab and I step into the gutter and stick out my hand.

London flies past in a neon blur, obscured by the raindrops chasing down the windows. I'm tired, I keep telling myself as the tears run down my face. Even though he's unreasonable, maddening and unfair, I still struggle to believe Alexander would string me along while sleeping with Valentina. But there's a small niggle there, as Valentina knew there would be, that makes me wonder. God knows, she was right when she said he does his duty. He'd definitely have no problem at all about finishing with me and telling me why, if he wanted to get back with her.

Yet, even now, I see his hand on her butt at the hunt ball, and the way he let her crawl all over him.

Fuck, fuck, *fuck*.

All the insight in the world isn't helping me feel any less shitty than I do now and I don't like the face that stares back at me from the window, miserable, unravelled and forlorn. That face is not mine; it's not *me*. I take a deep breath, and another, and try to calm down. By the time we reach Immy's flat, I've stopped crying and a new determination has taken hold of me. I'd like to say it was steely, but it's far too brittle to be called that.

I hand over most of the notes in my wallet to the driver and let myself into the apartment, thanking every lucky star that Immy insisted I have my own key when we first arrived.

I strip off my wet clothes, dry my hair on a towel and crawl into bed, even though it's past four a.m. and I wonder if it's worth getting into bed at all. Nine weeks ago, I landed in this city, ready to make a fresh start. Instead, it's been a term of angst and trouble. I hate the drama, the uncertainty, the lack of trust and the fact things are getting so serious that they have affected my studies and dreams for the future – yet I have to admit I can't quite get Alexander out of my head.

There, I admitted it, and I hate myself for it more than I ever have.

There's no point in trying to sleep while I'm in this mood so I switch on the light and sit up in bed, but that only makes my head throb like crazy. No wonder – I started on the booze at three p.m. I get out of bed and fetch a glass of water from the bathroom, trying to remember in which of my bags I put the Advil. After opening all the zippers of two bags, my brain feels like it's pulsating, but there's no sign of the pills. Finally, I resort to the trolley case. The pills must be there, in the compartment under the lid. My relief at finding the packet is overwhelmed by another discovery, one that temporarily eclipses the pain in my head.

The blister pack of pills is there, and so is something else: a small white envelope addressed to 'Ms Cusack' in handwriting that I know instantly. What I do not know is how this letter got in my case: not only did I not put it in, it wasn't here when I unpacked a few days ago. I know that because I now remember the last time I needed the Advil, for the period pains that seized me when I first arrived at Immy's. I took two pills and the letter was not there then, and nothing will convince me otherwise. Sleep deprivation and being hungover can't explain it.

Even as I run my finger under the edge of the envelope, sawing at the edge of the thick paper, my hands aren't quite steady.

Inside, there are two sheets of white notepaper, heavy and creased sharply so that each half is precisely the same size. Opening them in my lap, I flatten out the crease with my palm.

Alexander's bold script, sloping to the right, fills each side of the sheets. The words flow along in thick whorls of dark-blue ink. I picture the fountain pen in his hand and him sitting at his desk, writing the letter. Then I read on and realize it may not have been written at Falconbury at all but in some barrack room or hut.

Dear Lauren,

By now, you'll probably be back in Washington. Probably still hating the sight of me – and I can't say I blame you – because I wasn't the nicest person the last time you saw me. In fact, I may have behaved like a total shit.

May have behaved like a total shit?

Perhaps I should have phoned you to tell you what's in this letter, but I wasn't sure you'd take the call nor that we wouldn't have ended up shouting at each other again.

Closer to the truth is that I'm being a coward and find it easier to put what I want to say down on paper. Not that I'm given to this sort of stuff, as you'll see.

I've a couple of letters to write at the moment, because it's what we always do before we go on an op like this, 'just in case'. It's a pain in the arse and, as you can guess, it tends to

*sour the party atmosphere somewhat. However, it falls to me to
bully the guys into doing it and I'm supposed to lead by
example, so . . .*

*Here's the thing, Lauren. After you left, it occurred to me
how fucking ridiculous it is to leave off saying the things we need
to say until after we're dead. That is, as you might put it, 'crazy'.*

I shake my head and realize I'm smiling and crying at
the same time. I turn over the page.

*So, here goes. I suppose I owe you an explanation of why I kicked
off when I found out you knew Emma was still sleeping with
Henry Favell.*

Suppose he owes me an explanation! That's an
understatement. I rub my hand over my face, wiping
away the tears. No wonder he didn't want to phone me,
not that I'd have answered the call, of course. Of
course not, Lauren. Fuck, a tear splashes on to the
paper and I brush it away with my fingertip, blurring
some of the words. There's a few words missing but I
get the gist.

*I think you know that Henry and I were at school together.
He was two years above me at Eton, in fact, and it won't
surprise you to know that he was a grade-A tosser even then.
Cutting a long and sordid story short, he made my life a
misery, particularly so after my mother died. I was thirteen,
and when I'd recovered from the accident and was sent back to*

353

school, the nightmares started. Henry was in the same dorm as me and he made the most of it, taunting me for crying at night and calling me 'loony' and 'mental case'. There were other things too, but I'll spare you the details of those.

'Why? Why spare me, when you've started?'
I'm talking to the air here, but I can't help it. I want to know *everything*. I also have to stop reading and take a few deep breaths before I pick up the letter again, watching the writing grow smaller and tighter and the letters slope more steeply.

Now, I'd laugh in Cavell's face before I punched it, but back then, after my mother died, I simply couldn't handle it. I suppose I could have gone to the staff, but there was absolutely no way I was going to draw any more attention to myself and, of course, no one ever told on another boy, no matter how much of a misery he made your life. As for telling my father, I'll leave you to draw your own conclusions what use that would have been.

By the way, Emma knows nothing of the bullying and thinks I hate Henry only because he may be after her inheritance (which he is, of course, but that's another matter). There's something else too that I don't want to put down on paper, but let's forget that. All you need to know is that I don't want him anywhere near Emma.

After hearing all of this, you may wonder why Henry was at the ball at all, but the Favells are — were — old hunting friends of my parents. My father invited them, and he had no idea of what had gone on between Emma, Favell and me.

Are you still reading? Thinking I'm a coward and obsessed? Hating me, still, for the way I blanked you that morning?

In that case, there's nothing I can do, but I needed to tell someone — you — about my reasons and the way I feel.

I'll probably be home soon and regret I ever sent this. I may even be back by now, but if not, you should know that where I've gone and what I'm doing means they won't be giving me a medal — posthumous or otherwise — and you won't hear about it on the news either. So if my corner of a foreign field ends up being some dusty hellhole, be a friend to Emma for me, would you? Because I know, now, that you meant well, and I shouldn't have judged you so harshly. I do see what a difficult position you found yourself in, though I couldn't see it at the time.

I race straight on to the second sheet.

So, it seems I'm on to a second page, having intended to write only a brief note. Maybe I won't send the first one, maybe I'll only send this one. I don't know where you are right now, who you're with — if it's Scott, I guess I'll have to suck it up. I know he will.

But. If you're not with Scott, you'd better watch out.

Because if I ever get the chance again, I'm going to carry you off somewhere and lock the door on the rest of the world. I'm going to peel off those hundred-dollar knickers I know you're wearing, Ms Cusack, and have you until neither of us has the energy left to walk or speak or even think. I know you thought I was joking when I said I could break into your room any time I wanted and you wouldn't even know about it.

So, how do you think this letter got into your bag?

What? 'My God, you are unbelievable, Alexander Hunt!'

Ah, now I'm smiling because I can picture your face, hear your gasp of outrage and feel you bristling with indignation. I may be joking about that but this much is absolutely true: I want you so badly it physically hurts, and all I can think about is having you back in my bed, naked, probably furious with me, perhaps rightly, but there despite everything. Because I think you can't stay away from me, Lauren, and I know damn well I can't stay away from you.

The letter trembles between my fingertips, yet I can't tear my eyes away from the words.

I know you've hated me at times — perhaps most of the time — and especially now, but I swear this: if I ever get the chance, I'm going to make good on all the things I've lain awake promising myself I'd do.

Sweet dreams.
With love,
Alexander x

He hasn't quite reached the bottom of the page. There's still an inch or so of white space beneath the sign-off and the kiss. The solitary kiss.

I lay the letter across my lap, shell-shocked. I can see the blue marks on the page but I can't read them any more. The ink smudges and blurs and I have to push the paper away from me before his words merge into one inky blot and I literally can't read it. I ask myself the question: does this letter make any difference to the way I feel about him? Do I want to see him again? Touch him? Have him make good on his threat?

The answer won't come, or rather so many conflicting answers invade my head at once that I can't find the right one. Maybe there is no right one.

I get back into bed and lie down.

I'm going to carry you off somewhere and lock the door on the rest of the world.

The curtains are drawn; they're black-out curtains to shut out the neon-orange street lamp outside the window.

How do you think this letter got into your bag?

I reach for the rocker switch on the lamp and the room is plunged into darkness. Total blackness at first, but gradually my eyes adjust. I hold my hand in front of my face, turning my fingers this way and that. I think I can see the outline of my hand, or maybe my brain is filling in what my eyes can't see.

I strain my ears; of course I can hear things. This is London, an apartment block. Even on Sunday morning, through the double glazing, there is noise: cars in the street, birds singing, the creak of floorboards and footsteps above me. The world is waking up but I turn over and lie face down, the pillow soft against my cheek, the darkness absolute now because I have my eyes closed. *He said he'd peel off my knickers.*

I push my hands down the front of my pyjama shorts.

I touch myself, trying to remember how it felt to have his hands upon me, caressing my breasts. The ache in my breasts as he undressed me and the tight, almost painful contraction deep inside me when he looked at me.

I wriggle my pyjama shorts down my hips and press my fingers to my clit, now a swollen bud that blossoms under my fingers. In my fantasy, the door closes and the scrape of a key in the lock echoes around the room. Alexander bears down on me, the sensual intent burning in his eyes, while I back away. My legs bump against the bed and I know there is nowhere to hide or run.

All I can think about is having you back in my bed, naked.

He reaches out suddenly, grabbing my arm. I overbalance and cry out in shock when he pushes me down on to the bed, pinning my arms over my head, flattening me on to the duvet.

I'm going to make good on all the things I've lain awake promising myself I'd do.

Without warning, he sits astride me, pinning me to the bed, both iron-hard thighs planted either side of my legs. I'm saying 'no' inside my head, but the sound isn't coming out. He undoes the button of my jeans and tugs them roughly down my thighs. Then he gets off me, and I'm still paralysed, body and tongue, when he strips my jeans down over my legs.

He moves back on to the bed, kneeling beside me, so

swiftly; everything is happening all at once and some of it over and over. Before I can do anything, his hand is at my waist and finally I cry out at the sting of lace and silk being torn from my hips, at the ripping sound. Then I hear and see and feel it again, even more vividly this time: the brutal parting of my panties from my flesh, the destruction of the delicate lace, the exposure of my intimate parts.

As I replay this violation again, I squirm against the duvet, touching myself, imagining that it's him – longing for it to be him – stroking me, teasing me, bringing me slowly towards my climax.

The bed dips as the fantasy Alexander climbs astride me. I think he would tie me up – yes, with the cords to the bedposts. I'm helpless and blinded. I have some kind of mask on – he put it there – and the springs creak and the hair on his thighs brushes against the tender inside of my legs as he kneels between them. His erection is huge, hard, hot and thick. A voice keeps saying 'no' in my fantasy, yet I still open my legs wider, inviting him, teasing him, waiting for him.

'I'll have you until neither of us has the energy left to walk or speak or even think,' he tells me, nudging inside me.

He drives straight into me.

I screw my eyes tightly shut, and my body spasms and my orgasm overtakes me. It pulses through me, and just when I think it's over, it takes me again. It's half a minute before I open my eyes to find the room still dark, and the same workaday noises intrude again. There's no

Alexander standing by the bed, of course. It was pure fantasy, on his part and mine. There's no sound of Immy either, moving about in the bedroom next door or making coffee in the kitchen down the hall.

I get up to use the bathroom, take the Advil and crawl back under the duvet, hoping the world will just go away.

There's a buzzing in my ears. I'm not sure where it is or what it is, but I don't like it. It goes on and on while I pick clothes off the bed, looking for the source of the noise. I throw the pillows on the floor, pull open the drawers of the dresser, rip my dresses off the hangers. I can't find it and I know I have to. I have to find the buzzing noise or something terrible will happen. Just as I find it and realize it's my phone, the buzzing stops.

Almost immediately, it starts again and my eyelids flutter open. It is my phone, not a dream or a fantasy but real. It's right next to me on the nightstand, throbbing angrily, accusing me of ignoring it.

I make a grab for it, knocking it on to the wooden floor with a clatter. I scrabble for it and stab in the code.

'Immy?'

The phone's clamped to my ear as I lie across the bed, half in and out of the covers.

'Ms Cusack? Ms Lauren Cusack?' An English voice, crisp, female, unfamiliar, speaks. It's barely eight a.m. Who would call at this hour on a Sunday? How does this woman know who I am?

I answer slowly, reluctant to own up to my name. 'Yes, that's me.'

'I believe you know Captain Alexander Hunt, of Falconbury House, Oxfordshire?'

'Yes, I know Alexander, but who is this?'

'It's Sister Dixon from the Royal Infirmary here. I'm sorry to tell you that Captain Hunt has been involved in a serious incident.'

I'm still lying half on and off the bed, the blood pounding in my ears. 'What? What are you saying? Oh Jesus . . .' Icy fingers clutch at my stomach.

'Before he went into theatre, Captain Hunt asked us to contact you because his sister is underage.'

I scramble up on to the bed. My heart feels like it's going to burst out of my chest. 'What happened? How is he? Is he going to be OK?'

'He's in theatre at the moment.' *That's not what I asked you, damn you; I asked if he'd be OK.*

Her cool, crisp voice resonates against my ear. 'Is there anyone who can come with you to the hospital?'

'No. No one. No one but me.'

There's a pause, one that seems to go on for ever. 'I see. If you can get here, I think you should come as soon as possible.'

Acknowledgements

Once again I have so many people to thank for their help with the research for this book, including Leah Larson, John Schulze, Catherine Jones, Lizzie Forbes, Debra Ross and my US friends. Also many thanks to Nell Dixon and Elizabeth Hanbury for their continued encouragement, hugs and the coffee and cakes.

I also want to apologize for the fact that while I've tried to be as feasible as I can re military and Oxbridge ways, etc., this book is wholly fictional – which is why the Boat Race is two weeks earlier than in Real Life. If I've backed the wrong winner, I'm sorry.

Thanks to Broo, my agent, who is a gem beyond price, and to the awesome team at Penguin, especially Alex Clarke, Clare Bowron, Charlotte Brabbin, Bea, Emma and the energetic publicity, sales and marketing team.

To Charlotte and James, I couldn't have written this without you, and to John, I hope this one gets the neighbours talking again. ILY.